DRAGONBIRTH
Return of the Dragonriders
Book One
by Raina Nightingale

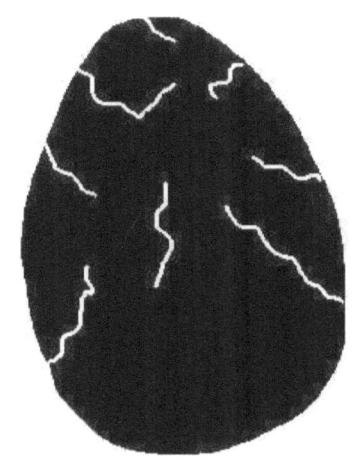

*Not yet available

DRAGONBIRTH
Written by Raina Nightingale

Paperback ISBN: 978-1-952176-06-7
Ebook ISBN: 978-1-952176-07-4

Summary: In a world where dragons are hated and feared, a young huntress' life is changed forever when she meets a dragon hatchling.

Cover art by MidnightRose.
Cover design by Raina Nightingale.
Maps by Raina Nightingale.
Interior Design by Raina Nightingale.
Illustration in chapter 8 by Raina Nightingale and Midnight Rose. All other illustrations by Raina Nightingale.

Published by Raina Nightingale
www.enthralledbylove.com

Author's Note

I first wrote *DragonBirth* when I was thirteen years old. For many years already, I had been writing stories – some very cozy, some very epic – about young women (often named Silmavalien) who bonded to albino dragons (often named Minth, and who often needed special care). When I was thirteen, several things tied all those concepts together and cleaned up, and I finally had a story that worked.

This is essentially that story I wrote when I was thirteen. All the major events are the same. The characters have the same personalities and motives, and the same themes are emphasized. Essentially all that's changed is that I cleaned up some flaws in the style, edited clunkier passages so that they flow better, cleaned up some unnecessary and awkward description and added a few details in other places to flesh out personalities (and a bit of the village's culture), and made some other things less confusing.

However, given the current climate, I believe the story merits a note that it did not occur to me it might need the first time around. Silmavalien and Noren come from a hunter-gatherer society, a tribal culture that's in transition to being more agricultural. The culture is original; it is not derivative of any earth cultures. But it was built with some knowledge about similar societies in similar climates and what they may have been like in the past of our own earth.

As such, people in this semi-tribal society are considered adults, and can and do marry, much younger than in modern societies (though still older than in some tribal peoples). If you are uncomfortable with that, you're welcome to put the book down right now. If, however, you'd be interested in a story that doesn't feel a need to present other cultures in a way that aligns with modern "civilized" norms, but without being about those differences, then be welcome.

If you'd like a slice-of-life dragon story, one with hints of the epic, but that really focuses on Silmavalien's journey to love her dragon friend and her struggle to survive with him through the challenges of day to day life, then I hope you enjoy this story. The most epic part of life isn't the climactic moments, but that day-to-day endurance, sometimes exciting and sometimes tedious, and I wanted to write a story to honor that.

The dragons will fly again,
-Raina Nightingale

Table of Contents

Map of Aneri

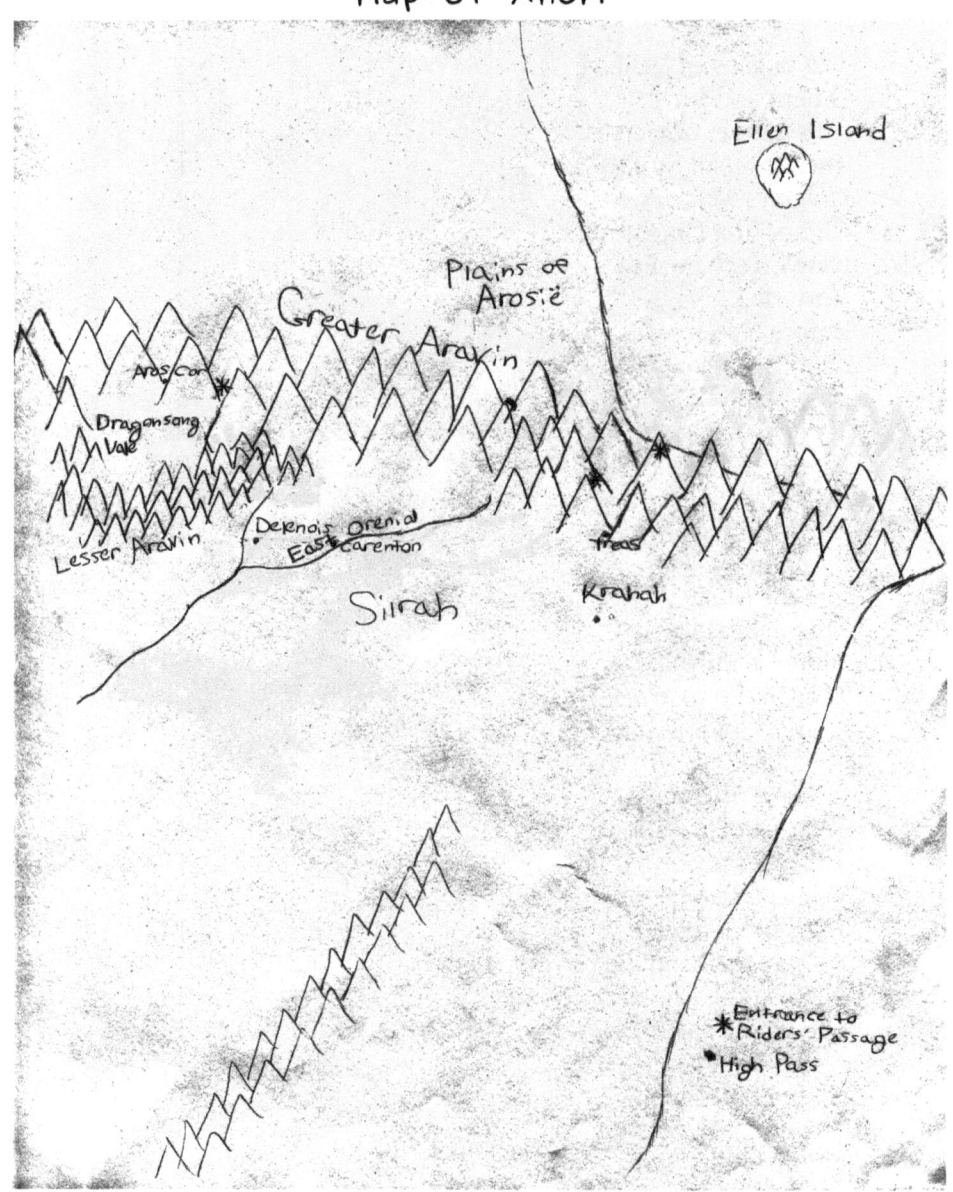

The Legacy of Valiena

Silmavalien put down the heavy basket of peaches in the shade of the shed, and stretched to loosen the knots in her muscles and get a little more wind flowing past her hot skin. She scanned the area covered by the shed, thinking about how much had already been harvested and how much there still was to do, and all the other tasks that had to be done. Maybe, after she got a drink, she could take a short break and then do something else.

"Sil! There's a bard coming! And his name's Gahnva!"

She turned at the sharp, excited voice before she processed the harmless nature of the words. Her younger sister ran around the copse of mulberry trees and skidded to a stop, waving her arms excitedly and twirling the long sleeves of the dress she must have put on in a hurry around each other.

"Sil, did you hear me?" she asked, when Silmavalien did not move or respond.

"Yes, yes." She stretched again and smiled. "I heard you, Rali. And I get this is very exciting, but I'm just hot."

Ralirilien gestured expansively. "There's time!" she said. "He's only just arrived and he's talking to the elders right now. You can dunk into the stream and be back in plenty of time for the stories to start!"

Her sister's exuberance provoked a tired laugh from Silmavalien. "I will." She would get something other than peaches to eat, too.

𝒮

A little less than an hour later, Silmavalien sat near the front row of the villagers, all of those who were assembled to hear the bard at any rate. She had taken another dunk in the stream, and she wished she had not so she could have gotten one of the spots in the shade. She shivered from the wet coolness on her skin, but the sun was fierce on her head and she would be hot again before the tale was over.

She hoped it would be something new and interesting. Sometimes it was, and sometimes it was not, and as she got older, the times it was not grew more common, though sometimes there was a new one that even the oldest had not heard before.

If it was an old one, the next best would be for it to be told by a bard who was truly a master. Like her younger sister, she loved the art of storytelling, and to hear an old tale told by someone who knew how to tell it to its best effect, and bring things out that she had never noticed before, was even better than a new one.

Gahnva raised his arms to indicate his story was beginning, then dropped them slowly and dramatically. He began to recite, and Silmavalien thought he was probably not the best she had heard, but not the worst either. He definitely put feeling into his words.

"In the obscure shadows of the past there lingers an ancient dread, ready to spring upon and devour the ignorant, known as Dragnor by some, or The Devil to others, or Maalok, or to yet others as Satein. To the Dragonriders, however, this King of Demons was honored and revered as Vïnra, the Soul of Fire. They worshiped him, glorified him, ruled and fought in his name, and even burned those of us who did not please them upon his awful altars. The souls of these victims will never find peace through all eternity because of this dark act of the Dragonriders."

Beside her someone fidgeted, but Silmavalien abandoned her previous assumption. The sorrow and anger of his tale burned in his eyes as he spoke. He was living the story and the emotions he was telling, and she was starting to live them, too. Even though this was an opening she had heard many times before, she held her breath in anticipation.

"At one time," the bard continued, "a city known as Truse was ruled by a king whom the Dragonriders honored: his name was Ris. While he was a young prince, Truse was ruled by his kind and noble father, Ken the Wise. During this time, Prince Ris came upon an emerald dragon egg while hunting in the woods. Immediately, he was captivated by its hellbound power and life."

The grief for what was to come dripped out of Gahnva's voice. "Great sorrow and doom was hatched that day for dragons are not the glorious, majestic, sympathetic, and beautiful guardians of chivalry their witch-riders portray them as, but rather powerful frightful demons of Dragnor, who revel in the suffering of others. From that moment on Prince Ris became ever more corrupt, but he retained the favor of his people for the few among them who were not witches of some degree were enchanted and blinded by the spells of the demons and their puppet sorcerers.

"Then, in time, Prince Ris, whose green demon Kris was now

full-grown, grew tired of waiting for the throne and power of his father. He poisoned the good King Ken, who was struggling against the power of the demons over his beloved city of Truse, and ascended to the throne. He ruled for many years, the dragon-demons and their witch-riders defending his kingdom as only supernatural powers can do. Evil wealth and riches of hell poured into Truse, and her foul Dragonriders conquered many cities through the most despicable of means. King Ris tortured and burned all who opposed the demons by whom he had been enthralled and corrupted. Only a witch-king could have committed the least minority of his atrocities."

Silmavalien felt the hatred and disgust, and the overpowering grief, as if she lived the tale the bard told. His words and his face told the story as if it were real to him, and she did not even notice that she shifted position to listen more intently.

"Truse became a mighty empire, and at the height of his hellish glory and arrogance Ris resolved to make the noble, wise, and beautiful Princess of Elagos, the only neighboring kingdom which had resisted Trusan intrusion, his queen. Her name was Valiena.

"There had been few before, and none since, Valiena who were so beautiful, so wise, so noble, or so courageous as she. When King Ris attacked Elagos and cities began to fall left and right before her, it became clear to Princess Valiena that it was desire for her that drove him and that only if she offered herself to him would Elagos be saved from his destruction and tyranny. Valiena told her family. She assured them that she would be taken regardless, but only if she went of her own free will would Eragos remain free. Finally, with much wailing and tears, her father and mother, the king and queen, allowed her to go, but all of Eragos mourned her, and her mother and father soon died of grief, leaving the young but honest Prince Tor, her brother, as king."

Gahva's voice cracked and Silmavalien felt a lump grow in her own throat.

"King Ris took Valiena, but was divinely prevented from further terrorizing Elagos. Instead, he terrorized his new queen, the brave Valiena. However, she was not left long at his mercy nor was he long permitted to continue tormenting those who resisted evil, for the High One looked with compassion upon Valiena's brave suffering.

"He sent his son, with an army of the angels of light, to overthrow the demons of Truse and bring Valiena to his palace in the heavens as a reward for her courage and love. The demons of Truse had no power to resist the forces of the High One. King Ris was killed and all his witches and his demons with him, and Valiena was rescued and brought to live among the angels of the high heavens. Those who had been enchanted were released and the slaves were emancipated, but Truse was leveled and her very stones crumbled to dust before the fury of the armies of light."

Silence reigned. For a moment no one breathed, and Gahnva raised his arms again, then brought them together in a circular motion, signaling the completion of tale.

Everyone around her sighed a deep breath, and Silmavalien leaned back on her arm, relaxing. It was a story she had heard before. Twice, she thought, but long enough ago that she had half-forgotten it and had not thought about it in a long time.

Beside her, her older brother drew his wife, Krielasoriel, half a year younger than Silmavalien, to his breast.

Kriela leaned against his chest. "Oh, Varkul," she sobbed, "That would be so awful." She shuddered.

Varkul rocked her gently. "That's fine. There are *no* dragons left. After the common people were released from their frightful bondage they killed every Dragonrider-witch and every demon-dragon in their midst. We can now live our lives in freedom, free from the bondage and fear of Dragnor."

Silmavalien rose to her feet. "That must be where the '-valien' part of my name comes from. I am proud to be named after Queen Valiena."

Kriela looked up from her husband's arms. "It is a name to be proud of, Silmavalien. I like it very much. I am so glad Valiena risked so much, even to everlasting agony, and underwent so much, even to the frightful abuse of demons so that others, ourselves included, could be free. And I am also so glad the High One had compassion to save her from all these horrors and the people whose Queen she had become, too.

Silmavalien agreed. "It was a brave and noble thing for her to have done. We are all indebted to her as our everlasting queen."

Varkul and Kriela exchanged a whisper below her. Varkul glanced up and said, "It is also so great of the High One to care enough about us, mere mortals, to send his army to deliver us. I wonder why. At any rate, through the valiant sacrifice of Queen Valiena and the undeserved compassion of the High One we can lives our lives in freedom. From this day onward, I swear by my honor that the memory and service of Queen Valiena shall be neglected no more!"

At this, Kriela stepped out of Varkul's embrace, even as he scrambled to his feet. Silmavalien stood still, not knowing how to respond.

Kriela held out her hand to Silmavalien. "You were named in honor of Queen Valiena. Will you join us in our mission to ensure the the honor of her royal highness is neglected no more, dear sister? We would be so delighted."

Feeling awkward, Silmavalien stammered, "Of course. How could I not, when she bought my freedom with her pain?" She did not understand why, or even what, she felt like. But the tale had moved her deeply, and a story like that, and a hero-goddess like Valiena, deserved to be remembered and honored. Not forgotten.

Her brother and his young wife inclined their heads. "Of course, Silmavalien. How shall we begin our service?"

"I –" stammered Silmavalien, "I don't know. I suppose we might start with helping others like those who were here and heard with us to remember her. To keep this memory alive by nourishing it and talking about her."

"Just what I was thinking!" exclaimed Kriela. "Oh, Silmavalien, this will be just great. Will you now speak to Noren about this? If he agrees it is worth it, as we may well hope, perhaps we shall then build a shrine to the honor of Queen Valiena."

"Of course," said Silmavalien. "How could I not?" She was betrothed to Noren. Their fates, their futures, their decisions were indissolubly bound together. Gathering what exuberance she had in the heat of the afternoon, she bounded off to find Noren.

Finding the fifteen year old boy was not hard. He was sitting under a tree, getting some leather ready to be cured. She wondered if he had been working the whole time. He had certainly selected a spot close enough that he could hear if he strained a little, and he had told her once that he listened better without too many people thronging around him and with something in his hands.

He looked up with a smile in his eyes as she bounded off, almost excited as her sister had been earlier. "Hi, Silmavalien!"

She sat down close to him. "Hello, Noren. I've been thinking about the story we just heard today."

"Oh?" asked Noren without glancing up from his work. "What about it?"

"It's – it's interesting," said Silmavalien. "Especially the part about Queen Valiena."

At this Noren *did* look up at her. "What did you find so fascinating, wild rose?"

"How the young princess gave literally everything up – her earthly happiness *and* her wellbeing in the afterlife, too – to save her people from the same. That's just …"

"Incredible," Noren finished for her. "And then the High One delivered her and her people by marriage. That, too, is amazing. Why would the High One care? Why would he even notice?"

Silmavalien nodded. "Very. We should remember, honor, and serve the High One of all creation and the courageous, noble, and loving Queen Valiena."

"You're right," Noren replied. He seemed to be concentrating on his work and Silmavalien, feeling more awkward than ever, did not push it. Finally, after a few minutes, he spoke softly. "If they exist. We don't actually know that it is true. It seems too … incredible … to be real. It's fascinating."

"Yes, it is," said Silmavalien. She scrambled a little to find words to respond to his strange doubt. "… Real things can be incredible too. And often are. What if it is true? What if we chose not to honor our deliverers who so nobly save us from our awfullest enemies? Who would deliver us, then, and why should the High One let us ascend into his heaven? Would we not rather be left for Dragnor and the demons? Who would send us good things and long lives and deliver us from our enemies and oppressors?"

"If you put it that way," said Noren. "I don't know what they would like."

Silmavalien hung her head. "Well, if I were Queen Valiena I should like to be remembered and thought about, to begin with."

Noren nodded, looking into her eyes. "What could be worse than being forgotten by those for whom you would sacrifice all? By the very one you love."

2

Omens and Love

Early the next morning, Silmavalien sat in her bed, gazing at the beautiful objects she collected, all arranged together on a shelf. A few years back, she and Noren had built it together for her collections, which had begun before she could remember.

Just last month she had found a beautiful oval stone, perfectly polished, that shone a rich emerald like the foliage of the trees. She never tired of the way multiple leafy colors marbled its surface. But she had another polished oval stone that she had found much longer ago, and still liked even better than the green one. It was smaller, small enough she could close her hand around it, completely covering it, and its bright pink surface was webbed with white veins. It was the intricate pattern that had caught her attention. She could almost lose herself in it.

A twisted and gnarled branch, which somehow still managed to be straight until it branched out at one end, lay over the stones. Its knots and twists drew her into them, singing in their soundless way of far greater complexity and life than she could ever understand.

Another of Silmavalien's treasures was a roughly oval, smoothed 'crystal rock,' seemingly composed of a frozen glow of intermingling peach and violet-lilac. She found it curious and interesting and inexplicable and had found it in the same brook as she had found the emerald stone beside it, only a few days earlier and a bit farther down the stream. Beside it was a whole host of ovalish stones of various colors and compositions, some sedimentary and some quite definitely formed from many different kinds of rock. One even looked to be of pink and white marble. She smiled as she considered it. Her 'starstone.'

Her eyes fell on her most recent treasure. It was

rather oval, smooth, soft, and shiny. The surface seemed to be of a smooth, oiled, white leather and, though soft, it held its shape. She had found it a few weeks earlier, taking a walk in the woods after a hot day and singing exuberantly a meaningless song of wordless syllables and nonsensical phrases to express how good she felt, while wandering about in the refreshing woods seeking a hint of edible food. The birds were singing happily as well, and a sweet breeze wafted through the forest, bringing a pleasant but confusing mixture of a wide variety of lovely scents to her nose. A ruby-throated hummingbird shot around her energetically as if the very spirit of her song, which he seemed to like.

Happening across a well-worn deer-trail, Silmavalien had followed it. She did not really know why, other than that she just felt like wandering along it. Soon enough, it led her across a wide open glade. She beheld the slender, towering pine trees, rising to the sky like a spire of prayer ascending to the High One, with a certain sense of wonder and awe. Then her eyes fell upon the living, breathing treasures of the glade. A young buck, his antlers small but quite definite, touched noses with a young doe. Both deer were strikingly beautiful and Silmavalien longed to touch their fur. There was just something about the subtly different shades of gray on their backs, and their white underbellies – and their fur just looked so silky and smooth.

But most of all, their eyes captured her. Their eyes! The dark, liquid brown, dark as night but brown instead of blue and wells of such emotion and inner beauty!

A flicker of motion. Her eye followed it to the young doe standing knee-deep in a clear pond that the stream flowed into. The doe was staring right at her, holding her eye almost, and just on the other edge of the water stood an older fawn, likewise watching her, motionless.

Suddenly, looking at them, she realized she did not want to eat deer, or any other animal, really. She decided she would try not to eat more of them than she had to. All creatures had been given the wonderful gift of life. Should she take away such a wonderful, precious, beautiful thing – leave a voice of empty, worthless decay, death – merely so that she might eat what she liked best? Certainly not!

She could not tear her eyes from the deer, until finally she noticed how late it had gotten. She took a last, long look and turned to go home.

That was when she found her most recent and strangest treasure.

A shimmer of white had caught her eye. What looked like an oval white stone lay at the foot of a young cedar. She knelt down to pick up the rock and, cradling it in her arms, found that, though its interior was firm, its exterior was a little soft, and certainly leathery.

She still wondered what it might be.

She had shown it both to Noren and her parents, all three of whom agreed that it was interesting. None of them, however, had forbidden her from keeping it, so she was able to put it with her other treasures instead of hiding it somewhere. She delighted to run her fingers, or any patch of her skin which felt irritated, inflamed, or even merely hot, over its surface. As far as she could tell everyone else had completely forgotten about it by now.

She never talked about it, but she had definitely not forgotten about it – or any of her other rock treasures for that matter, either.

S

After breakfast that morning, Silmavalien returned to the fields to help with the rapidly ripening harvest. That work was best done while the morning was still cool, and other things could be done in the heat of the day, but a reflective mood drove her to work a spot where there were few others, and drift away from them as she worked.

She pulled her hair out of her face and glanced over her shoulder, to see who was around. A moment later, she put her basket down and straightened. Noren was walking through the rows, and in his arms was a shiny, oval white thing that looked just like her treasure!

"Do you remember that 'leathery stone' you found a few weeks ago in the woods?" he asked her, before she could say anything.

"Of course I do!" she replied. "How could I have forgotten it? I say! That's not the one in my room with my rocks, is it?"

"Not at all," he responded quickly. "I found it, as best as I can tell from your description, near the spot you found yours, this very morning."

"Oh!" she exclaimed. "I have often wondered what it is."

"It *is* strange," he agreed. "It is even stranger that we have both found one as we have done ... Tonight, can I see the rest of your treasures?"

"Of course." She paused to concentrate on picking the fruit. Noren moved in to help her. After a few minutes she said, "It is strange indeed, the rock-things we've found."

They worked in companionable silence for another few minutes, before he asked, "Silmavalien, do you have any idea what these things may be?"

"No," she answered, then laughed. "We are to be married, are we not? And we do love each other, do we not? Maybe they are our eggs, and when we find them joined into one it will be the sign of our eternal unity given us by sacred Monra." As she spoke the name of the goddess of love Silmavalien twisted her right hand against her heart and Noren, when he heard it, bowed his head and murmured, "Sacred Lady, Sacred Love, curse me not, but bless or take our lives."

After a moment of silence Noren said, "Perhaps. It would be a beautiful, wonderful thing, and too good to believe, for her to so treasure us as to send us such a glorious omen."

She nodded solemnly. "It would be, but can you think of any better explanation?"

"No," Noren replied, "but then, to me, even that is not a very plausible explanation. I could as easily see it as an omen of the opposite, though I would not accept that as truth, so earnestly and so whole-heartedly do I desire our unity."

At that she and Noren embraced each other. "As I," she said.

S

Early that evening, about an hour before Gahnva was going to deliver his night-time narration, Krielasoriel and Varkul sought out Noren and Silmavalien. "Hello!"

Noren replied, "Hi Varkul. Hi, Kriela. How is it going, today?"

Kriela drew herself up. "We found the stone, a curiously shaped slap of colored marble. When we came upon it I thought, 'Surely this is the place. Here we are to consecrate to Queen Valiena and raise her a shrine.' Then, when I laid my hand on the marble I heard of voice of such beauty and courage I knew it must be the Queen, and she said, "Yes, this is Aralien, this is my altar and the place where my shrine of shrines is to be, my dear child."

"That is interesting," said Noren. Silmavalien looked down at her hands and was silent. Once again she felt awkward. Embarrassed. Nervous. What was wrong with her? She glanced at Noren. He did not appear to feel so awkward.

Noren asked simply, "Did you, Varkul, hear as Kriela did, as well?"

"Yes," answered Varkul. "I saw a huge, brightly colored butterfly that appeared from nowhere and disappeared into nowhere above her head, and I heard the voice of unrivaled beauty, love, courage, and sweet strength speak to Kriela, though I could not distinguish the words."

Kriela smiled a radiant smile and said sweetly, "I and Varkul have sworn to spend our lives in the service of Queen Valiena. Would you as well, Noren and Silmavalien? She loves us all intensely, but she is, after all, a great queen and a goddess, to be served and not refused."

Silmavalien felt trapped. She did not know why; she just did! She did *not* want to make such a vow, but she felt she could not refuse. She glanced at Noren, wondering if her betrothed had a way out.

"Omens of the unknown," he whispered, but she did not quite get his meaning. Then he said, "We will pray to all the gods above and especially to the High One for fourteen days. Then, when they reveal an answer, we will make this decision of to whom to pledge our lives."

Kriela curtsied. "Very well. And we will pray for you, that you make the right choice, in confidence and desire. Farewell! Be blessed."

Silmavalien felt hot anger welling up in her being. As Varkul and Kriela turned away she turned to Noren. "What is it?" she asked.

"I forgive you," he murmured. Totally dumbfounded, she was silent. After a moment Noren said, "I don't know. Gods, goddesses. I've never been too interested in the Higher Powers." He shrugged. "As if they've even noticed me. You aren't too interested in them either, are you?"

Silmavalien shook her head. "Not really."

3

A Reminder of Curses

This time, the bard was to tell the story at night. Silmavalien rushed to get there early, so she could get a front spot. She relaxed, waiting while the rest of the village – everyone, she believed, this time – gathered around in a rough sort of circle.

Then Gahnva raised his arms and lowered them again, the gesture a bit rougher than his story-telling. But this time Silmavalien held her breath in anticipation. He had not revealed what story he was going to share tonight, but even if it was one of the most common ones – perhaps especially if it was one of the most common ones – she would be thrilled to hear it. She hoped her singing was like his story-telling.

"Once there was a woman named Faeri," he began. Not a story she knew, Silmavalien remarked. She did not recognize the name, unless it was a variation she had never heard before.

"In her time she was honored, respected, and obeyed. She had for her companion a beautiful black and white dragon whose name was Chrysanthemum. Faeri was not good, as everyone believed her to be; rather she was evil and a terrible witch. For many years she traveled throughout what is now Silrah and the surrounding kingdoms, giving gifts to all who asked from her and many others besides. But they were not good gifts. Oh no, not at all.

"For a time Faeri's gifts brought great prosperity and health. Those who had them became strong, rich, healthy people, and for a time it seemed as if all the evils of this world were over. Faeri's gifts had well nigh extinguished poverty and sickness and all kinds of suffering. Women no longer died in childbirth. Children no longer died of disease. It was rare for men to die from injury, working on the farm or hunting. People seemed to be living far better and longer. But, in the end, Faeri's gifts brought about the complete destruction, both spiritually and bodily, of those on whom they were bestowed. They were curses in disguise."

Gahnva spoke softly, earnestly, building anticipation and wonder for what would happen next. "One city, high in the mountains, Vata, and many of the towns gathered around her, refused Faeri's gifts. They remained poor, haunted by death, sorrow, and suffering, but they largely escaped the corruption of the era and the souls of their inhabitants remained pure and free. In the mist of pain and grief they retained true life and true joy. Were that all had been like them, but they were laughed at and looked upon with scorn. Those they sent to tell others of the truth were persecuted and killed."

Now his tone dropped with sadness for the life damaged and lost. "Faeri's gifts enchanted their keepers, keeping them from seeing Vala's Truth, and for long decades they seemed justified as they dwelt in peace and prosperity. But, in truth, they were slaves of an evil power who was, even in the midst of their prosperity, condemning their souls to everlasting torment and death. Even in their comfort their spirits agonized."

Gahnva paused for a moment, and when he began again hatred battled the grief for dominance in his voice. "The witch Faeri bestowed her foul gifts, curses in disguise, upon kings and emperors, queens and nurses, knights and slaves, peasants and nobles, merchants and farmers, thieves and criminals – anyone at all, anyone who would listen to her – throughout the world. She was praised and revered as a great heroine everywhere she went. Finally she disappeared, leaving behind the false reason that she was a humble soul who had no desire for all the glory of fame or for power.

"But it was a lie. She was a proud soul who greatly desired both power and all the glory of fame. At any rate, she vanished.

"When Faeri and Chrysanthemum learned that it was now time to disappear from the world at large, they retired to an obscure little mountain village known as Skyre, which is no more. She gave all the people who dwelt there her twisted gifts and installed herself as their queen. In time she married one of them and lived there in peace for a few years."

Again Gahnva paused for a moment, while everyone waited in breathless anticipation. When he began again it was in a slow monotone. "Then, accursed Faeri gave her signal. The most dreaded of demons swamped the village. There were the Fire Shades, dreadful beings composed of shadow and flame who wielded whips of burning anguish. There were the Medusar, foul women whose hair was of snakes and the sight of whose faces turned men to stone with a twisted longing of love and fear. There were the legions of Imps, lesser demons of shadow and fel fire who hurled this flame without restraint. There were the Abysstreaders, spirits of shadow and nothingness who dissolved whatever they touched. There were Ghouls, abominations who had taken possession of the corpses of the fallen and fought with them. There were countless other horrors, but no one can mention them all.

"The demons swarmed throughout Skyre, destroying all but flowing harmless around Faeri the witch and her dragon-demon, Chrysanthemum. That was a horrible day, one to be mourned by the whole world and all the peoples forever after."

The sorrow in his voice built to a crescendo. "Then, Faeri rode Chrysanthemum into battle and the awful demons destroyed all who had received her gifts, both in body and in soul. Even the people of Vata grieved for the atrocities of that day, and nature herself moaned in torment. The gods looked on, even they, in helpless rage and sorrow.

"Keep this tale in your hearts, all you who hear, so that you may not repeat the mistakes of the past nor receive the gifts of the Evil Ones and their curses in disguise, but may truly live fruitful lives."

Silmavalien rose to her feet far too quickly, even before Gahnva had finished his closing gesture. Doubt tore at her heart. Her shimmering white treasure. Could it, too, be a curse in disguise, another ploy by the "Evil Ones" upon the same old theme? Another beauty and treasure which would, ultimately, lead to unimagined suffering and evil, even though seemingly innocent, pure, good, even, perhaps, helpful and useful?

How? How could she know? For not all omens were veiled harbingers of evil, but some could be omens of good, as well. She felt totally confused and bewildered. She shook her head to clear the buzz and the fuzz but it only grew so that she felt like fainting.

Noren noticed and quickly got to her. He put his arm around Silmavalien, who swayed and slumped against him. "What is wrong, my rose?" he asked comfortingly and compassionately.

"I ... fe-ee-el li-ike fainting," she stuttered, then was silent for a moment. "I'm ... so-o-o-o ... co-o-o − confused. My trea-easures. Are the-they − are they omens? O-o-o-omens of ill? Wha-at does it mean? A-are my clo-o-o-o ... safe? I-if it see-ee-ee-ee ... ms to be nice ... or an i-improvement, is it da-dangerous? I − I!"

"I can't understand you," said Noren, apparently unperturbed. "Let's take you in and get you some warm food. Perhaps you'll feel better then, my dear Silmavalien." He kissed her.

S

About half an hour later, she had told Noren what she was feeling and he had told her he did not even really believe any of the old stories, which was not really that much of a surprise after all the strange comments he had occasionally made – since they were children, she realized.

They were sitting across from each other on the floor of her room with the door open. Then, in walked her brother and Krielasoriel. "Hello," she said. "Please forgive us for the intrusion. We had to."

Noren held out his hand to Silmavalien and she took it. Neither of them answered Kriela's speech.

Varkul and Kriela came and sat down on the floor, close to but not right next to Noren and Silmavalien. Kriela said, "We came to tell you about your shiny white ovals."

Still, Silmavalien did not answer, though she wondered how Kriela knew about Noren's oval. His manner when he had told her did not sugest he meant to tell anyone else.

Still gazing into Silmavalien's eyes, Noren unemotionally, almost mechanically, stated, "Go on."

"Queen Valiena caused the tale Gahnva told a little earlier this night to stir our hearts – for your sakes. We know the shiny white ovals are an omen, but of what we do not yet know," Kriela told them.

Silmavalien closed her eyes and asked, "Kriela, have you eavesdropped on us?" Noren gripped her hand tighter, as if in warning, but she did not heed it.

"We have never!" asserted Kriela, but the gleam of anger in her eyes was but a passing scorn, instantaneously replaced by compassion and serenity. "Queen Valiena herself lead us to hear of this and inspired us to speak to you that you may learn what your omen means and be appropriately wary. We hope you have heard an answer to your prayers."

Silmavalien clutched Noren's hand lightly, hoping for support. He answered, "The gods do not often answer either quickly or lightly or clearly." All four of them inclined their heads.

Kriela asked, "May we see and handle the shiny white ovals?"

Silmavalien was silent, hoping Noren would see how to handle the situation. After a few seconds of seeming thought he said, "I would like to hear what you have to say first. Then, by the grace of the gods, I will weigh and judge it myself. If I am to led to see it as worthwhile and important, I will yield the ovals to you."

Disappointment fell on Kriela's face. "Your answer is not what I had hoped, but by the grace of Queen Valiena it will do. Nor are you to blame for your suspicion. I am confident our gracious queen will forgive you on account of your good will –" This kind of talk was really getting on Silmavalien's nerves. She shifted restlessly and edged closer to Noren. He noticed her agitation and his eye met hers. "– We are glad to present you with an escape to your predicament with your ovals."

"Oh. And what might that be?" asked Silmavalien sharply.

"The easiest and simplest is for you to give us the ovals. We are confident that, in the event she fails to reveal their meaning to us, our queen will nonetheless protect us from any ill they may bring," said Varkul. "The second easiest and simplest would be for you to visit the shrines of great and revered gods and goddesses and make them a sacrifice, requesting that they would, in turn, reveal the meaning of the omen to you. The best would be for you to enter Queen Valiena's service and request her protection, which she will not fail to grant."

Silmavalien sidled closer to Noren. He replied, "Thank you very much for your time and concern. We are indebted to you for your good will. The rest I do not now know. We will consider what you have said and pray to the gods about it. May the gods bless, comfort, and guide you. Goodnight."

Kriela and Varkul rose to their feet and left with a wave or good night.

When the two had gone, Noren kissed Silmavalien and released her hand. Then he, too, stood and yawned. "Bless you," he said. "Goodnight." Then he walked out.

Silmavalien took a small drink and then threw herself on her straw mattress and wrapped herself in blankets. She slept.

4

The Obsidian Stone

A few days later, Silmavalien was walking through the forests below the village. Conifer trees of many sorts intermingled with the deciduous oak trees. Here and there were groves of wild roses, their simple flowers delightful and pleasant in a way no other could be, their scent sweet and lovely as she had found no other. She walked through meadows, often with a little stream running through them, almost knee-high with fresh, green grass and scattered throughout with thousands of wildflowers of all sorts. Beyond she could see the high conifer ridges of the upper mountains.

It was strikingly beautiful. As she walked through the woods, in search of herbs, she softly sang an old song:

> Borne on wings as old as time
> My choice, my love, has chosen me
> Our souls made one, our hearts must climb
> Evermore one we must be
> You are my great desire, to ever see.
>
> Closer and closer we draw together
> Ever since the day of your birth
> My soul's desire is to know you ever
> To soar with you above all earth
> To share in your, unknown heretofore, mirth.
>
> Dear, you are my closest heart
> With you alone I find life complete
> Without you, empty is my part
> With I'm freed, no longer bound by feet
> But with you I'm truly freed 'n fleet.
>
> Come bright wings, be my light
> Carry me to the world I've never seen
> Show me what it is to see, shine bright
> Lift from my eyes the dusty screen
> So I can see the world beyond me.

She felt certain that was not the end of the song, but she could not remember it despite a strong, inarticulate desire to do so. There was more to it ... more. As if those few verses were just the beginning of a symphony, greater and more beautiful than anything they could ever have hinted at. She intensely wanted to hear it and to understand what it meant ... and more. To be part of it, to join in it, to ... she could not know what.

A flicker of movement caught her eyes, even as she was struggling to remember the song. She stopped dead in her tracks, and then jumped back. A rattlesnake writhed across her path. It coiled, clearly threatened, but did not rattle.

Noren had been teaching her to shoot since their betrothal. Now, when she went walking in the woods she always kept her bow and quiver on her shoulder, and while her accuracy was not what a true hunter must have, it was good enough at close ranges.

Now, once she took a few more steps back from the snake, she pulled the bow from her back and strung it. A rattlesnake should rattle. If it had, she would let it live. But since it did not, it would make good food.

She fit an arrow to the string and took the stance to shoot, thinking of how Noren would correct her, then let the arrow fly. It struck the snake, not quite where she had intended, but at this range the power of the arrow sent it all the way through the snake, deep into the ground. The creature writhed in what must be agony.

Frantically, she searched around for a stone, one she hoped she could crush the snake's head with. She doubted she could hit it again with the arrow, writhing as it was. It was not long before she found a stone and ran back. Heart in her throat, breathing rapidly, she stood as near the snake as she could, watching its movements, then hurled the stone.

She struck true.

The rock rolled off the crushed head, and Silmavalien approached, drawing her pocket-knife from its small sheath on her belt, to cut off the snake's head. She kicked it into the bushes and buried it under a bit of dirt and leaves, then turned back to the rest of the snake.

She smiled grimly to herself as she stood over it. Without a doubt, Noren would congratulate her on her first kill, her first hunt. She may have – or, just possibly, not – lost one of her precious arrows pinned in the ground, but it would still be a wonderful achievement for a girl like her. She knelt to pull the arrow out of the ground and collect the snake.

Then she continued on what was not only a search for herbs and food to gather, and not a pleasant walk. The snake had startled her, and she could tell that she was not going to relax any time soon. It would have been too easy to die there. She could not help keeping her eyes constantly scanning the shadows, noting detail with a sharpness she usually did not experience.

Several times she fancied she saw a snake but, upon closer inspection or a brief pause, found that it was only a stick or even a cute harmless lizard.

Soon after, she walked out into another wide meadow, fringed with wild roses and further out, among the free grasses and lone trees, were acres of lupines and other wild flowers, from peacock orchids to daisies to lilies of the valley, and other yet flowers yet. A deep stream ran through it, flowing through many shallow pools, keeping the flowers and the grass green, even in late summer.

As she walked into the meadow, peace descended over her. Her nerves relaxed, the startled fear passed, as if the place felt safe and secure, a haven of the gods. Song welled up in her breast, and then she found she remembered another verse of the song she had been singing earlier:

> Sweet, sweet heart of mine
> Together, away we shall fly
> To lands more fair and fine
> Than any we have yet come by
> Amidst the beauty and wonder of that sky.

Still the song urged her on with an unfulfilled, unknown, inexplicable desire, that seemed connected to knowing the song better. Another kind of excitement from that of the snake grew in her breast, one that exulted at the butterflies of all sorts that fluttered around her, monarchs and little yellow ones and lavender ones, and the honeybees that went from flower to flower.

For a few moments, she stood still, watching the winged dance and hearing a sweet call which she was unable to understand. "What is it?"

She continued walking along, right through the meadow, following the inarticulate call. She came to where the little stream, crystal clear, flowed over pebbles. A few river weeds grew out from between the pebbles and a few colored fish swam in it. A brilliant iridescent green hummingbird flitted past her on her way to the lilies of the valley, just down the stream.

She knelt on the bank for a moment and let the cool, refreshing water flow over her hands. Then she stood, intending to turn around and follow the trail back up towards Treas, but something caught her eye.

A glint of shiny black, through a haze of violet lupines and green blades of grass. No matter how hard she tried she could not tear her eyes off it. Silmavalien tried to walk away, reasoning that she did not want to be captured in any more omens, but she could not look away.

If she walked away she would have to do so blindly for her eyes could focus on nothing but the black stone. It would be so easy to step into a den of snakes before whatever-it-was released its hold on her and be bitten and die there.

Instead, she carefully drew near to the glint of black. Her heart pounded with frantic fear and her blood seemed to surge with a chill, fiery energy, but she did not feel she had any choice about the matter. At last, she knelt before what looked like an ovalish lump of polished smooth obsidian.

Silmavalien tentatively reached out and touched the stone. It was cool and smooth, hard as marble, yet it had a strangely glassy sheen. A lump here and a dimple there marred its otherwise nearly perfect symmetry. She felt a strange thrill or vibration run through her fingers and into her blood as she touched the stone.

Terror coursed through her blood in stark contrast to the peace of the meadow, but she did not know what she feared. Then she felt magic touch her mind and heart and knew she would be unable to speak of the matter to another living soul. She felt both freed and isolated, as if at once and by the same object or action. Then she felt impelled to pick up the stone and carry it home.

This time, she obeyed without fighting, and picked up the stone. It was a little longer than her forearm and about half as wide, but it weighed lighter than she thought it should. She wondered what it was as she stood with it, and then cursed it for attracting her and forbidding her to communicate about it, in any way, with another human being.

She did not mind not being able to tell her family, but she wanted to tell Noren very much indeed, yet knew she would not be able to.

The obsidian stone glittered at her, as if communicating something. Why would it care?

As she was climbing up the last ridge below her village, the stone suddenly rolled from her arms and vanished. As it rolled out of sight, she found herself wondering where it came from, what had happened. Suddenly, it was all vague and cloudy, and she could only remember that something strange had happened that she could not speak of. No matter how hard she tried, nothing more came to her.

She put the matter aside and sought out Noren to show him the snake.

As she had expected, he congratulated her and so did many others. All day, though, she felt uncomfortable, as if there was something she very much wanted to say but was unable to remember or put to words. When she was alone images of the obsidian stone flashed in her mind but she could not recall where or when she had seen something like it or why it made her so uncomfortable. Nevertheless, she felt laughed at by something.

Then, at night after everyone else was asleep, Silmavalien remembered the obsidian rock and cursed it again, as she lay in her bed. She wondered where it was and if there was any way to destroy it. If she could find it again she would seal it in a bag and take it to the forge in Kranah and ask a blacksmith to hammer it in a bed of burning coals until it was scorched and crushed beyond all recognition.

She heard a voice in her mind:

"Would you then kill me though I have harmed no one? I am yet unborn, one of a scattered handful of the last few remaining members of a persecuted race. I know that you know not what you do, but nonetheless I warn you: if you kill us we will still burn you. We have not forgotten the blood of the dragons and we will be their Avengers and our own, O privileged Silmavalien."

Terror and fear ran through Silmavalien and she whispered to herself, "I am cursed by the gods. I have gone insane." When she woke the next morning she could recall nothing of the night but a vague sensation of unease.

5

Dragon's Mystery

The bard had gone that day and left behind the stories of Faeri and Queen Valiena, written on hides, to add to the others the village of Treas kept. Silmavalien lay in her bed, shifting uneasily.

Then something squeaked. She tensed but did not move. It sounded like it was in her room.

In the silence that followed she could hear the beating of her own heart and the rhythm of her breath. It irritated her more and more, as no other sound broke the silence. For a long time she waited, lying on her elbow, consciously controlling her breathing.

The shrill squeak pierced the darkness again, higher and clearer than before. It rang in her ears and she found it intensely irritating and even a little painful. It resembled the screech of unoiled steel scraping past unoiled steel and continued on until it passed from her hearing, making her want to squirm the whole while.

Her heart beat frantically. She was excited but not afraid and she felt weak, weak as she had never felt before, and yet, for some reason, she felt as if she had always been this weak. Totally confused she sank back into the straw mattress and fell asleep before she could think about how strange that was.

Overpowering desire startled her back into alertness. Something she had secretly desired all her life was so close. It was as if an essential part of her that was yet indescribably more and other than herself was about to touch her, or else was within her reach and she had only to reach out to touch it. A new weakness, that was yet present from her first, least articulate memories, held her back, stood in her way. Held by such desire, yet in the midst of such weakness, she felt desperate. Just beyond her lay all the meaning of her life, all her heart's desire, and yet she had no strength to stretch out her hand and touch it.

Her voice soft and strained, she sang:

> All I desire is with you to be
> Yet I am without any power
> To reach out, I to you, you to me
> Desperate and helpless, call out to the Higher
> All then perfected, outside and the Inner

She sat up in her bed, rocking restlessly. She felt like all her life her heart had been a still, quiet valley in which dwelt a few silent forms of life endlessly seeking something wider and more. Now, all that was gone in a chaotic whirlstorm of confusion and emotion. Would it shatter the walls enclosing, and sheltering, the little valley of her heart? Would it shatter the valley itself? When it was gone, would enemies pour through the broken walls and lay waste all that she was or desired? Or would it let in the Higher, to totally transform and fill her?

Wrestling with her emotions and fears, a soft thump on the floor behind her startled Silmavalien. She twisted around and first beheld the white light of the silver moon streaming through her window and flooding her room with pale and colorless yet strangely beautiful soft and white luminescence. At first all in her room seemed to be just as she had left it.

Then, she saw that her shiny white oval was not in its place on the shelf. She searched for it frantically, and found it, just a few feet away from her, shining softly in the moonlight and riddled with a webbed network of thin, inky black lines.

Cold, icy fear surged through her. Even her heart seemed to stop beating. She did not think. She did not move. She did not hope or guess. She waited, yet with neither patience nor impatience. Fear annihilated all else.

Then, the shiny white oval split, revealing its true nature.

A few feet away from Silmavalien, sprawled what could only be a dragon. A long, thick, clumsy tail uncurled itself on her floor. A thin neck, but nonetheless short against both the body and the head, supported a large, awkward shaped, rough and squarish-triangular head. Large, bulging eyes glowed a dim minty color and whirled slowly. A spiny ridge ran down from the forehead to the nose, where wide nostrils flared revealing molten depths which seemed almost to glow with dark red slumbering flame.

The dragon splayed four stumpy legs out around its body and looked too thick and clumsy to properly walk on them. The claws were a pale color, faintly transparent. Rather too small, much-crinkled, crudely shaped wings were splayed around the contrastingly lithe body. Everywhere the skin shone white in the pale moonlight.

Though she thought that the dragon was despicably ugly and even repugnant to look at, Silmavalien felt a strange thrill of excitement as its birth. She felt strangely affectionate and drawn to it as, overpowered by its hunger, it twisted around and began to eat its egg-shell. She felt its hunger and helplessness in herself. Despite its ugliness, the dragon fascinated her.

When the dragon had finished its egg-shell it twisted back around and creeled mournfully. The plea touched her heart. She recognized it! She knew it, from the very bottom. All fear and reluctance suddenly gone she reached out and touched the dragon.

The instant her fingers touched the dragon's skin icy fire coursed through that contact into Silmavalien's blood, bringing with it both burning, excruciating pain and a strong sense of pleasure, which, mingling into each other, made the whole sensation even more unbearable. The dragon screamed a piercing screech which hurt her ears.

Reflexively she shrank back, but it did nothing to the fire burning through her soul. Already her heart and soul and the dragon's were uniting, becoming one. Their minds were linked. Neither of them could do anything to that anymore than Silmavalien could revoke the fact that she had, of her own conscious will, touched. Her heart was already melting and breaking so that it could truly bond to the dragon's. Perhaps that is why dragons are born so ugly; an attraction to something based in any way whatsoever upon beauty cannot serve as a foundation for such a bond.

Slowly the pain melted away. She lay beside the dragon, conscious of his name though she could not remember learning it.

Minth. Unbearable ecstasy of joy, excitement, and wonder flooded her being. She drew Minth into the mattress with her and kissed his ugly head. Joy and love surged through her.

Silmavalien's eyes fell on the dragon and she loved him. The beat of her heart harmonized with his. The rhythm of her breath merged with that of his. Their whole bodies vibrated with the same force and energy as they stared into one another's very different eyes, the one having dark brown irises and black pupils, the other a dim, pale minty glow. They were so different and yet they were so close and the differences served not to separate them but to draw them closer together. It was wonderful, impossible, totally new.

Silmavalien smiled and drew Minth close to her breast. She kissed him on the nose and stroked the smooth skin on his neck and shoulder. The unbearable, inexplicable, unbelievably wonderful had happened to her. She was freed and bound. She had been born with Minth, but she still felt quite confused.

Indeed, she now felt more confused than ever. A dragon. The dragon. Minth himself was with her. She loved him. She wanted him. She wanted to be with him. She wanted things she knew she had never wanted before, but what it was she wanted she did not know. She had been instantaneously thrust into the wide new world of the undiscovered and the unexperienced and of another being's emotions, experiences, and personality.

One thing she did know. She and Minth were eternally bound together. Bound by love, bound by joy, and bound by desire. Their very lives, too, were joined. She felt his breath and his heart beat in her even as her heart beat in him. Without putting into words or knowing how, she understood that they were already bound by a bond stronger than fear or death.

Acceptance, love, gladness, and quiet marvel filled her heart. This was the foundation on which all truly wholesome bonds are set. The fear, the terror, and the panic of just a few moments before seemed to have no place at all in the whole world and all the worlds. Indeed, it was very nearly forgotten in the love and goodness of their bond.

In time she sank into a soft doze, not really all that akin to sleep, as she lay about Minth. Desires and images such as she had never known before and can hardly be described flooded her dream-consciousness. New emotion and new being flooded her mind.

A song rang through her dreams, one that told of and was told in the language of the new world that opened around her, but in words it was something like this:

> Swift and fiery, wind immortal,
> Running beyond all mortal sight,
> Now made one, undying in unity eternal
> Beyond the everlasting fire and light.
>
> Before the worlds were born
> This was and is a world of its own;
> Only those to love forsworn
> Know this world to which no eagle has flown.
>
> Now see and behold, lo!
> This world more deep than eyes may see.
> Come and find what no mind may know
> Where all may dwell and as one be.
>
> The streams here are pure and clear.
> The winds are born with a flame living.
> Never can one come to the end of me here.
> There is fulfillment and yet no end to the seeking.
>
> Come and find all your desire
> To be made one ever closer.
> Soar on winds of fire,
> Fly beyond all you ever were.
>
> This is where your heart can learn to fly;
> These are the lands of true flight
> Where there is no end or limit of beauty and sky
> And you can race flame, soar on light.
>
> This where you may run
> As fleet as deer;
> This where you will soar to the sun
> Find there is no fear.

Swim through the rivers,
Ride upon the crest of the waves of the sea.
The winds here are stronger
Than all you can ever be.

Yet there is no harm;
Even pain will be life in love.
Find only peaceful charm,
Join the joy of all winged life above.

Do what you cannot do.
Race the wind swifter than you.
Find her in your heart, too
In strangest ways all your desires come true.

The song seemed to soar forever without end, telling of and told by that world where everything is stronger than oneself and yet nothing is impossible, the world of fiery winds and tides and rivers and healing and the joy of love incarnate. She did not understand even half of what she heard in it, but she knew that she and Minth were together in a way that more real and intimate that she had ever imagined. She knew her life was changed forever. She no longer was, and yet she was just beginning to be.

"I love you, Minth."

6

Choice of a Dragonrider

A few hours later something jolted Silmavalien back into the realm of normal alertness. After a moment, she identified it as ravenous hunger. It could not be hers; it must be Minth's. She crawled out of bed and Minth looked up at her. He squealed pitifully.

The light in his pale, minty eyes touched Silmavalien's heart. "Stay here," she told him. "I will be right back. I'm just trying to get you a bite."

A dim acknowledgement came from Minth, as he felt her meaning through their connection. She quietly stole from her little room and into the main room of the house. She cut a hunk of cheese and then, always careful to be quiet, sliced it into small slices, before returning.

The dragon ate the cheese, bit by bit, from her hand, while she sat in the straw, trying to think. Horrible thoughts passed through her mind, and she cringed.

She was, undoubtedly, a Dragonrider. As a Dragonrider she was doomed to a certain and horrible death. Dragonriders were believed to be witches, and witches were burned alive. She closed her eyes, trying to stem the tide of awful images her imagination was forcing upon her against her will. She flinched.

She faced an awful choice, which was not really a choice at all. The only alternative to an awful, torturous death was to hand Minth over to the same fate. The very idea made her nauseous. She could not do that! To lose Minth, worse, to kill Minth, would be akin to killing herself. Not only was murder wrong, the dragon was so close to her that to do such a thing was to deprive her life of all meaning, all purpose, all satisfaction. It would be like trying to cut herself in half and then go on living as if she had never been whole, never destroyed the half of herself. No. She could not do that. Nothing would make her do that. She would rather die than let Minth die.

Hate and fear churned in her soul. She was a Dragonrider, but she knew that she was by no means any sort of witch. Minth was a dragon but no demon. The stories about King Ris and Queen Valiena and about Faeri and Chrysanthemum, along with many others, were at least partially false, if not entirely so. Her world was shattered.

What *was* true?

She could no longer trust the old stories. She wished she knew more truth about the dragons and dragon-raising, and at least something of the true history of the Dragonriders. She remembered what had been told her several days ago when she wanted to destroy the obsidian rock:

"I am yet unborn, one of the scattered handful of the few remaining members of a persecuted race ... We still remember the blood of the dragons, and we will be their Avengers as well as our own ..." Somehow, she knew it was not Minth who had spoken to her then. She asked, *Who are you who spoke to me? I no longer wish to destroy you. What can you tell me?*

Silmavalien waited quietly but she received no answer. Hate and fear boiled together in her stomach. She felt a helpless rage. She wanted to destroy the slayers of the dragons and the Dragonriders. She wanted to know the truth and she wanted to kill the liars who stood in her way. But, there was only one of her. Quite possibly, there was no one else in the entire world, except for Minth and the guardian of the obsidian rock, who would listen to her or even care. There were hundreds and thousands who would fight against her.

Again she called out with her mind and heart: *O Obsidian Guardian, have mercy on me! Forgive me for my unthinking hatred of you before I learned the truth about the dragons – or at least the beginning of it. I still wish to learn more of the truth. I want to join forces with you against the dragons' enemies. Will you protect me, a new Dragonrider, as you seek to avenge the blood of the dragons and their riders?*

Finally the reply came, a faint whisper in the back of her mind. *"I can't. It is not yet time."*

Silmavalien looked at Minth, hopelessness welling up in her heart. They were alone. They had to survive together with none but themselves. She knew she had not the skill for them to survive if they ran away into the woods. Not yet, at least. How could she hide Minth for long enough?

Not even Noren would believe her, Silmavalien was sure. At the present he did not believe in Higher Powers, gods, dragons, demons, or witches. But if he were to see a dragon? Would he not, perhaps, believe the whole thing and all the stories? Or else, that he had gone insane and was imagining the whole thing? She wondered what she would have thought and felt if she found Noren to be a Dragonrider before she bonded with Minth? Would her belief in her fiancé's essential goodwill have triumphed, or her belief in the old stories and the 'gods'?

Noren, too, had a dragon egg. The 'shiny white ovals' were dragon eggs. When would his hatch and would the dragon bond with him? Would he, like herself, be too afraid to tell her when it happened – if it ever did? How long would she have to hide Minth's existence, along with the absence of his egg? Could she? *How* could she?

Silmavalien speculated wildly. She would leave as soon as she could with any significant chance of survival. Meanwhile, what would she have to hide and how?

She counted on her fingers. No one could learn the egg was absent. No one could see the dragon. No one could learn about his waste products. No one could learn about his food. No one could hear him. Ouch! Perhaps they were already discovered! Silmavalien put aside the thought for the moment. It was not like she could do anything about it. What *could* she hide?

Silmavalien decided that the first thing she had to do was not invite people to her room. In fact, to try and dissuade people from even thinking about it. If she were to deny entrance to her room, what might people think?

She got up. Carefully and quietly, working mostly by feel in the darkness, she moved her shelves and all the treasures on them into a corner. Then she took one of her bed spreads and hung it over the shelves from a couple of catches in the wood wall. She sat down, back against the wall, and sighed.

Minth waddled over to her and lay down in her lap. She looked down at him affectionately and scratched his head. She closed her eyes and rested her head against the wall. She had fixed one problem, but she was really quite tired and it was already early morning. *How can I do this?*

Sitting there, cradling Minth, she struggled to think straight. She would … she would be as involved in outdoor activities as possible, spend as little time in her room as she could … to avoid any suspicions about what might be going on. That way … that way, if someone were interested in talking to her, or anything that might lead them into her room, she could easily say, "I don't feel like that. Let's go walking in the woods," or something like that.

Then … then … no, she still had to figure that out … no, it was not that. What was it? Silmavalien could no longer even remember what she was trying to think about, let alone think about it straight and take reasonable factors into account. A feeling of troubled fear and discontent wafting around in her mind, Silmavalien dozed off without even crawling back into her mattress or covering herself with a blanket.

Several times she drifted into a state of half-wakefulness and shifted her position. Between the cold of the hour before dawn and the hardness of the clay floor on which she was sleeping no position remained comfortable for long. Her fear and worry increased her restlessness, contributing to her poor sleep. Once she woke up terrified, directly from a nightmare, her heart pounding, every fiber of her body read to fight and run. It took her what felt like an hour to get back to sleep.

She never remembered that nightmare or, if she did, she never learned to connect it with that night. But she remembered the intense sense of dread, fear, pain, terror, even panic, and of loss and desire and hate. She wondered if the nightmare was an effort on the part of her mind to conjure up what it would be to lose Minth, to feel her dragon die. It permeated her mind through the morning, making her sleep uneasy.

Whenever she woke up and looked at Minth her heart burned with love and fear. Love and fear which she physically felt in her blood and throughout her being. She loved him. Therefore, she feared for him. That was all Silmavalien now knew, all she had to live with and build on, find meaning in.

7

New Life, New Fears

A ray of warm sunlight poured through the window and made her body zing with pleasant warmth. Eventually, it woke her up.

She opened her eyes and saw the world with new eyes. Somehow, colors were subtly different. Patterns of light possessed a meaning concealed from her till now. It was like seeing the world and the daylight for the first time.

It was with new ears that she heard the world, too. A world she had not heard before. The chirruping voices of the birds in their morning songs was clearer now. She heard parts of it she had never heard before and these missing parts, now suddenly there, made it fit together more smoothly, allowing her to hear more of it and its meaning. She smelled sweet scents she had never known before and others more keenly than she would have believed possible.

Silmavalien's eyes fell on Minth. Since their bonding she had not forgotten him even for a moment. A love of a quality she had never before imagined poured through her and seemed to permeate her senses. It was almost as if she could see, hear, smell, taste, and feel the love between them. She sat up, feeling as if this vitality and love would kill her. It was too much, too wonderful, lovely, full to be borne or lived with for long.

As Silmavalien sat there, cradling the weak dragon in her arms, the sound of voices startled her into full awareness. Every one of her senses perked, her muscles tensed, her heart pounded, her breaths came faster. Cold fear poured through her, freezing her heart. Both she and Minth were in mortal danger. At any moment some unsuspecting relative, who had up till that moment been her friend, might open the door and see the dragon. Then everyone she had ever known, even perhaps Noren, would turn against her in fear and hate and have her burned alive. No one would or could help them. There would be no escape, no life, no dragon and rider.

Her heart clenched with panic. Minth screamed before the pictures and feelings flowing from her mind into his, a high, cold, thin, wailing sound, piteous and desperate that momentarily shocked her out of her dumb panic. She impressed upon his mind a need for total silence. *Any* noise would mean *death*. He did not understand what death meant, but he did understand it to be something very horrible and to be avoided. His scream died away into silence. He stared into her eyes, his own pale and quivering with fear, and she did not know how she would endure this. It was so horrible and unfair!

Minth was a hatchling, an infant. He should not have to deal with such fear and danger. It was too cruel and he was so weak already. Would he die? Tears streamed down her cheeks but she got up and placed him under the curtain. Again she impressed upon him the need to stay where he was. Then she left him, knowing that to stay with him would inevitably mean both their deaths. Still it hurt her to leave him so alone, so young. How could she?

She quickly discovered that the voices she had heard were not from her family quarters. Everyone there was still fast asleep. She grabbed a couple more slices of bread and meat for Minth and then went back to her small room. She fed him the food and hugged him. Then she changed into more appropriate clothes and left. She wanted everyone else to believe she was not all that interested in her room or in anything she kept there.

Silmavalien wrote two short notes. One read, "Keep out. You won't find me here. Went hunting." She hung that one on her door handle. The other read, "Went hunting this morning, Noren ~ Silmavalien." She put that one in Noren's window. Then she gave Minth a goodbye hug and kiss, told him with pictures, as best as she could, to stay where he was and make sure he was not found, took her bow and a hunting knife, and left.

It tore her heart to leave Minth. As she ascended the trail leading upwards, her thoughts turned to him again, how she loved him, what would happen to him – and her – if he were found while she was away hunting – mostly so that she could feed him. As the distance between them increased she expected to lose contact with him at any moment.

She did not. The link between their minds was still as clear and strong as when she had lain with him that morning. She could sense him paying attention to her, curled up in her clothes on the shelves behind the curtain.

Nonetheless the separation made her uneasy. The feeling that at any moment Minth might be discovered and she was not there to protect him terrified her. The fact that even if she were there to protect him it would not do much good did not give her any comfort. A fire burned in her muscles, making her feel as if her entire purpose and life was bound up in nurturing and protecting a dragon, Minth, her soul's partner. Her uneasiness flowed across the bond and made both of them uneasy and twitchy.

She noticed when a robin flitted across her visual field. She flinched at the sound of nearby voices through Minth's ears. He could not tell from what direction any sound came from his enclosure because he did not know which direction was which. Thus, neither could she, through his mind and ears. Every fiber of her felt as taut as tensioned wire.

A squirrel dashed across her path. At any other time she would not have been fast enough nor her senses keen enough to hit it. As it was, she had barely identified it before she had her bow over her shoulder and an arrow on the string.

S

Silmavalien got a rabbit as well, and then stopped on the outskirts of the village. She wanted to use hot rocks to cook the squirrel for Minth. She gathered some rocks and tinder and kindled fire. While it warmed up she skinned the critters and gutted the rabbit. When the rocks were hot she banked the fire and buried the squirrel in the hot rocks and dirt to retrieve later. Then she returned to the village with the rabbit to show for her hunt.

She ran into a group of men standing on the edges of the fields talking to one another. As she drew closer, carrying her rabbit, she could hear what they were saying. They were talking about some strange sounds some of them had heard during the night. She tried to conceal her fear, which would too easily give her away, under a blank expression. Fortunately, the men noticed her, acknowledged her, and moved aside a little to give her room to pass out of common courtesy, but did not question her or even try to talk to her. She acknowledged them with a nod and passed on.

By now everyone was moving about, getting ready for the day's work. It was past the usual breakfast time and Silmavalien's stomach rumbled loudly. After finding the rabbit a suitable place so that it would be cooked sometime during the day she found a plate and served herself the remains of breakfast. Then she went and sat down outside, with her back against her room and the outside of the very corner where Minth was, and enjoyed the morning while she ate. She relished being close, if not exactly next to, Minth.

It was not long before Noren came across her. "Hello, Silmavalien!" he greeted her. "How are you?"

"Fine." She smiled at him, trying to act normal despite the fact that she was not. "Thanks. I got a rabbit this morning."

"Awesome." He smiled at her and sat down next to her. "Yes, I read the note you put under my window. Speaking of which, I came here to see you before I leave today. I will be going on the three or four day hunt preceding my ritual entrance into manhood before I can marry. I don't have a problem with it, gods or no gods."

Silmavalien nodded. She chewed and swallowed, then said, "Goodbye. I'm a bit sorry. I would have liked it if you didn't have to go. Anyway, I suppose I'll just have to deal with it. I'll be fine. Good luck."

"You do know I might have to be gone that long hunting for us when we have a smile," he said with a smile. He kissed her. "Happy days,"

I do hope Varkul and Kriela do not bother me, thought Silmavalien.

She extended her thoughts to touch Minth's mind. The tired, weary dragon was asleep, but she sensed a dim uneasiness in his consciousness. Part of it was due to a half-articulate longing to be physically with her and in his rider-guardian-mother's arms. Part of it was due to the dread of a mysterious, unknown danger.

A pang of pity and guilt passed through her. Should she not have imparted this sense of fear and danger to safeguard him from it? Yet it was wrong not to do everything she could to protect their lives which, even so, hung in such a fragile balance. What was there left to hold on to? Her bonding with Minth had shattered all her beliefs, her entire sense of identity and purpose in life.

There was only one thing she could still – and had to – live for: Minth, and the love between them. Yet what was that? A weak, fragile thing, to be twisted and distorted by fear and danger and, finally, annihilated by death. It was all she had. It was essential to all she was. If she lost Minth, lost their love, she lost herself and all meaning in life. Aware that she could not sit and ponder much longer she got up and got a drink. Then she had to get to her work.

Silmavalien had yet another thing to hide in order to avoid suspicion and discovery: her disbelief in almost everything she had once believed in. How *could* she avoid suspicion and discovery from all these different sides? Talking was dangerous, lest she reveal her disbelief. Not talking was dangerous, lest she arouse suspicion, for why would she not talk? A-a-ah! Who would help her? To whom could she call for deliverance? She and Minth were alone.

S

Silmavalien tried to avoid Varkul and Kriela. She tried to pick fields or portions of fields where she did not except to run into them to work. She spent a lot more time in the company of Noren's household, people who did not know her so well as her own but whom it would seem sensible and natural for her to be around.

Whenever anyone passed near to her little room where Minth was hidden, she would flinch. She tried to cover this by working hard in dense areas where she would be running into branches and twigs anyways.

Half on purpose, half because their fears and anxieties flowed uninhibited across their bond, Minth came to see anyone other than Silmavalien as a deadly and dreadful danger. Whenever anyone passed near where he lay he shrank into his corner and as deep into her clothes as he could, shivering uncontrollably and cowering. Silmavalien felt sorry for him. Once when she was moderately alone on her way to get a drink and short rest she felt Minth's fear run through her. She was sick and tired of things. She felt as helpless as he did. She looked up into the sky and whispered in exasperation, screaming in her mind:

"Is there no one who can help us? Why are we endangered and persecuted as we are? Who are you that you could, and still can, allow the dragons and Dragonriders to suffer this? Do something!"

No answer came from above but only the chatter of a bird.

8

Nurturing

Silmavalien bit into her lunch and then froze. "I was just at the other end and there's a strange stench there," someone said. "It's like nothing that I've ever smelled before."

Terror and fear raced through her and her blood ran with cold fire. Her muscles quivered. She felt suddenly cold and sweat profusely. She knew where it came from and what it was.

Trying to be inconspicuous she left the house with her lunch. She quickly found a tree to hide the lunch in and then grabbed a shovel and pan. She wandered around the edges of the forest before heading straight for her room. Minth knew she was coming, so he should not be startled.

She opened the window and climbed in. Immediately a strong awful stench, not quite like any other she had ever smelled, filled her nostrils. Minth had relieved himself. She hurried in and set about cleaning the place up. She tried to do it quickly but without making too much noise. Meanwhile, she thought to herself, *I really need to do better. If clues like this keep on escaping soon enough people will put two and two together and discover the truth. I* can't *let that happen. Minth is far too weak and helpless for us to run away right now.*

It was not easy to clean Minth's mess up. She left as soon as she had gotten the bulk of it. She dumped the smelly stuff on the outskirts of the woods and refilled the pan, this time with pine needles and dust. She carried it back into her room and put it in the little covered corner where she hid Minth. That way he could relieve himself in dirt next time and it would not be so messy. She gave him a hug and a kiss and cradled his trembling body for a moment. Then she left, thinking to herself that she would find pine needles and sage and mint to cover any stench and fill the little place with a pleasant scent, purifying and protective.

She burned to be with Minth, and yet she had not only to stay away from him but to hide all her uneasiness and desire and every way in which she had changed during the night. She began to feel more and more smothered and suffocated as the day went on. Every time Minth made any appreciable noise she impressed upon him a connection between noise and discovery. She was in constant fear of discovery, and soon he was in constant, though less articulate, fear. She felt bad about her soul-partner's fear but knew of nothing to do about it.

Finally the sun set, but still she kept herself away from Minth. She went to her room, but only to get a cloak to keep herself warm. She felt like all the chatter she engaged in was meaningless and yet she had to find it interesting lest she arouse suspicion and hand out even more clues; she had already let out more clues than she could afford. It was nearly agonizing.

At last people began to go in and get dinner. Silmavalien went in, too, and got dinner for herself, then went outside to eat it under the stars. She took a bag with her in with she hid a few fragments of her dinner. Then she went to the forest's edge and retrieved the squirrel. It had cooked during the day. She also took a few pine needles and sage leaves and went down to the stream for the mint, then headed back.

When she returned everyone was getting ready for bed and she had not been missed. She told her parents she would be going to bed and then went to her room. At last! She could be with Minth now.

She scattered the aromatic leaves around the dark room. Then she sat down on the edge of her mattress and invited Minth to come out now, assuring him it was safe. Immediately he began stirring and the curtain rustled. He gave a small squeak, soft and piteous.

Immediately she impressed upon him the same message. Any noise was a way to invite death upon them both. The poor dragon cowered and shrank back. She again invited him to come to her, assuring him that leaving his little sanctuary – and not making any noise – was now safe. He tried to waddle out to her.

The small, weak dragon struggled to cross the distance between them. The sight smote Silmavalien's heart. She leapt to his side, picked him up, and carried him to the bedside. She let him down on the mattress and poured out the contents of her bag. Then she sat down next to him while he devoured the food as fast as he could.

Silmavalien placed her hand on the young dragon's shoulders. As she watched him she smiled. For some reason she felt comfortable with him. She stroked his neck and put her arm around him. He seemed amazingly fierce engaged in eating, yet he was so weak and helpless. He touched her heart again and again, ugly as he was. She loved him in ways she had never dreamed it was possible to love.

As Minth ate a soft, quite rumble, almost a purr, emanated from his throat. It vibrated through him and Silmavalien felt it in the arm she had around his shoulders. It was so quiet and so endearing. She did not silence him or tell him that 'purring' could easily mean their deaths. She felt so bad imparting such fear to him so much of the time. She was unwilling to now, even though she did perceive it as dangerous.

Silmavalien gazed out her window at the uncounted multitude of unwinking stars, twinkling high above in that chilling autumn night with its hint of biting frost to come. Even in that one tiny patch of the sky were more stars than she could have counted in a thousand years. They looked down on her like otherworldly eyes, full of compassion and understanding. She looked up at them as though through pinprick holes in the dark canvas of night into the endless expanse of heavenly radiance beyond, which is more than mortal flesh can know or endure. Or yet still, they were like bright beacons of hope burning through the dark haze of fear and danger and desperation. There was more to reality than the little world where she lived and the experiences of her life. Did her and Minth's lives have a reason and purpose?

Weariness closed in her as she pondered that question. The events of the previous night and then of the following day had left her exhausted. Silmavalien had no strength with which to wonder what the stars really were or whether the lives of mortal, earthly beings had enduring purpose. She drew Minth close to her, pulled a warm fleece blanket over them both, and was soon fast asleep.

$$S$$

Silmavalien woke early the next morning by the cold light of dawn. Birds chirruped their song all around. Minth stood on the edge of the bed in plain view from the window. His over-large, bulky tail twitched as he

watched the sunrise. He looked weak and vulnerable. Her heart skipped a beat. She reached out and pulled him into the covers with her, ignoring his weak protests. Images and emotions flowed from her mind to his as she warned him that to place himself in a position where he could so easily be seen was more than extremely dangerous. Their position was already more dangerous than either of them could understand. It was tantamount to inviting an unpleasant death upon them both.

Minth cowered under the blankets and she crawled over him to comfort him. She cradled him in her arms and rocked him back and forth, humming softly to him. He rested limply in her arms. His fear and helplessness touched her heart and she yearned to change it, but was completely unable. They were one, not only in their love, but also in their fear and helplessness.

Once Minth had calmed down a little she set him down. Then she squirmed out from under the blankets and surveyed the room. Not one scrap of Minth's meal the previous night had been left. He had eaten even the bones and the organs. She reached her arm under the blanket and scratched his head. Then she peered over the edge of the bed and noticed the disgusting mess on the dirt floor. At least he had gone on the floor, not the bed.

"I'll be right back, Minth," said Silmavalien in little more than a whisper. She got up and climbed out the window. She got the tools she had used the night before and cleaned up Minth's mess.

Then she reminded him to relieve himself in the pan she had left last night. She hugged him and kissed him between the eyes before leaving the room to get the poor little dragon a small breakfast. She sat with him while he gobbled it down and put her arm around him. They just enjoyed the little time they got to have together and each other's companionship.

Too soon, she knew it could not go on much longer. Discovery was just around the corner, and Minth had to eat. Already he weighed noticeably more than he had when he hatched. She picked him up and kissed him. There was loneliness that pierced her heart and fear in those pale, minty eyes that looked up at her as they read what was about to begin that second morning of their life in that world. She picked him up and carried him to the drawers-corner where he hid for the day.

Silmavalien used the same notes she had used the previous morning again that day. As she walked up into the woods, with her bow in her hand, she contemplated her difficulties.

She tried to keep her new fear from reaching Minth for it could do him no good, but she was certain she would not entirely succeed. She knew nothing about caring for a hatchling dragon and there was no one to whom she could go to learn. For all she knew there was some food vital to a dragon's health that she did not know about and Minth was, therefore, missing out on. She did not know if they were exclusively predators, or if they needed to eat plants as well. Minth might be going to die on account of her lack of knowledge.

She decided to pluck portions of as many plant varieties as she could find and offer them to Minth. Samples of each she would offer to him whole. Other samples she would make into tea and then offer to him. Still others she would leach in cold water. Anything he ate she would do her best to find and get him more of. It was not certain to work, but it was far better to work for providing him with the necessities of life than doing nothing at all.

So Silmavalien took leaves, bark, and stems from every different variety of non-poisonous plant she came across. She debated that choice with herself. Minth was a dragon. He was not a human, he was not any kind of creature she knew how to care for. There were things birds could eat and liked that humans couldn't. There were things that humans could eat, like onions, that many other animals did not. In the end, she decided it was better to be safe, at least for the first few weeks of his life, and give him only things that were not poisonous to any species that she knew of. Probably, the egg he had eaten would take of most of his nutritional needs for a little while.

She took great care to make sure she remembered from which variety she took which sample for many plants had parts which looked very much like those of other plants. She also gathered flower parts or the seeds or fruit of a plant. For all she knew dragons hatched at a particular time of year so that they could get a particular nutrient only available during that time of season. As she went she sent Minth a hopeful and encouraging message along with a cautionary reminder to stay still and quiet and out of sight.

9

Before Noren's Return

Silmavalien gave Minth his dinner and pulled him under the covers with her. He had hardly begun his meal before she was fast asleep.

That night she slept long and deep. She was wakened in the morning by warm, bright sunlight shining on her body and her eyelids and by the sound of voices. Minth was cowering, his poor little body shaking with fear. He had pressed himself as close up against her, and even under her, as he could. Silmavalien almost panicked. She barely held onto her sanity with Minth's fear in her veins.

Silmavalien hoped she would neither scream nor freeze with fear. She sat up when someone knocked against the door and next moment the door handle started to turn. Minth fainted. Springing out of bed, she tossed the blankets so that they would fall in a jumble on top of him, careful to make sure they hid every part of him.

Next moment she crossed the distance between her bed and the shelves in a single step. Trying to force her voice to remain calm she said, "Wait a second, please. I just got up and I'm getting dressed."

"Okay. No big deal." It was the voice of Lenalorien, Noren's sister.

When she was dressed Silmavalien carefully and quickly carried the still unconscious Minth to his place in the corner under her shelves. She kissed him, then walked to the door and opened it. "Let's have breakfast."

Outside both Lenalorien and Krielasoriel were waiting. Silmavalien tried not to reveal her dismay at seeing Kriela too. She managed a bright, "Hello, both of you. How are you today?"

"Fine," replied both young women. "How are you, Silmavalien?"

"Well," replied Silmavalien, "I slept in today. Probably comes of having gotten up so early these past few mornings to hunt rabbits. Other than that, no, I couldn't be better."

"Good," said Kriela. "Lenalorien tells me that you have been spending most of your time working and what you haven't spent working you've spent with her household."

"That's right," said Silmavalien, "and not for scorn of you, my own family. You see, I've wanted to help cover the cost of my bride gifts and also be a good wife to Noren, really accepting his family as my own." It was plausible, and it would have been true had she not bonded to a dragon, thus becoming a virtual outcast and being so changed, inside and out. In fact, she still *wanted* to do so. She still wanted to marry Noren. She knew she could not, but she hoped against all probability that they would be able to, someday. After all, he too kept a dragon egg. Hopefully and probably it would hatch sometime.

A little later, Silmavalien was sitting outside on the grass having breakfast with Lenalorien. Minth recovered enough to take stock of his surroundings, then, when he realized she was not with him and he was alone, immediately fainted again. *Oh, poor baby.*

"What's up?" asked Lenalorien. Evidently it had happened too quickly and Silmavalien had not managed to conceal it, to keep it from finding expression on her face.

"Oh, nothing," she said and then added, at the persistence in Lenalorien's eyes, "I ... I was just thinking how awful it would be ... if ... if Noren were injured in the big Hunt."

"He won't be," Lenalorien assured her, "but I know how you're feeling. My brother is so strong, you needn't fear. He could wrestle a bear or run up a tree and shoot down a wolf pack, and he has others to guard him. Take heart, Silmavalien. He *will* be fine."

She managed a smile. "I'm glad ... thanks, Lenalorien."

Lenalorien tittered a little. "Of course. It is truth and my pleasure, Silmavalien."

After breakfast, Silmavalien tossed a little bread and some cheese through the window. Unfortunately, she had no meat to offer Minth that morning. Then she took a drink and got to work. During the day on various occasions she got to offer Minth samples of different foods. One time she gave him a peach and on another a plum. She tossed him a full cob of corn. Another time she showered in on him a dish of beans. She also gave him some nuts. She wondered if dragons could eat these things raw, since after all dragons are dragons not humans, but then she realized that in all the stories she knew of them they breathed fire, and they also bonded to humans. They might need their parents or their riders to cook their food for them.

Or they might need nutrients that were destroyed by cooking. She could only offer Minth samples of both and see which he preferred.

That evening Silmavalien had to figure out a way to do a lot of clean-up in her room without being noticed. She thought about how she could possibly hide and protect Minth until he was old enough and strong enough to flee. He was definitely gaining weight and his belly was getting round and plump but he could only barely waddle about. He would eat ferociously for the first couple of minutes and then nibble away at the rest of his meal, yet he ate every scrap she gave him.

For his dinner, Silmavalien was able to get Minth a few strips of meat. Then the two of them curled up together and went to sleep. She hoped she would be able to wake up early and hunt well. She was certain that Minth, being a dragon, needed to eat a fair amount of meat. She hoped to get at least two kills for him.

According to her intentions, Silmavalien woke by the cold light of an early dawn. She again used the same notes. After getting Minth a small block of cheese, she took her bow, quiver, and knife and left for the woods.

That morning Silmavalien shot two pigeons and a rabbit as well as gathering more of the plants Minth had liked. While she was out the autumn morning fog overhead thickened rather than dissipating. Soon it began to rain.

Since the rain was still light, Silmavalien kindled a small fire under a large, sunken boulder. She sat next to it while she did the cold and disgusting job of skinning the rabbit and plucking the pigeons' feathers. She buried the pigeons in the coals to cook and gutted the rabbit. She did not want the people of Treas to know she could get such prey as pigeons or as much as she could, but she also did not want anyone to think she had not really been hunting or was keeping her prey for the gods-know-what, so she brought them the rabbit and kept the pigeons to feed to her little dragon.

As she entered the village many of her closer friends came out and gathered around her. "Silmavalien," they said, "it's raining. Have you found any traces of Noren in the woods? How was it, hunting in the rain?"

Silmavalien did not know why hunting in the rain was such a big deal. She replied, truthfully enough, "I'd already got my rabbit and was on the way home before it started raining hard enough for me to really notice. Why?"

"Just, you've never been out hunting when Vorli – to receive such honor as mortals can give for all ages – has her hand on the weather and her countenance mirrored in the skies."

To Noren, and now to Silmavalien, that was just a fancy way of saying "while it is raining." She smiled. "It was fine. Let's work on the harvest. This rain probably won't, but it's a sign that it may hail soon. We want all the harvest in before that happens."

"Yes, we do." A woman came forward and took the rabbit from Silmavalien. "I'll go and cook this," she said.

"Well, can I come with you and get some breakfast before helping with the harvest?" asked Silmavalien. "I went out hunting without a bite."

"Of course, girl," said the woman. "C'mon. I'll serve you some."

As the day wore on the light showers became a heavy rain. Silmavalien became cold, tired, hungry, and drenched. Minth's discomfort only served to further deplete her strength. She was both relieved and afraid when evening fell. Then she remembered. The light was failing fast and she left without telling anyone anything. She went to the edge of the woods to retrieve the birds and herbs for Minth.

Unfortunately the birds were only half-cooked, but they would have to do. Minth was very hungry. Besides, he was a dragon and dragons could probably eat raw meat without any problem at all. Though once again, she thought about the fact the adults could breathe fire.

By the time she returned, soaking wet, it was almost totally dark. She had a good excuse to go to her room and give Minth his dinner: she needed to change into dry clothes and hang her wet ones up to dry. Then she kissed Minth and told him goodbye before leaving her room and going to get her own dinner.

Silmavalien ate with everyone else in the common dinning room. She told everyone it had been a long day and she was too tired to stay awake, so she would go to bed, even though everyone else was too excited about the rain ushering in the new year.

Because she had gone to sleep so early the previous night, Silmavalien was able to wake very early that morning. It was still very cold. She hid Minth in the corner again and wrapped him in her clothes. Then she changed back into her wet clothes and cleaned up Minth's messes. When she had done that, she got her bow, quiver, and knife and went out to hunt for Minth, this time keeping it a secret from everyone but the dragon.

The cold wetness, and the darkness, made it her most unpleasant hunting experience so far. Silmavalien also wanted to make sure no one discovered her absence, which meant she had to get back before the others – who were probably sleeping after staying up so last night – woke. She gathered some blackberries but only managed to shoot one pigeon. As soon as she got the bird she headed straight for the village, plucking the feathers along the way. It was not very much, but it would have to do, since it was better to play it safe.

Silmavalien did get back in time. It was still before people usually woke up, so the likelihood that anyone was awake and would notice she had been out was very unlikely. She went back to her room and slept with Minth a little longer. She was awakened by people's voices. She told Minth good day and left him the uncooked pigeon. She had to show something for having gone to bed so early so she helped out with breakfast, which was a big affair because of the rain.

Other than that, and the dancing and singing that everyone did in the rain to thank Vorli, this day was fairly like the last. The rain was cold and quickly re-drenched everyone's hair and clothes. Silmavalien was always glancing up to the woods, trying to find Noren. This was something like the fourth day since he had left for the Hunt. For some reason, or reasons, she only partially understood, her desire for his return was strong and intense. At one point Lenalorien noticed this and reassured her that he would return that evening. The rain would probably give them some trouble with their ceremonies but, other than that, all was quite well.

Later, her thoughts turned from Noren back to Minth. She was always afraid when people passed near where he lay. She felt more uneasy away from him than with him though she knew she had no power to protect him for long, only to ensure her own death with him if that feared, but probable, event were to occur. With every day that passed her fear that it would occur, her fear of it, and her hope that they would be spared that doom, increased.

She constantly wondered who and what had created the universe and why. Was the world she lived in, and maybe the stars, the accidental and perhaps temporary effects of some other purpose, or did whoever created the world have some purpose in mind for her world and those who lived in it?

The question troubled her, and she wondered if Noren also was plagued by the same doubts.

10

Last Night Together

Lenalorien had spoken truly. Noren returned that evening. He was tired-and wet-looking and had over his shoulder the carcass of a buck which he held by the antlers. His hair was shaved off and wet ashes coated the top of his head like a cap. Silmavalien ran to greet him. The rest of the villagers followed behind her.

Noren held out his arms to Silmavalien and the engaged couple hugged and kissed. "Nice to see you again," she whispered.

"And it shall be nice to be back," he replied. "It is certainly nice to see you again and to know there is nothing now between us and marriage in a few weeks. Would you like to know my true name?"

They both knew what name he was talking about: his secret, ritual, 'true' name as a man. He did not believe it held any significance and now neither did she. "Yes, that would be nice. Thank you," she said, despite that fact.

"Very well," he replied. "'Grace-and-Strength-of-the-Buck. His grace is in his feet and his strength is in his antlers.'"

"You like it," said Silmavalien. "I do, too. It is grand and noble."

𝓢

Silmavalien and Noren spent a fair amount of time together. She treasured it, for she knew these might be the last weeks they would ever have together. She waited for a subtle difference in him, perhaps one that mirrored the change she knew existed in her, to indicate that his dragon had hatched and he was also a Dragonrider. Then she would talk to him about it and tell him about Minth. They could run away together. That would be wonderful.

She continued her habit of hunting in the morning. She kept what excess kills and edibles she could obtain in a special place where Minth could not get to and devour them. She knew they would want to have as much as they could while Minth grew large enough and strong enough to hunt for himself and, hopefully, for her too. They would need it especially at the beginning. She had no idea how they would find a place large enough and temperate enough for them to survive the winter and far enough away from people to be safe.

People in Silrah were afraid of the high mountains. Supposedly all kinds of evil and fantastic creatures lived in their depths and bad luck fell on anyone who wandered far and wide in them. Many who did so did not return, or so the stories said. Silmavalien knew it was a risk she would have to take. There was no other direction to go where there would not be people all around to hunt and kill her as a witch. Even if there was, she did not know how to survive anywhere about the woods. Her only hunting experiences were here and she only knew about the plants here. The village of Treas was in the foothills, at the edge of where it was still believed to be safe, in the Greater Aravin Mountains.

She spent every bit of time she thought was safe with Minth. Even so, she got to spend far less time with him than she liked. Days passed, but he did not seem to get any stronger. He certainly grew and his belly was round and plump. A few days after Noren's return she thought that he weighed almost, if not quite, twice what he had at hatching. In about a week he had doubled in size.

She fed him everything she could get or believed she could spare from the 'savings' stash she kept so that they would not starve when they fled. Even so, he was always hungry. Silmavalien felt sorry for the poor dragon. She wondered how long it took for dragons to grow up and how much grown dragons needed to sleep. He spent more than three quarters of the time sleeping. Almost all the time he was not sleeping he was eating. Human babies were like that, too, but she did not know how they would travel and flee if he had to sleep so much.

When he was doing neither it was almost always because he had been abruptly wakened by the presence of other humans. Then, he would shiver and cower with fear. When the danger of discovery seemed particularly great he would faint. He also fainted if he expected her to be physically beside him, or at least near, and she was far away.

Silmavalien wondered if he remained so weak because there was something crucial in his diet he was missing or if it was normal and natural. Were dragons supposed to be like kid goats, who grew up quickly, or like human infants, who were helpless for months and years?

As the weeks passed Silmavalien grew more and more uncomfortable. Every day that passed brought the day she and Noren were supposed to be married closer. She did not see how she could keep Minth a secret through the marriage ceremony and in marriage. Every day brought the awful day when they would have to flee for their lives one day closer. Minth did not seem to be growing stronger, though perhaps he was, only at a snail's pace. Bit by bit, day by day, his waddle grew a little steadier.

When Minth was about two weeks old he had grown considerably, and Silmavalien thought he weighed a full twice as much as he had at hatchling. He was still wobbly, quite slow, and sometimes he fell down when he walked. She hoped he would grow more slowly and become steadier and faster. Soon he would be too large and heavy for her to carry, yet he was still too clumsy and weak for him to walk or fly on his own. She decided that if he kept growing at such a rate she would flee with him within three weeks.

At about the same time, she noticed sores she could not explain on Minth's skin. Rashes of reddish, flaky skin developed. In some places his skin became dry and split and cracked. Some of these cracks bled. In other places wide patches of skin flaked and then oozed. She had started to notice such drying and flaking a few days after he hatched, and dismissed as insubstantial. She had far too much else to take care of to waste time worrying about little skin conditions.

Then, one night, he was in such an awful shape she felt it could be ignored no longer. He was covered in the sores, which cracked, bled, or oozed whenever he moved. The blood loss was not substantial, but he was in constant discomfort. She shared in the discomfort and simply could not bear it any longer. He was only a hatchling. It was unbearably cruel that he should have to suffer such loneliness, such danger, such fear, and, on top of all that, this new nuisance and discomfort. She felt sorry for him and would do everything in her power to stop it.

She hated the cause of all this pain, whatever or whoever it might be.

That night, it took Silmavalien what felt like hours to find sleep. She lay, tossing and turning, considering every possible cause of Minth's skin ailment and every possible cure. She ruled out causes, made lists of possible cures, and considered which were feasible. Eventually she fell asleep, exhausted by the days and her partner's own weakness and weariness. She forced herself to get up early the following morning and get a jar of oil. She meant to rub it into Minth's skin, especially the dry, flaky, cracking patches. Perhaps it would help coat his skin and keep it moist, helping it to stay fresh and pliable. If that did not result in skin improvement in a few days she would have to find some way to wash him and see if that helped.

Naturally, applying the salve required her to touch the tender sores. Throughout the process Minth let out occasional low, soft moans. He tried not to and kept what noises he did make as quiet as possible. Nonetheless, it was more than she would have liked. She hoped everyone else was still fast asleep.

After kissing him goodbye she took her bow, quiver, and knife and went out again. She wondered how she would get an appropriate salve for Minth's skin out in the woods by herself, always assuming the oil worked.

During the weeks that followed Minth did not only grow in size. His proportions began to change, to grow more fitting, natural, and beautiful. His entire body was developing. He still looked awkward and a little ugly, but he was much better. His tail was a little less bulky. His neck grew longer and a little thicker. She thought the size of his head did not change as much. His triangular wings, one side of which grew out from his side from shoulder to last rib, were somewhat larger comparatively and more shapely. His legs were somewhat less stubby, his feet were taloned like a bird's, and a row of talons spread themselves out along the back edge of his wings. A small ridge, almost like a chicken's comb, ran up his forehead. Like his fangs and talons, this was a semi-transparent ivory-like substance. His ears, which were on the side of his head, were covered and protected by something of the same basic structure as his wings but curved in on itself like a horse or wolf's ear, though a little flatter, wider, and longer.

Noren seemed to have forgotten about his dragon egg, which doubtless he did not know to be a dragon egg. Silmavalien suspected this forgetting of the dragon egg was not because it had hatched and he did not want to give the fact away but because he had too much else to do to care about it. But that day, he invited her to his room so he could show her what he had and talk to her a little. She saw the dragon egg – or 'white oval' – he kept was still whole and lay on his floor in one corner. She wondered when the dragon within would hatch and to whom he or she would bond. She wondered how that was determined. Was the new Dragonrider whoever first touched the dragon or whomever the dragon chose or was it determined by still some other factor?

The next morning, Silmavalien noticed that Minth's skin was starting to look better. His sores were barely less sensitive to the touch. The cracks and splits in his skin were reopening to ooze and bleed less. No new rashes or flaky, cracking patches had appeared and patches where it had just begun were now smooth, soft, moist, and pliable. She worried about how she would get enough meat grease to successfully treat his skin condition, alone and out in the woods.

She started trying to separate the fatty portions of her kills and cook them in such a way as to get the grease out of them. Meanwhile, she rubbed small quantities of oil into Minth's skin every other night to keep it in good shape.

As Minth grew, so did the messes he inevitably made. Soon, she spent all of her 'secret' time – except for hunting and sleeping – cleaning up his messes and taking care of his skin.

Silmavalien suspected she would want to sew things sometimes once she was out and, except for Minth, alone. She managed to obtain some spare clothes and a box containing a couple sewing needles and several yards of thread.

Among her greatest difficulties in keeping the little dragon hidden were her brother and his wife. They lived in the same household as she did because Varkul was her brother – and, of course, Silmavalien was yet unmarried. Varkul backed everything his wife did, and Silmavalien secretly believed that Krielasoriel was off in her mind. Kriela still wanted to start a new order in the honor of Queen Valiena, and she constantly badgered Silmavalien about what she was going to do with her white oval and when *would* she take it to be shown to an oracle of one of the gods? She finally came to understand that Kriela believed that she herself was a, *the,* priestess of Queen Valiena. She wanted Silmavalien to present the white oval to her and make a 'sacrifice' to her goddess-queen. Not only did she not want to do so, she could not. Finally, she went to Noren and asked him to tell Kriela to let her think about it in peace. He did so happily, but that prompted Kriela to denounce Silmavalien as a traitor to the new order to which she had pledged herself.

Her little sister, Ralirilien, was less of a nuisance. In some ways, Silmavalien was most concerned about her because there was always the possibility that she would breach her manners and look into on her older sister's room, but it did not seem likely. Ralirilien spent most of her time outside playing or learning or working with the other children of about her age. While she was friendly to Silmavalien and often excited to see her and share a bit of news with her, watching her soon assured Silmavalien that Ralirilien was like that to many others, and was not particularly concerned with her. Certainly, Rali did not seem to notice any change in her or care about it.

S

At last, the evening before the marriage ceremony, Noren and Silmavalien sat together under the moon. She was so uncomfortable that she could not relax, and she knew Noren felt the tension in her, but he thought it was because she was nervous about tomorrow. She did not give him any reason to suspect otherwise, but she knew that it was because she was disappointed that the dragon egg he kept had not hatched and so they could not run away together. That, and she was anxious about the flight she was to attempt last night and what it would come to, whether she would be captured and burned alive, or whether she would starve in the mountains – or against all odds, survive.

Noren put his arm around her, and she leaned into him. "My lady," he said, "I do not know what to say about this. At last, the longed-for-moment is near."

"Yes," said Silmavalien. "I do not know what to say, either."

"This is why we live," he said, kissing her on the forehead. "It is no wonder no one can find any words with which to adequately express it."

"Perhaps," she said, leaning against his breast. She wanted to go to him for comfort but was afraid to do so. Always she had to comfort and protect Minth. To whom could she go, herself? She was in love with Noren, yet she had to flee from him, too. If he knew about Minth he might too easily turn against her or be pressured into doing so. *A-a-a-ah!* She could not risk that.

"I love you, Silmavalien," said Noren, "O Sweetness of the Wild Rose."

Silmavalien looked up at him with tears in her eyes, That would be the secret 'true' name she would take as a woman and his wife. She felt torn in two. Torn between her love for Minth, the sleeping dragon to whom she was irrevocably bonded, and the man beside her, with whom she had fallen in love. "I love you, too," she whispered. She wanted to say "I'm sorry," but felt she could not. It would give away what she still needed to remain a secret for a little while longer. It was then that she resolved to send him a note that very night, that he would someday find, to reassure him of her love and desire to meet again and marry him then, and to explain something of her flight.

Noren squeezed her lightly. "Silmavalien, you will be safe. I will let no one and nothing hurt or harm you, ever."

She leaned into him, resting her head on his shoulder. If only she could really believe that. Almost, she wanted to. How good it would be to unburden herself. Not to fear him. To have a partner in him.

But she could not risk what might happen. To be rejected by him. For Minth to burn.

11

Last Farewells

Moonlight poured in through Silmavalien's window and flooded her room, making it light enough to move freely. She had waited, pinching herself to keep awake in the silence of the night, until the hour when everyone would be asleep and her movement would go unnoticed. Minth lay beside her on the bed. As usual, he had fallen asleep shortly after eating.

Silmavalien walked to her shelves and threw back the curtain. She pulled it down and carefully folded it up. Then she stuffed it into her large traveling bag. She would need it as a curtain no longer. But she would certainly want it as a blanket, out in the mountains alone with Minth during the winter. She hoped he would be rather bigger by then.

Then, she took all her stones and sticks and other treasures, which she could not carry and for which she would have no use, and lowered them out the window. Many of the harder, heavier objects made quite a thump, and sometimes a clack, when they landed and bounded, and she hoped no one would notice. Then she climbed out the window and carried them, the heavy objects one at a time, into the woods. In less than an hour that part was over and done.

Then she went out and got a scrap of paper and a pen. She was about to write the note she had conceived hours ago and the last words she would write in years, perhaps in her entire life. This is what she wrote:

Dear Noren, I love you. I long to be with you. Were that this moonlit night were indeed the eve of our marriage. May we one day be married and live our lives and die as one. This is indeed my prayer.

However, on this night I am forced to admit that cannot yet be. There is something I must accomplish and hastily. I will tell you one last hint: Both white ovals hold the secret of my mission. May it be yours as well. Keep your white oval and guard it carefully.

Farewell, love of my heart. May yours be a happy life of fulfillment
~Silmavalien.

Upon writing the note Silmavalien left her family's house and stole carefully to Noren's window. The moonlight shone, bright and clear. Only one night in her previous life could be compared to this one, in danger, in potential, in feeling. That night was the night Minth had hatched for her and they had bonded as rider and dragon. This was the night she left behind all rags of her previous life, all she had ever known, and faced a new danger and a new life as a Dragonrider. She did not yet know what that would be, only that she had to go forward.

Tears came to her eyes as she stood there, still and silent in the moonlight. She shivered with the autumn cold and also with emotion, with love and fear, with loneliness, with she knew not what. The hand in which she held the note to Noren trembled and the moonlight glancing across the quivering surface of the white paper with stark black lines had much the effect of clear water, rippling over sand, under the sun. Only the latter was all of day, but the former was about the night.

Silmavalien looked up at the cold, unwinking stars overhead and wondered if anyone else in all of Aneri and the vast heavens above even knew about her and Minth or really cared at all. It was a lonely existence. Then, stirred out of her deadly musings by a deep longing to be truly known, understood, and loved, she walked right to Noren's window and slipped her note through it.

The piece of paper lightly fluttered to the floor and landed. As she watched it, with longing in her heart, Silmavalien felt that its fluttering fall was like weak, fragile wings trying desperately but vainly to halt their descent and rise to something greater. Feeling sick at heart, with even Minth asleep and unable to offer any rag of consolation, she turned away.

First, before she went too far, Silmavalien glanced over her shoulder and through Noren's window. For a moment her eyes alighted on her note lying on the floor next to his bed of straw like a puddle of ink-streaked moonsilver, shimmering yet shadowy, eye-catching yet hard to really see. She desperately hoped, as if such hope could really act of itself, that he would find and read the note one day, soon enough but not before she was well away and safe.

Once again, Silmavalien turned and stole quietly back into her own family's house. The next minutes were desperate and fearful. Her heart pounded almost painfully. The alertness of her ears to the slight sound that might give her away or give her a hint of what she might be able to do to avoid being given away was uncomfortable in itself.

She grabbed a large knapsack and – always careful to be

absolutely quiet – packed it with as much as would not spoil and would fit. She paused often to listen but heard nothing but the frantic pounding of her heart. She found herself praying to gods whose existence she did not believe and who, if they did exist, would surely be her enemies, for she had scorned them and, worse, become a Dragonrider.

Once she caught herself in the act of such a prayer and asked herself, *Am I going crazy? Is all this a mere figment of my imagination or is that constant, dreadful fear and the conflicts of my heart and love driving me insane? What am I? What am I supposed to do? Oh, someone, help me! I am alone, lost, and utterly confused. Please!*

Soon she began to imagine she was hearing things. She still had some measure of sense left, but this further increased her concern that she was losing touch with reality. Her muscles began to spasm and, despite the cold of the night, she sweat violently. She feared that she would suddenly lose, at least for the moment, all rationality and self-control and just panic and bolt, messing the whole thing up and losing everything she cared about.

She prayed to the unknown that she would not.

Finally, she finished packing the sack. She gave silent thanks that she had not panicked and fled like a crazy lunatic. She crept back through the passage between the sleeping rooms and entered her own. There she laid down the precious provisions sack and suddenly remembered they would need water, too. Her heart pounded with fear more than ever. She stole back the way she came and grabbed a water skin. She could always fill it in a stream and boil it so it would be safe to drink, so she did not waste any time filling it.

Silmavalien sat down on her straw mattress to relax for a few minutes. Her heart was racing frantically and she feared that, if she tried to attempt any more right, that her fear would result in idiocy or clumsiness. She took long, deep breaths in an attempt to calm herself. It did not seem to be working.

For one thing, she was very tired. If she relaxed too much she might fall asleep and the whole thing would be ruined and Minth inevitably discovered. She could not bear that. Never in a thousand lives. She had to stay awake, and since she was very tired that meant she had to remain tense. She had to keep her sense though, and that meant she could not be too afraid. So, how to reconcile the two? How to succeed?

Finally, she decided she had to keep on moving, scared out of her senses or not. Otherwise, she would fall asleep, and that was at least as bad. She got to her feet, yawned and stretched, then fell back to the ground to avoid fainting or falling. When the giddiness passed she rose to her feet again and continued her preparation.

She stole cautiously through the house, her heart pounding like a drum in her bosom, but somehow calmer than she had been. Perhaps the decision to go on, fear or no fear, resulted in a sort of calm acceptance. She went to the room where the family treasury was kept and carefully searched for and found her bride gifts. She took them out and inspected them in the moonlight. A pile of silver coins glinted beautifully by the light of star and moon. Under this treasure was yards and yards of colored yarn, two knitting needles, and a crochet hook. The yarn was wrapped into balls stuffed into clay pottery. Lying on the side were several spoons and forks. It would certainly come in handy sooner or later.

Silmavalien did not want to risk going back through the house and between the rooms of sleeping relatives another time. Instead she walked around and climbed through her window, her bride gifts tucked under her arm.

When she climbed back in through the window of her own room, Minth woke up enough to yawn and gaze at her with those dimly glowing blue-mint eyes. She smiled. He was so adorably cute. She just wanted to love him and hug him close. He did not stay awake for long, though. A few thoughts of recognition and love and drowsy excitement passed between them while she worked. Then, the little dragon dozed off.

She smiled and set to work on the last of her preparations. She wrapped the bride gifts up in her sleepwear. Then she stuffed it in the bottom of her carry bag. She also wrapped up her own food reserves, made of mostly of her kills but also consisting partially of berries and nutritional herbs she had gathered or otherwise saved. She carefully folded up each item in her wardrobe so they would all fit in her bag and be possible to carry. She was sure she was going to need them in the winter to keep herself and Minth warm. She had only been two years old and did not remember the last time it had snowed in the village eleven years ago, but according to the older adults that was a higher unusual weather pattern, and she had heard plenty of stories about snow.

The fluffy, very cold, white power which turned into water when it got warm fell many times a year deeper in the mountains. Even in the warm recent years, the hunters reported it, and the snowline could often be seen on the hills rising above Treas.

Up there it would blanket the earth in a coat that was feet, or even yards, thick. She had no idea how she and Minth would survive that if he was not yet old enough and large enough to breathe fire or fly away with her on his back. She was not sure how she would be able to ride a dragon bareback, either. Being rocked by the winds so high in the sky would be terrifying. She thought it might cause her to faint and fall off. Still, she need not worry about that, yet. She had enough to do and worry about just making sure they survived the next hours, days, and weeks. Otherwise, there would never be any need to worry about it at all.

Silmavalien packed her little candle, which she would have to use sparingly, and other likely-to-be-needed accessories. Finally she folded up her blankets and put them in, too. Lastly, she got herself ready. She put her own pair of warm pants and shirt on under her robe, then slipped into two cloaks and pulled both hoods over her head. Finally, she belted on her hunter knife and slung her quiver over everything. Almost ready!

She slipped her feet into her warm skin-and-fur boots and packed her sandals in the little remaining space in the pack. Then she pulled the food sack over both shoulders much like a backpack. Finally she dragged her own bag over and helped Minth crawl into its warm, cozy, soft and comfortable enclosure.

With all of that accomplished, Silmavalien paused for a moment to breathe a sigh of relief and take a last look around her room before the last or first – depending on which way one looked at it – step of the daring adventure. There was nearly nothing left in the room to tell of her, her personality, interests, age, accomplishments, her life.

"Now, for it," Silmavalien whispered, taking a step forward. Minth stirred in his bag and peeked his head out at her, watching and learning. From now on, he would be her only companion and friend. The best one in the entire world and worth all the cost. So believed the infant dragon's young Silmavalien.

12
Through a Black Night

Silmavalien struggled to get the heavy bag into which she had helped Minth over her shoulder and stand. She hoped the little dragon would not mind being carried this way.

He was quite awake now and both excited and eager. She was not excited. She was tired and did not at all feel like doing what she had to. She knew that it was with an effort that Minth kept himself from blurting noises to express his excitement after life's silence and fear. He was still as weak as ever but he was very excited and his joyful excitement gave her the energy and will to carry on.

She struggled to get her leg over the window sill without tearing her over-robe, with everything she was carrying. She reached up and grabbed the top of the sill to help ease herself through. Her arms burned with the effort and her fingers rubbed. She thought she might have gotten a splinter or two. She managed to get both legs over and fell through, landing on her hands and knees. She was glad she had packed so much soft stuff, like blankets and clothes, around Minth to help cushion and protect him against any impact. She was also proud of him when he did not squeak.

She felt his rush of delight at her pride.

Silmavalien was still afraid of discovery and she was sure her fall had not been noiseless. She hurried away into the night, as quickly as she thought she could sustain with the burden of carrying Minth and their food. Guided by the stars and moon she hastened northwest towards the higher ground and conifer woods. Soon the black shapes of the tall, ancient trees rose up in front of her, cutting off the light of the stars. The bright full moon, still rather high in the sky, cast its light on them for a while longer and it was still easy for her to see the ground under her feet. She walked quickly, despite the difficulty, while she could. Soon the trees would block out nearly all the light and she would have to walk carefully, and dangerously.

It seemed longer than ever to the forest's edge. Far too long before they reached it the towering trees cut off the light of the beginning-to-descend moon. Silmavalien had to walk gingerly, and several times her nerve almost failed her. She was afraid of snakes, even though she reasoned she should not be as it was rare for one to be out this time of night at this time of year, but then again it was so dark she might accidentally slip into a den.

And she was so tired. Even walking gingerly she tripped a couple of times and fell once. The load she carried did not help.

Minth remained quiet, but Silmavalien sensed his growing desire to express his exuberance. She did not believe it was safe yet; the village was still within easy earshot. Added to that, she would not want to attract any wolves, especially since it was dark and so she would be unable to see or to defend them.

Now and then Minth peaked his head out of the bag, and when he did so he shared his eyesight with Silmavalien. It was far superior to her own, though not satisfactory. By the light of a few stars or his own eyes he could see what she could by a crescent moon. It was different from her own eyesight and she found it confusing.

The trees closed in all around her, cutting off all light except for the occasional star peeking through the canopy or a gap in the trunks around them. Silmavalien crept forward in nearly total darkness, occasionally turned to gray twilight when Minth poked his head out. At first this light was confusing and she tripped and fell more often by it than in the total blackness, despite their previous familiarity with each other's senses. But she quickly learned to understand Minth's eyesight as well as her own and moved forward confidently when he chose to grace her with it.

Throughout the journey Silmavalien grew ever more grateful that Minth was well-cushioned in his carry-bag. Neither of them was cold. She was wearing a lot of clothes and he was wrapped in layer after layer of cloth.

She tripped often, over tree roots, or stones, or mere dimples in the ground, even her own feet. More often than not, she fell. During these falls she gained many bruises and scrapes; Minth would have gotten even more bunged up if not for his protection. As it is, he got only one minor scrape on his head one time when he had poked his head out, and she had fallen before she grew accustomed to her eyesight.

Often, too, she walked straight into trees. She snagged her clothes on branches. Then she had to stop and carefully de-snag herself. She did not want to tear her precious clothes within a mere hour or so of climbing out the window with Minth. Soon she learned to use her hands and the feel of the ground not to run straight into trees very often, but she still got caught on branches. She took great pains to make sure she did not end up trying to walk straight through bramble or branches since this would tear her clothes and carry-sacks, as well as her skin.

She knew she tripped so much not just because it was dark, but because she was tired and burdened. Often she stumbled forward, yawning, while she fought to turn uphill, towards where she wanted to go, instead of downhill, towards what she was fleeing from. Often she suspected that her vision would be fragmentary and gray had there been any light to see by, let alone daylight.

She was continually assaulted by a dread and fear of strange, nightmare creatures and demons stalking her through the darkness, making her want to panic and flee back where she had come. At times, the one thing that kept her from doing this was that she did not know the way; she was totally lost. If she just tried to flee down she could easily run off a cliff or fall in a pit – the perfect place to be caught by such a creature.

She feared that she was walking around in circles, though she knew this was not the case since she was almost always going at least a little uphill.

Sometimes she walked through glades and glens where she could see the black spires of pine trees rising in a circle around her, outlined against a sky shining with a thousand thousand glittering stars. Then the moon would shine down on them, giving them some longed-for light by which to see. Silmavalien would sit down and let little Minth out to relieve himself. While he did so, she would look around for any berries to eat. Once she found some late blackberries, enough for a few mouthfuls. The glades made her want to sleep, they were so beautiful and peaceful, and so much nicer than the darkness where she stumbled so much.

As the night wore on and the moon sank down she lent her light to these glades less, though the stars continued to shine down clearly, and Silmavalien found the glades less pleasant. She wanted so desperately to stop and rest, and even much of Minth's excitement had worn out as he grew tired and sleepy. But she was still much, much too close to the village.

It became more and more difficult to stay awake in the dreary all-the-same blackness of the night-time conifer woods. Minth and their provisions seemed ever heavier, and she had to pause and rest against a tree to recover more and more often. Always she had to fight to get moving again.

Then she came to a steep slope, or at least it felt very steep. She was not sure she could tell anymore, her mind foggy with exhaustion and her body burdened. But she knew it was not as steep as it felt. She was forced to crawl forward on hands and knees, but under other circumstances she knew she could have walked up it comfortably.

The way became steeper still; she did not know how quickly. By now, except when Minth poked his head out and offered his light, there was no way to tell time. Everything took an eternity. Everything was blackness. Everything was just the action. She did not think anymore; just went up and up, tired, burdened, and through endless blackness.

The moon was low in the west, down behind the trees and ridges of the mountain. She could see gray shapes, sometimes deceiving in both shape and distance, about a foot, sometimes three feet, in front of her face. She would reach out and clutch tree roots or wrap her arms around trunks and pull herself up. She would bring her knee up under her, wedge her foot against a tree or a little bump in the ground, and push herself forward. It seemed to take forever to get to the ridge top.

Finally, she simply had to rest. She was afraid she might have to let go and slide all the way to the bottom and be forced to go around. At best, she might be able to curl around a tree in her way. Just then, she found a flat, soft bed of pine needles. Exhausted, she dropped down, sprawled out, and panted.

Silmavalien lay there for a while. Eventually, Minth woke up and poked his head out. When he saw that it was not so steep he crawled out of the bag and began to waddle around and explore. The sight of him revived her a little. She sat up and held her arms out. He came to her and cuddled in her arms. She picked him up and went on, walking along the ridge line.

She walked for a long time, as exhaustion wove a dreamy mist around her. Eventually, she sat down and helped Minth back into the bag, then rose again. A rosy flush crept into the eastern sky, heralding the approach of dawn. They began to feel more than a little cold now, as it was the coldest hour of the day, the dark before the dawn, and they were no longer working hard enough to keep themselves warm; they no longer could. The earth or grass under her feet was soaked and the stars began to be obscured.

When she woke out of the dreamy mist, she found herself walking up a valley rather than a ridge. She could hear a stream running close beside her. Minth was awakened for a moment by the sound of running water. He made an ugly, discordant chirp of excitement before dozing off again. Though the moon shed no light on them Silmavalien could barely see variations in the greyness around her. The rock walls squeezed her nearer to the stream. She was forced to cross it. The whole night felt surreal, hardly real. She took off her boots so they would not be soaked, rolled up her pants, and carried the hem of her robe. She plunged first one foot in and then the other. It was very cold and numbed her feet, but it was neither too deep nor too swift for her to cross safely. She let her clothes down and put her boots back on.

Then she followed the stream up the mountain on the other side. Little by little, the light increased.

13
Unacceptable Vanishing

"Noren!"

The voice was his father's, and it came with a knock on the door.

Noren had woken early that morning to prepare himself mentally, emotionally, and bodily for the marriage ceremony. All morning, while he was dressing and mentally reciting his parts, his thoughts had been on his love and bride-to-be, Silmavalien. He had chosen her to be his wife only because she also wanted to be his wife. If she had not said "yes," when he asked her if she really wanted to marry him, he would not have wanted her as his. They loved one another.

"Yes, Father! I am ready!" announced Noren, striding to his door.

His father opened the door and stepped in. There was no joy, but anxiety, fear, and anger on his face. "Noren, my son, there can be no marriage ceremony. Silmavalien vanished, during the night."

The news made a shiver run down Noren's spine. Could it be true? Silmavalien would never flee from him and marriage. They loved each other. They fervently wanted to marry each other. It could not be! *"No!"* exclaimed Noren. "She would never. How *could* she? How *would* she even?"

"I don't know," said his father. "One thing is certain: no one can find her."

Noren would doubt his own father before he would doubt his love, her devotion to him and their love for each other and mutual desire to be married – or her word on anything of which she could be expected to have any knowledge. That was the level of trust between them. He *could* trust no one more. He had to see for himself if the unbelievable were really true. "She couldn't," he declared. "I must see for myself." He strode out, brushing past his father.

As soon as he was out in the open Noren ran. To lose Silmavalien … worse, to believe that she had lied to him, had run away from him … was something he could not bear, could not do. He had trusted her more than the rest of the entire world. He had loved her. To experience such a thing was akin to dying. It would be to have all that was worth it in life, all purpose, torn away. If such trust and love even *could* be betrayed and denied, where was there any meaning in the world? What was life about?

No. Silmavalien had not lied to him, had not run away from him. *If* his father had not lied to him, some greater power of evil was at work. It was this that had taken Silmavalien and potentially destroyed their future together. Like the heroes of legend it would be his duty to hunt down and subdue that evil, whatever it was and however strong it might be, and rescue his love, his proper bride.

It was still very early in the morning. The sun had risen less than a quarter hour ago and shone with a deep golden radiance through the heavy mist. People were running here and there, trying to do Noren had no idea what. He still believed he would find Silmavalien in her room. Clearly in his mind he could see a picture of her sitting serene, happy, and expectant on the heap of straw that was her mattress.

No one seemed to notice Noren as he ran across the village square, dodging around people who, he presumed, must be attending to their morning chores and the ritual preparation for the wedding to take place that day. Of course they would not notice him. They were busy. Too busy to look him full in the face and realize he was that day's bridegroom and was not going about the wedding preparations like they were. It was perfectly natural, out here.

Then Noren turned a corner and entered the house of Silmavalien's family. Now, he could not run. It was even more crowded in here, again as was natural and reassuring. There was even more bustle, with people moving here and there and chatter such as Noren wondered that anyone could hear anything – he certainly could not – as everyone busied themselves with preparing the weeding feast. Again no one noticed him as himself in particular, occupied as they were with their own tasks.

Finally, he got through the maze of people and turned into the hallway between the personal rooms. Now, at last, he could run again. He did, and soon came to Silmavalien's room. Here, at last, he came to his first hint, apart from his father's declaration, that something was wrong. The door was wide open. He halted.

He did not consider the situation before raising his voice expectantly. "Good morning, Silmavalien. May I come in?"

Noren paused and waited, but there was no answer. His nerves were beginning to tingle and he felt a little uneasy, but he continued to hope and did not begin to doubt. After a few moments he cautiously stepped forward and glanced into her room. A terrible sight met his eyes.

His beloved's room-home was in total disarray. Her shelves had been moved from under the window, which was wide open, to one of the corners. He remembered she had kept many treasures, including the white oval, on it. Now it was totally bare. Not one of her treasures remained. Not even clothes were strewn on it in her usual manner. It was totally bare. But that was not all.

Her straw mattress which she liked to keep neat, full, and smooth so that it would be comfortable and afford easy sleep was roughed up and much of it strewn on the floor. Uneasy, he stepped in and looked. Nothing was left where Silmavalien had kept it. Her bow was gone. Her quiver was gone. Her knife was gone – so much time he had spent teaching her to shoot and hunt and how well she had sought to learn from him! It had been joy to them both! Both her pairs of shoes were gone. Her sewing-box was gone. Her gloves were gone. Not one movable item had been left.

Shocked, and at the same time drawn by curiosity, Noren softly walked further in. He examined the bare room and all that had been left in it. He was careful to examine it closely, for anything that might give a clue as to the cause of his beloved's mysterious disappearance. He walked around and walked around. He knelt down and closely examined the straw, the floor, the walls, the bed frame, and the shelves. A lump formed in his throat, and he wanted to collapse and cry.

Though he knew that it could do no good, tears pressed at the back of Noren's eyes. One escaped to run down his cheek. In the clay floor he had found no clue but only the prints of bare feet exactly like Silmavalien's. He knew her form very well. Drawn to her eyes, her voice, and her personality, he had been captivated also by her physical form. Then, he found something a little strange on her floor. A smelly, orange-brown goo around a black, sticky-looking glob. Looking at it made him feel nauseous and sniffing at it made him seriously feel like vomiting. He wondered what on earth it could possibly be.

Noren moved away from the disgusting thing and began to hunt for more clues. If he saw such a thing or smelled such an odor again he would recognize it, he was sure. He needed more clues, though. Could he get them?

Encouraged, Noren searched the entire room carefully and scrupulously, looking for even tiny or trivial details. His hunt was rewarded. He found scratch marks, as if made by claws, on both the bed frame and the lowest shelf. He also found orange stains on that shelf. Scattered throughout the area around the shelves were pine needles, dried bits of leaves, and loose bits of dirt.

Noren's hope collapsed as he sat down on Silmavalien's mud floor, struggling desperately to fit together the clues he had found in her room and explain her sudden and mysterious disappearance. They simply would not go together. He tried and tried, but he could find nothing that would leave all the traces he had found without leaving other, more significant ones. In his concentration, he became totally oblivious to the world around him and the passing time. He had been forced to accept the unacceptable, and he was fighting with everything he had for a solution.

Finally, loud shouts got his attention. People were yelling his name. Noren started up. Let no one think he was lost too, now! He ran through the now-empty house and out into the open. "I'm here! Noren, here! I'm not missing!"

Everyone quickly gathered and crowded around. "There you are," someone shouted. There was too much loud talking and Noren felt like he could neither hear nor speak. "Be a little quieter, please!"

Suddenly everyone was quiet. Surprised, he realized they wanted to hear from him. Perhaps, they wanted to know his view on the matter and how he felt about it. After all, apart from Silmavalien, he was the principal individual the matter concerned. While he considered how to begin, someone shouted, "Where have you been?"

Noren immediately answered the question. "When I heard the news of my beloved's disappearance, I went to her room to see with my own eyes its truth, which otherwise I was forced to disbelieve, and also to glean any clues as to why. I found some, but they are incompatible. Any others?"

Everyone started talking and Noren raised his voice. "I cannot hear you all! Please talk one at a time!"

Silmavalien's father stepped forward. At his side was his son, Varkul, and his daughter-in-law, Krielasoriel. He stated, "Dealing with this mystery, we must use any clues we can find, however insubstantial and insignificant they seem at first glance. Ours are these: we heard footsteps and thumping during the night. We also heard a screech. We did not take notice at the time since we were half asleep and they could have been, to any one of us, imaginings or dreams or that someone needed to use the outhouse and was surprised by a bat. They could still be signs only of the latter. Nevertheless, we heard them. Consider them as you will." With that the trio retreated back into the crowd.

Silmavalien's mother stepped forward. She said, "This morning while I was preparing everything for the wedding we believed would be held today, I found her bride gifts gone. It was my first hint that something was amiss." Then she too stepped back next to her husband.

Someone called out, "Noren, you mentioned that you have clues. Tell us about them."

Noren simply related what he had found in Silmavalien's room.

Then the oldest of the elders of Treas stepped forward. He said, "These are weighty news and dark clues. We all deeply regret whatever happened during the night. However, we cannot let the consideration and mourning of it keep us from our work, for that inevitably mean our deaths, too. Let everyone weigh the clues in his mind while he works and see if he can guess what happened to our dear Silmavalien. Meanwhile, let us work hard that we may gather in the harvest and survive the winter. We will meet again after sunset to discuss our ideas about what may have happened and, if we can get that far, what to do about it. I now disperse this meeting. Everyone should have breakfast before beginning his day's work, but be quick and take care that grief and thinking do not cause anyone to dawdle." With that, he walked away.

Noren sank to the ground. He felt that he would be unable to eat. His stomach gurgled with hunger but threatened to reject anything he might stuff into it. He felt that there was only one thing left for him to do. If he succeeded, all might be happy and wonderful. If he could not, he may as well – nay, it was his duty to – die trying. He must either rescue Silmavalien – which would be happy and wonderful – or avenge her if she had been killed. The later was sickening but not so awful as the thought that she had betrayed him. Nonetheless, if it were true he felt that there would be no life for him to live once he had avenged her.

Noren chose to hope and believe that he would be able to rescue her. Not only did he want to, he could think of nothing else to do while he tried to figure out a way to find and rescue her. First, he needed to know something of her captor.

Noren scrambled to his feet. He may as well work while he sorted this riddle out. Hopefully, working would even help him clear his mind, coordinate his thoughts, and thus solve the riddle. He certainly could not dwell on himself and how his life had been turned upside down. That would do no one, least of all Silmavalien or himself, any good.

He walked away and got himself a drink. After the morning's excitement he was quite thirsty, as well as quite hungry and just as unable to eat. When he had drank he went back to his room and changed out of his wedding clothes into his working clothes. While he did so, he tried to put together the new clues he had just learned to figure what sort of captor had carried off Silmavalien and what might happen to her.

He was getting very afraid, for it felt to him that a totally new power and evil had invaded his life and carried off the one he loved. The fear everyone else in the village possessed of the nightmare monsters of the mountains was probably why the elder had given that sweet speech but rather discouraged than encouraged any attempt to put search parties together.

Besides the fact they were not likely to do much good against a monster that could appear and vanish like that with its prey. What could one even do?

Terrified at what might be Silmavalien's fate and his, if he tried to rescue her as he ought, Noren looked up at the sky and clenched his fists. *If only we could have been married before. If only I could been beside her on this accursed night. If only we could have bidden each other our last farewells and promised our undying love properly. If only I could know that this is not the end. If only I could be sure that we* will *meet again. Whatever I know, I* must *hope and believe, or I shall go mad. O Silmavalien … O my love … can you hear me? Please, hear me. O Silmavalien, my love, my Sweetness of the Wild Rose, I love you. You love me.*

14

A Dragon Song

The morning light softly illuminated the little valley down which the little stream ran and up which Silmavalien and Minth crept. The sun had not risen over the crest of the mountains and its light filled the crisp morning air. All around and above birds were flying, darting from tree to tree and chirruping their sweet little song about the morning as if this were the first morning the world had ever known and with it came a joy never before dreamed in all existence.

Silmavalien, tired and weary as she was, felt that joy spring up in her. The night was over. Morning had come, bringing light. She and Minth were finally free, if not exactly safe. Against this, weariness and hunger were placeless and powerless. It was a glorious morning.

Minth woke up at the singing of the birds and instantly picked up on the new air in the world around him and his partner's fresh state of mind. He began to make noise, and Silmavalien did not tell him not to, though she found the sounds ugly. As ugly as he had been when he first hatched. As she had loved him then in spite of the ugliness of his form, so she loved him now in spite of the ugliness of his voice.

She thought it was so ugly, at least in part, because he had no practice making sounds and, due to the physical changes of growth, had lost much of the vocal instinct he had been born with. Now, most of his noises were still high in pitch, but both the notes and the shapes of the sounds came out, more or less, randomly, Sometimes he would try to make a sound or alter his pitch and over correct drastically.

The result was ugly, and Silmavalien was saddened that he had lost so much, and she almost felt bad for discouraging him from making sounds, even though that would have meant death.

Yet she listened happily. Minth's joy filled her, overcoming her discomfort at the sounds he made. He was so happy and so excited to be able to make noises at last. He was not in the least disappointed about their quality either, and so she tried to banish the unhappiness and guilt she felt. To him, it was all fine and natural, and she did not want to damage any more for him. As it is, he had no preconceptions about what noises should come out of his mouth, but only wanted to sing with the birds. He was just so happy and exuberant: to sing and crow, at last!

After a few tries, Minth grew comfortable with his voice, and then loud. Often she cringed at the volume of his sounds. She did not know how far up the mountain they were yet or how far west, but she wondered if Minth's jubilant crowing could be heard all the way back in the village.

She figured that, even if it was, they were safe. Though doubtless they were still low enough that the villagers would not be afraid to ascend to where they were, Minth could not possibly be loud enough to be noticed that much there, and no one would want to climb the mountain to find him. They would think he was the demon of the mountain. Even if they did seek him out, it would take a while even for hunters to reach their elevation and, by the time they had, she and Minth would surely have moved on. At least, Minth would have quited down long ago for no other reason than because he felt like it.

The echoes would be confusing, so he would be very hard to trace accurately. Though their current elevation and position were not safe, they were safe, at least for the time being.

To Silmavalien's surprise, the birds were not all that frightened by the dragon's loud declaration of his presence and life. They were somewhat bewildered and spooked at first, but soon decided that it was no big deal, or at least not one to be worried about. She could not hear whether or not it was a cause of joy since Minth was crowing too loudly for her to hear anything else at all.

She could not help smiling at him. Despite her exhaustion, her smile grew so big and bright that it quickly grew uncomfortable. She could not help it though and, against her weariness, hunger, scrapes, and bruises, it was nothing.

Little by little, she came to find Minth's singing – or crowing – less irritating. Whether it was his vocal coordination or her eyes or mind that caused the difference she did not know, but she was glad to be disliking it less.

Now and then she heard notes of birds' song when Minth paused for breath. The volume of his sound was definitely not constant. Sometimes he could crow a series of loud, ear-splitting notes, full of jubilation. Then, he would crow or sing more quietly, perhaps to have to breathe less, perhaps to give his rider's ears a rest. Perhaps both together

It was not long before his joy flowed over into her, and she too felt like singing. It was the first time she had really sung to Minth since he hatched, and he soon became silent to listen to her voice. Tired as she was, only one song would come to mind, so she sang it, and then sang it over again:

> Lead me back to the vale in which I belong
> Where I was born and for which my heart does long;
> There is my love, my soul's one true desire
> Who stands and watches, for me waiting ever.
>
> Even from world to world and age to age and forever
> To return to that green vale is all my desire.
>
> Carry me to the sweet valleys of my birth
> On wings of gold, smelling of heaven's earth;
> There is the only land of true life and worth
> And the valley of all yearned-for joy and mirth.
>
> Even from world to world and age to age and forever
> To return to that green vale is all my desire.
>
> Back to the happy vales high above
> And with me all I've learned through yearning to love
> To our joyous home and origin in the sky
> And with wings to soar and fly.
>
> Even from world to world and age to age and forever
> To return to that green vale is all my desire.
>
> Lead me back to the vale in which I belong …

By the time Silmavalien began the song for the third time Minth was accompanying her, though volume was the only thing he was able to reliably control and mostly his song was a toneless crowing. Nevertheless, his was the only accompaniment that really mattered. They were singing together, and that was the whole point.

Overhead and from the boughs birds chirruped their song, too. From dens and boughs squirrels chittered happily as they scampered about, though Silmavalien heard very little apart from his noises except for when he took a breath.

As he sang on, his voice, long disused, grew more scratchy and creaky. It cracked, wobbled, and grew steadily worse.

Minth did not seem to mind or even notice. Being still a hatchling he did not have many expectations and, even if he had, he was too happy to be safe, free, and finally making sounds to notice, let alone care. But it grew more and more cracked, and soon Silmavalien could not ignore how she disliked it, no matter how much she tried for the sake of not damaging Minth's joy. It constantly irritated her and scratched at her ears. She felt like it would drive her crazy.

Exhaustion had also returned in full force. She felt all the weight she carried again, and all the hours she had been awake as an added weight, and even a few minutes seemed to take an eternity. She just wanted to stop, sit down, make a fire to boil water for drinking, put down everything she was carrying, and eat. Though, really, all she wanted was to lie down, cuddle with Minth, and never get back up.

However, the valley up which she walked and down which the little stream flowed was thin, hard, rocky, and without any clear, flat spaces. There were sourberries, wild grapes, wild blackberries and raspberries, blueberries, strawberries, huckleberries, and other plants and herbs along the water's edge and the walls of valley. Weary, thirsty, and hungry her singing faltered.

Minth was silent. He snaked his head out and looked into her face. It was as if he were asking her why she had stopped singing. He wanted to listen to her song and sing with her. Why had she stopped singing? The sense of what he meant, what he felt, came across clearly through their bond.

"Minth," she said, speaking out loud for no particular reason, "I can't really. I have been awake, working, since yesterday morning. It has been a long time and I still want to get farther up and away today, and hunt some food for us so we don't starve."

Minth opened his mouth and crowed what had to be an affirmative though it did not exactly sound like one. It was a strange, clacking, drawn-out noise. He understood how Silmavalien felt in a way far deeper and more intimate than her words could ever say or hint.

After a few moments of peaceful, watching silence the chirruping note of a brightly colored bird as he flew overhead caught the attention of Minth and, thus, Silmavalien. The baby dragon let out a loud, sharp, squeal of excitement and recognition. He paused for a moment, then squeaked again.

Minth's voice echoed and rebounded across the mountainside. It seemed as if the entire mountain and forest were singing with him, declaring unchangeable joy that a dragon lived again. Silmavalien smiled, captivated. He was so cute, sweet, and different. The way he looked at and heard things seemed so innocent, strange, new. In scattered moments, it overwhelmed her aches and weariness with incredulous joy, and gave her the strength to keep on moving.

His singing, ugly as it was, was inexplicably endearing and captivating, perhaps because she loved him.

15

The Morning Day

All the while Minth was singing, she wearily searched for some flat, level ground where they could stop. Make a fire and cleanse some stream-water to drink. Have breakfast. Spend some time recovering so they could continue on, catch some food, and put a few more miles between themselves and the village of Treas, which already seemed a world away. Though Silmavalien was rather lost and had no idea how to find it had she wanted to – or at least she thought she would not be able to find it – she knew it was not very far away yet.

Now she found the place she wanted. It seemed that she had been searching forever, but it could not have been that long. The birds were still singing in full chorus and the sun was only rising above the mountains. She could see mountains slopes high above them just being kissed by the golden rays of its light.

The narrow valley opened out into a little forest dell. On one side of this dell ran the stream, flowing through a series of cataracts and down little waterfalls. At the base of the last of these, at the far end of the dell, it ran through a little pool carved in a basin of molten red and black rock. Here the icy water was crystal clear and still fresh from the clear, high airs and snows of the mountain top. The sloping basin rose above the water's edge since it was autumn, and the water was at nearly its lowest, only a little refreshed by the recent rain.

A little ways from the banks of the stream grew several apple trees. Pink blushed fruit hung from their branches and lay about their feet, and the sight of the delicious fruit poured weary delight through Silmavalien.

The center of the dell was clear and thick with tall meadow grass, but all around the edges and on the stream side grew a variety of berry plants. Wild grapes, still bearing a few small purple clusters, climbed several of the trees, clothing both apples and the towering conifers with their greenery. On the edge of the valley-dell a huge sequoia, larger than she had ever seen before, grew at the foot of a rock slope, and all around, on the edges of the wood and in open, were beautiful wildflowers, many of them new to her.

The mountains were even more beautiful than she had dared dream! And this was a good place to stay for a moment, with plenty of food and probably plenty of animals to hunt with relative ease.

Without a moment's hesitation she walked forward and bent down. She laid all her bags in the springy, pine-needle-covered earth at the base of one of the larger incense cedars trailed by a grape vine. Even as Minth crawled happily out of her bag, she rose, relieved to be free of all the extra weight.

She reached up to pluck the few grapes still on the plant and within her reach. They were overripe and a little winey, but she liked them just as much that way. Perhaps because she was tired and hungry, she nonetheless thought them the best grapes she had ever tasted. Meanwhile, aware of the pattern of Minth's thoughts, she said through a mouthful of grape, "Go and do that somewhere off on the right, where I won't have to see it, or smell it either."

Still clumsy and awkward, Minth waddled off to the edge of the dell. Silmavalien called after him, "You can dig a hole and bury it if you like. That might be easiest. Just make sure you do it somewhere out of the way where I'm not likely to step on it." The images that flowed across their mental connection told him what she meant.

At the sound of her voice Minth looked back at her. He lost his balance and rolled over. She laughed. "Just practice, and you'll be doing so much better in less time than you'll know."

Minth winked at her. He was so adorable, lying on his back, belly exposed, wings splayed wide, talons held out. He made her just want to hug him. Then he rolled over and scrambled back onto his feet. He looked at her again and flicked his ears. Then he trod on.

Silmavalien pulled her bow out of her quiver and strung it, then kept an arrow handy. Out of one of her bags she took a small sock to carry any food, fruit or otherwise, that she got. She walked across the dell to the apple trees and started eating apples. Unlike the grapes, they were not the best.

While she was still eating apples and a few berries, Minth came waddling over to her. Every few paces he would slip or stumble and fall, since the ground was rough, wet and, in places, rocky. She sensed his appreciation and recognition for how she walked with relatively few falls through pitch darkness.

She smiled. She did not consider her falls to be few. Besides, she told Minth, she had had years to practice walking. He had only been alive for about a month and he had very few opportunities to practice. She had not been able to walk at all at his age.

Minth tilted his head in another gesture that tugged at her heart. Then he carefully waddled and crept down to the water's edge and drank. Silmavalien leapt forward, cursing her inattention. "Oh, Minth, I'm so sorry for not boiling you some water. That water might get you sick, sweetheart!"

As she sprang towards him Minth lifted his head and looked at her, puzzled but acknowledging her. He turned away and began to crawl back towards the dell. Just then, he slipped and fell into the stream with a terrified scream.

Suddenly Silmavalien's weary body suddenly shivered as renewed energy rushed into her blood. It was positively terrifying to hear her dragon's desperate scream and see him caught, helpless, in the current. Feel his terror.

Silmavalien flung herself down on a rock and reached half-way into the stream. Her chest and shoulders were beyond its edge, and she stretched her arms out across the stream. In a few moments Minth was upon her, lying on his back, wings outstretched, still screaming against the current.

She understood only too well how cold he was. Already violent shivers racked his small frame. She was afraid, had she time to think, that he could already be in danger of death from the shock of the cold water. It had quickly numbed her feet just earlier, and only her feet and ankles had been in it. Minth was a fraction of her weight and his entire body had been submerged. She caught him in her arms and half-pulled half-wriggled the two of them safely back onto the land. She cradled the cold, shivering dragon against her chest. His wings were numb all through. So were his legs and tail and the ridge of his neck. Afraid, now, she kissed him. "Minth, are you okay?" she asked, aware that he could not answer her. He could not know himself. "Oh, live, please. Please, don't die! Please!"

Minth nuzzled her face and rubbed his chin on her shoulder in an attempt to be reassuring. However, he was unable to reassure her. He continued to tremble violently in her arms. She wondered if that was a good sign or a bad sign. Kissing him on the comb of his forehead, she asked lovingly, "Would you like me to put you in the sun for it to warm, and meanwhile kindle a fire?"

She received no definite reply through their connection, but she decided she would have to try it anyways. It was the only thing she could think of to help him more than simply cradling him in her arms.

She stood and carefully carried him back to the open clearing. She shook her outer cloak down on the wet grass in one open patch of sunlight, then laid Minth down on it. She hugged him, kissed him, and went to gather tinder and fuel for a fire. It took her much longer than she would have liked, and by the time she got back with it Minth was somewhat inadvertently telling her about how much his wings, tail, and limbs hurt from the thawing.

That was an encouraging sign.

Quickly she tore up a bunch of grass so she could build a fire more safely. She stood and took a step back to assess her work. The grass was green and wet. It would not catch fire too easily, and she thought she had done enough.

Once she had the fire going, she got the one large metal bowl out of her bride gifts. Filling it with water from the stream she placed it by the fire to boil. Remembering that Minth must certainly be hungry again, and food would help him to warm up as well, she gave him a chunk of roast to chew from her food sack, and ate another apple while she waited.

By the time the water was boiling and she took it off the fire to cool, Minth no longer felt frozen. But, he shared with her, he was very hungry. She gave him a bit of cheese and got herself a bit of bread, and when the water had cooled enough, both dragon and Dragonrider drank it up.

Then she got more from the stream. Their water-skin needed to be filled.

S

After a good hour of rest, she felt much better, but she still knew that much, much more distance than she liked still needed to be covered that day.

In a few minutes, she found a smooth slope where Minth could walk far enough from the stream that he would be in no danger of slipping in, and they continued, Minth walking beside her now. She was far too tired to carry him any more.

The little dragon sniffed at everything, and continuously stopped to rub himself on leaves or dirt that smelled interesting, and even occasional tree trunks. He tried to prance, excitedly to be walking himself, and then tripped. She had to regularly remind him they were trying to get far away from danger, and even so he was always distracted, sometimes ambling off into the bushes to look at something that caught his attention. But while he could not keep the fact they were still fleeing in his mind, she did not have to remind him not to wander far from her, or not to get too close to the stream. Falling in had scared him, and her presence felt like safety to him.

Even when he was not distracted, Silmavalien had to move very slowly to match herself to his pace, as he could not do much more than waddle, and he tripped and stumbled on almost any obstacle, no matter how small. But the slow pace meant she could keep an eye for small game and hunt while they walked, even tired as she was. She kept her bow strung and an arrow on the string, but she only shot one pigeon and one quail; arrows were hard to make and she could not afford to waste too many, so she could not risky shots, and weariness made her reflexes slow.

They walked for a while, as this part of the valley was rather easy-going but Minth soon grew tired. It was not long before he walked more that day than in his entire previous life. Though he was so excited to be walking that he was willing to keep going on long after he was tired, she was nearly too tired to go on herself any more, let alone carry Minth further on top of everything else she had to carry, and he was stumbling more and more often. She did not want him to hurt himself on a stick or a rock, so she started looking for a place to spend the night.

Before she found something good, Minth simply could not go on anymore. She let him lie down under a bush, where he soon fell asleep, while she searched the surrounding area for shelter. Finally, she found a spot with rocks and boulders not far from the stream, but on the other side of it from where she had left Minth. She let her bags in a big tree where she hoped they would be safe for a few minutes, and mentally called to Minth as she headed back to cross the stream.

Her call woke him easily, but he was still too tired and too sleepy to come to her. She realized he was right. She would not even want him stumbling through the forest without her. In the end she went to him and walked alongside him until they reached the stream, where she had to carry him across. By this time, she was so tired that, especially with his added weight, Unfortunately, she had to carry him across it, and by now, she was so tired she could barely keep her footing on the rocks. Twice Minth screamed with shock and fear when she stumbled, and that did not help her to stay calm and keep her footing.

But they reached the other side safely.

16

Firelight

They reached the shelter of rocks in the little clearing between the big trees safely. Silmavalien's bags were still safe, and she took off her quiver and knife as well, and left Minth there, along with the pigeon and quail.

Then she went to gather firewood.

It took her far longer and farther away than she would have liked, and even so she got mostly grass and twigs. She knew she would have to gather more if the fire were to last even half-way into the night, but she returned anyway. She wanted to get the fire going first, before leaving Minth for however long it would take for her to drag some bigger sticks over.

He was already fast asleep at the foot of the large conifer where she had left the bag he had stayed in. He was so cute, with the clothes and blankets pulled out of the bag and gathered around and underneath him, and she smiled. It was good to see him safe and comfortable.

After she got the fire going, Silmavalien looked for the birds to get them ready to cook. But she did not see them, and she walked around the clearing trying to think of where else she might have left or what might have happened to them.

Finally, she realized Minth was lying down on top of them. She knelt next to him and woke him gently. "Wake up, Minth," she urged. "I need to get our dinner to cook it. C'mon, Minth. Move on over."

Finally, disgruntled and confused, he woke up enough to move over half a foot, lie back down, and go to sleep again without even realizing what she was asking.

She pulled up the clothes he had dragged out, and shook them out, looking through them. There were still no birds. Perplexed, she gave it up for lost, and went to get a drink and eat a bit of dinner herself. A slice of bread, a little cheese, a few berries, and an apple. Then she cut up the rest of the berries she had picked in the morning and spread them out on a tray to dry, before going to get some sticks for the fire, though she did not put them on the fire yet, instead letting burn down. Then she stumbled over to where Minth lay, and collapsed on the ground next to him, asleep almost before she hit the ground.

It was very dark and cold when she woke. Only one star glowed, like a radiant gem, through the sky-born mist. The fire was but a few embers glittering in the darkness, and her blanket was stiff with frost. She sat up and rubbed her eyes.

She went to the fire and added branches to it, stirring it back to life. Soon, it was blazing and flickering, illuminating the little clearing with dancing orange light and shadows.

The flickering light woke Minth. He turned to look at the light, and she was immediately struck by the way the fire fascinated him. He had never seen fire in darkness before, and the hazy, flickery curtain formed by the flames awed him. Through their bond, she shared in his awe and wonder, gaining a new appreciation of the beauty, as well as the peril, of fire, even as his understanding of its nature astonished her.

Slowly he crept forward to the fire, drawn by its warmth, and lay down at her feet. She sat next to him and put an arm around him, and together they enjoyed the crisp warmth and light Excitement tingled through him, worming its way into her heart and soul.

Firelight was certainly like no other light.

For a long time, Silmavalien watched the intricate and indescribable patterns of the flickering flames with new eyes, as Minth had shared the secret of seeing it with her. She had no idea how he had such an affinity for it without any previous experience, but she wondered if it was because he was a dragon and, as such, a creature far closer to fire than she, or any human. Dragons breathed fire.

Minth snuggled up as close as he could to her. He took his gaze from the fire, and their eyes met and locked. Mutual love, appreciation, and understanding passed between them. She felt that her heart would burst with her love for him. Something simultaneously unbearable and exclusively worth anything burned within her. It was akin to fire, its danger and power to destroy, and its beauty and power to create and sustain, that were somehow one and the somehow.

Yet it was totally unlike fire, too. Or was it? What was it?

Overhead a gray-white blur with a silent whirring of wings passed, almost invisible in the foggy sky, except for the firelight gleaming on the white feathers of its underbelly and broad wings. It hooted as it passed over them.

Silmavalien stroked the ridge on the top of Minth's head. A thought flicked between them, made up of and threads from both their minds and personalities. *Fire is a wonderful thing.*

He nudged her leg with his snout, affectionately. Again, a thought from both of them. *Sing!*

The song that came to her was the one she thought of as the Dragon Song, since it seemed closer to the song of her dreams the night she and Minth bonded than anything else. This time, with Minth crowing accompaniment, she remembered two more verses.

> Borne on wings as old as time
> My choice, my love, has chosen me.
> Our souls made one, our hearts must climb;
> Forevermore one we must be.
> You are my great desire to ever see ...
>
> In joy we are ever-bound, new,
> In His gift, truly together,
> One another now able to love and know.
> Yea, this is like life's very fire,

And the ever-living, pure, clear water.

It is so glorious and lovely
To as one soar together there
In bliss beyond what could be
In those heavens so fair
Where healing and life is ever in the air.

As the last note of her song sank into silence, so did Minth's last, loud, jubilant crow. For a few moments, the entire mountain seemed to echo and re-echo that last note.

Her thoughts dropped into silence that followed, as she thought about how she remembered the verses. In some strange way, the song was coming true in her life, and that was the only reason she could sing it. Perhaps there was still more, and when it came true, then she would remember it.

Then the clear, pure, ringing, yet somehow soft, notes of a night singer floated out into the night, from a nearby tree branch. She realized the illusive bird's beautiful song had blended into her and Minth's voices the whole while she sang, and now he sang alone, as if though she had no more to sing, he knew the song, or at least his part in it, and that still went on. As if he were continuing to sing that they might learn their parts in listening to his.

Silmavalien invited Minth to crawl into her lap and snuggle up against her skin. He wrapped his tail around her, she put her arms around him, and they cuddled together, listening to the nightingale's song and watching the firelight. On one side, the crisp warmth from the fire made them almost too hot. From the other side the cold chill of the nightbreeze blew against her back, making her shiver a little, even with the heat of the fire on her face.

She pulled her cloak all around them and kissed his head, "Shall we go and get some more covers, and cuddle between the fire and the rocks together, and sleep there, do you think?" she asked softly.

He snaked his head around, tearing his gaze from the tongues of fire, so they could see each other's face and look into each other's eyes. They were truly partners. Their relationship was to each as the fire, both of the sun in the sky and the burning sticks before them, and all the vastly various waters of the earth were to the lives of all.

Silmavalien was still too tired and sleepy and, besides, it was far too cold, for either of them to want to move. But after staring at the fire for a few more minutes, she decided they would have to move to go back to sleep. She gently pushed Minth, who was already dozing, out of her lap and stood.

She yawned wide; her head felt sleepy-fuzzy-fizzy as if she might fall down again, and she could not see through the fuzziness. Once she felt steady enough to move, she was already shivering, though the firelight on her skin still felt too hot. She took the blankets and another cloak and laid them out by the rocks, then managed to convince Minth to move over with her. There they lay down and snuggled together.

17

Under the Mist

It was relatively early in the morning when she woke for good. Her blankets were frosty, but the light was a soft, dim gray that told that the sun had risen over the edge of the world. The rock against which they had lain had radiated most of the heat it had gathered during the day into the night and was no longer warm to the touch.

Above them, conifer trees stretched up into the sky, the tops of the taller ones lost in the white morning mist that kept the sunlight from turning their world golden. The morning felt quiet and peaceful, but though still tired, Silmavalien was wide awake and she was not going to fall back asleep.

She sat up and reached her hand under the blankets to scratch the base of Minth's head. When he did not wake easily she rose and piled the blankets around and over him to keep him as warm as possible. She needed to get ready for the day's journey upwards and get more food.

As she turned from Minth, she noticed small white bones and scattering feathers near where she had lain her bags. Kneeling down to examine them, she identified them as a few bones of some small bird, with the marks of sharp teeth all over them.

Suddenly, she realized what had happened to the pigeon and quail that had disappeared the day before. Minth had eaten them both, raw and whole. There was no other explanation, and it also explained why he was not very hungry.

She had not noticed the obvious because she was so tired.

What Silmavalien did not know was how to deal with was Minth's voracity. He ate more meat than she did, and he was so much smaller. He was only going to grow more, and it looked like it would be a long time before he could hunt for himself.

How was she going to feed him? How quickly would he grow if he could eat as much as he wanted, as babies should? Was he so weak because he had not been getting enough food?

There was nothing to do about it except to hunt right now.

Silmavalien grabbed an apple to chew, got her bow and knife, and left. She was not worried about Minth waking up in terror of her disappearance, because she would know at once and reassure him that all was well. She would not be even as far away from him as she had been while keeping him in what had been her room. Never yet, since the day Minth hatched, had they been unable to feel each other's minds.

The mist was thick and low, and it did not burn off as the sun rose higher. Fortunately it was not as thick down on the ground where they were as it was even a little way off, so Silmavalien could see a fair distance through the trees to hunt, even though their tops were lost in the whiteness. But she was worried the mist might be descending, so she was very careful about where she was, since she did not want to get lost in it.

Today, perhaps she was still tired, her hunting did not go so well, and she failed to get a good shot the first time around and had to chase down the wounded rabbit with her arrow in it. But it was a rabbit, and that meant a bit more food than the small birds. She got back to the clearing, which was now hung with tatters of descending mist, with the rabbit and a few more sticks for the fire just as Minth woke up, and wondered where she was.

The reassurance that she had just gone hunting and was almost back was more than enough to make him happy.

She hung the rabbit where Minth could not get it, and then stirred the night's coals into a fire. While the water boiled, she sat down next to the fire to skin and gut the rabbit. Minth sat next her, and she relished his quiet companionship. He gobbled up everything she threw away, even though she told him not to. She did not want to take the chance of him getting parasites or something worse, but he insisted that he was too hungry, and she could not really stop him anyways. She could only warn him, and then not worry about it.

After all, maybe dragons needed to eat the things she was throwing away.

When she was done, Silmavalien tossed the rabbit meat into the boiling post. Minth looked up into her face and asked her why she bothered cooking the meat. It took so long and didn't she like it raw? It tasted lovely, raw and bloody! He shared the memory of a raw bird he ate with her, as well as was possible even across their bond. She smiled, unable to dispute it; he really did like it that way.

"Well," she explained out loud, "that's all right and great if you like it, but I couldn't eat it that way. For one thing, it might make me sick. For another, I don't personally find it tasty. I don't even like the smell. And it's too tough for me to chew. So, I am cooking my meat. When you can catch your own, you can eat as much raw as you like.

Okay?"

He clicked his tongue in acknowledgement, but she felt his emotional belief that she was being preposterous. He said nothing about it, but she felt his quiet amusement anyways. A thin wisp of smoke trailed up from his nostrils.

Watching him with a quiet smile on her face, she realized something looked wrong with his skin. Something different from the flaky patches.

Larges areas of his skin were reddish, burnt, irritated, as if he had sunburned, but he had not been under direct sunlight very long at all, and it was autumn, not summer.

Looking closer, she realized he needed another oiling. Suddenly, she remembered why she had not wanted him to eat the rabbit skin. She needed the grease for *his* skin. "Oh, Minth," she exclaimed. It was part scold, part expression of pity.

"Don't do it again," she said, and explained why with images and feelings. He nodded his head and told her yes, he understood, now.

Today she would just have to use the grease she had brought from the village. While she went to get it out of her bags, she wondered how she would get enough grease for his skin once he had grown big.

Minth lay down and spread himself out for her. She used the grease sparing and tried very hard not to waste any. She carefully rubbed it into his skin, using only one of her thumbs to avoid getting anything stuck on her own fingers which had no need of it, and She used it at all where his skin was still undamaged, instead applying it with special care to his sunburnt or cracking patches.

When she was finally done she asked him to try to rub and scratch himself as little as possible. Minth readily acknowledged her and assured her he would do so. He understood the effort she took to take care of him.

Though tending to Minth's skin condition had taken far longer than ever before, the rabbit was still far from done, though it was beginning to smell tantalizing. To pass the time, she took some of the cloth she had and measured out Minth. Then she started to sew him a blanket to protect most of his body from the sun so he would not burn so easily, making it a bit too large so he would not outgrow it too quickly.

It took a while, though she had plenty of practice sewing. By the time she was done, the rabbit was ready, and the mist still hung very thick around them. She was both very hungry and thirsty by now, so she and Minth drank from their water skin before having breakfast. She split up the rabbit to give Minth the larger portion.

Then she told Minth to stay put, and went out to hunt again. She was still certain they were not entirely safe at their present altitude, but they needed more food and she realized she was not quite so desperate to get deeper into the mountains anymore. Actually, she wanted to get over the mountains and down the other side before winter arrived, but she was not certain that was possible. She knew nothing about crossing mountains at all, during the approach of winter or at any other time of year. She did not know how long it might take, nor where the passes would be found.

She doubted now that they would get over the mountains this year.

As Silmavalien wandered looking for game, she took note of good fire wood to collect. Deer trails abounded, but she did not think she was ready to try deer yet. Instead, she had to look for a rabbit trail or a flock of birds.

She still had not caught anything, when it suddenly started to get darker. She fought back panicky fear and tried to keep a calm and level head. Back in the clearing, Minth was fast asleep and quite oblivious to the descending darkness and to her terror.

She realized she should start running back, while she still had enough light to do so.

But then she noticed a squirrel hiding behind a tree. She still had her bow and an arrow in hand, as she had wasted no time unstringing her bow. She stopped to shoot the squirrel, then ran off the trail to retrieve it and then back to the trail with it.

Deeper and deeper fell the darkness. Soon Silmavalien was sweating with fear and yet so out of breath that she could run no more. She had lost her calm and overdone it.

Now she was forced to a rapid walk, holding her hand to her burning side and hoping against hope that the light would last for her to make it back, though she did not expect to make it.

When it was almost too dark to see the ground in front of her feet, a low, red light illuminated the forest, making the shadows miles long and every needle sharp as a knife. She looked over her shoulder for a moment, to see a red sun, resting as it were on the great western ridge of the mountains towards which she had been climbing ever since the night of her flight.

Just above the sun hovered a dark storm cloud, as if the smoke of a dying day. She knew what it meant. A storm was brewing. She also knew that these would be her last few minutes of light.

In spite of the stitch still present in her side, she ran again. It would be too dark too soon. If she did lose her way she would have the stream for a reference point. She had only to search up and down along its length to find her clearing.

As she ran, the light faded rapidly. This time it was even more sudden and frightening. She chanced a brief look over her shoulder, but there was no longer any hope of another guiding light. The red rim of the sun sank behind the mountain ridge and into more dark, stormy clouds.

In a few moments, there was total darkness. It was like the night of her flight. Then she felt herself sliding down. Terror engulfed her. She had done something wrong and was sliding down a cliff. She was going to die. What would happen to Minth now?

Just then, she saw herself sliding down a slope in near blackness. It did not look like she would have expected herself to look, but somehow she knew it was her. Her terror had wakened Minth, and he had once again told her what he saw, as accurately as only their connection as Dragonrider and dragon allowed. This time, to comfort her.

"Thank you!"

18

Mountain—Rain

The previous night, Silmavalien had used stick to move the coals under the rock outcropping of Minth's sight. Then she had started the squirrel cooking, moving her bags under the rocks as well, and worked on getting all the grease she could out of the squirrel skin.

Now, she looked out from under the rock where she and Minth slept, and was surprised to see that it looked much like any other stormless early morning. A bird chirped, calling his mates to join him in greeting the sun and celebrating the dawn. In a few minutes the forest was filled with the song of a full orchestra of birds, Minth crowing along with them. She noted that his voice was already more coordinated and his tones sounded a little more like a tune.

Silmavalien got up to look around and see where the storm had gone. A few puffy white clouds lingered in a clear blue sky, and behind the mountains to the west lurked a cloud which might have been the storm, but she could not tell because most of it was on the far side of the mountain from her.

"Don't do anything with the squirrel," she told Minth. "For one thing, if you try, you'll get burnt on the coals. Also, try to stay out of any direct sun until I come back and put your blanket on." Then she left to hunt again, and of course to gather anything else she saw, like berries most of which she ate on the spot, and sticks for the fire.

This time it was not long before she got close enough to a flock of quail to shoot one. Desperate for more, she shot another arrow as the quail started and missed. She ran off after the arrow to find it before she couldn't, and when she returned she found her initial shot had not killed the first bird.

She really wished she could stop shooting things without killing them, as she approached the frightened, wounded thing with the knife to kill it. She did not mind hunting, but it was an offense to cause more pain and fear than necessary.

Since one quail was not very much meat, especially with Minth's appetite, she did not turn back until she noticed the birds had suddenly stopped singing.

She glanced around, wondering what was wrong. Then, she noticed that it was overcast in a clearing only a couple hundred feet away, and the line was rapidly moving towards her. A glance up at the sky showed her storms clouds were rapidly gathering overhead. She saw forked lightning, but the trees hid half of it from her view, and she could not see whether it struck the ridge or was sky to sky.

Immediately she turned west, towards the storm, the stream, and her clearing-home.

A few moments later, she heard the thunder, very loud and close. The rain was falling in sheets and her hair was soon soaked, dripping water down her face and neck long before she got to the stream. She had to cross the cold, icy, foot-numbing water in the pouring rain to get to Minth and the clearing. She ran across the clearing to get under the rock with Minth as quickly as possible.

Then, she noticed that he had carefully knocked the metal bowl and pulled it over, all without touching the coals or somehow burning himself. Then, he had eaten the entire squirrel, bones and all, and as much of the sauce as had not boiled away and he had not spilled.

She glared at him. "You naughty dragon! You ate my breakfast as well as yours, and I did *not* forget to tell you not to!"

Minth cuddled up to her, in a way that was so naughty, yet appealing, innocent, and almost piteous. She had told him not to eat it because he might burn himself trying, but he had carefully figured out how to get to it without burning himself, he told her. How and why could she possibly be mad at him?

She laughed, and bent down to hug and kiss him. "Oh, Minth, you silly dragon!" Of course, she had told him through their mental connection. He had known full well that she did not want him to eat it because she wanted to eat, too. If it had been okay for him to eat it all, she would have paused a moment to take it off the coals so he would not have to be hungry. She had left it there precisely because she wanted an extra incentive for him to leave some of it for her.

He looked up at Silmavalien and growled playfully. There could be no doubt that he was feeling better, better perhaps than he ever had before. "No," she said, firmly. "You could hurt me too easily, trying to play with me like that. Look at me. I don't have claws or teeth like yours, and, besides, I really ought to make more arrows."

Minth did not contest her, but she felt his emotional disagreement. He crept to where she sat, lay down on her feet, and nuzzled her. She smiled and stroked him in return. Then, she pulled her feet out of underneath him and stood up, as well as she could under the rock. She had to stoop, with her back bent and head down to avoid banging her head on the rock overhanging.

Bracing herself, she stepped back into pouring rain to collect a few straight sticks, whose points she would sharpen against the rock before fletching with quail feathers. By the time she got back to their little shelter, every bit of clothes she had on was thoroughly soaked and she was shivering from the cold wetness.

She changed into warm clothes, then convinced Minth to lay down on her feet and not smother her while she worked on making her arrows. Noren had taught her how to do it, though she wondered how well her quail feathers would do. As she rubbed the first arrow against the stone, she found herself missing him so much. She wondered how he was doing, how much he missed or feared for her, and whether he had found the note she had left him. She wondered if the dragon egg he kept had hatched yet. If it had, he would know what had happened to her, but would he be afraid a wild beast had eaten them? She found herself both afraid and sorry for him. What might happen to him if he set out to rescue her? How awful might he feel?

Minth looked into her eyes, as she sharpened the arrow point against the stone. He knew all her feelings, and she understood that he wanted her to forget about Noren. After all, was he not the person who gave meaning to her life? Was it not he who was her greatest love and chosen one? Never mind, there had been no choice.

Silmavalien kissed him tenderly, then returned to her repetitive yet attention-demanding work. She replied silently. Yes, since the day he had hatched and forever he was all that and more – unless, it were possible, she were bonded to another with a still greater bond. Nonetheless, she had others she loved, too, and once, before he had hatched, she had thought those same things about Noren. She could never forget Noren, just as she could never forget Minth himself.

S

It rained continuously all day, but Silmavalien was able to finish two arrows. Then she changed back into her wet clothes to get some more sticks for the fire. This time, the wood was wet, but the coals were hot enough to make it burn easily.

In the morning it was still raining as hard as ever, and she realized she would be forced to hunt and gather in the miserable cold rain. The sooner she started, the better, so she ate heartily to keep herself warm, then changed back into the wet clothes again, leaving off a layer. She would be a little colder, but the wet clothes weighed a lot too, and she hoped to keep warm enough moving, and then warm up afterwards.

Silmavalien did not want to be lost in the blackness, away from shelter and Minth, and she knew how easily that could happen from the previous night. The need to keep track of the time, since in this weather nothing but her own internal senses would tell her, kept her tense as she hunted.

As the hours passed, her feet and fingers grew numb, except for the way they hurt, and she had trouble tripping over her feet. The rain never let up for even a few minutes, and she slipped on the wet slopes and had to splash through huge puddles. Sometimes, the canopy overhead would keep a little rain off her for a few moments, but all in all, it was a miserable experience.

Nonetheless, hunting went well, perhaps because she spent all day on it. She had a rabbit, five quail, and even a few berries by the time she thought it might be late enough she should go back. She doubted it could be anywhere near nightfall, but she did not want to risk it, especially since it might take longer than she expected to get back.

S

The rain-storm went on for several days. Though she did not enjoy it except for the fact that Minth enjoyed, Minth certainly enjoyed it – except for the fact that she did not – because she spent so much time hunting that he was able to eat as much as he liked.

She hated it both because she believed they were still too close to the village, and because it made hunting miserable and difficult. It was a challenge to keep her bow dry. Though it delighted her to feel Minth's full belly and to see him growing, she grew more irritable every day, until she found herself snapping at Minth, despite her love for him. She had had enough rain at one time!

19

Dragons' Dream

She woke up to the chirrup of a bird.

The rain storm was over for good. It was more than just a longed-for lull. "Yes!"

Her exclamation woke Minth, who instantly told her he had been awake for a few minutes, earlier. In the dark before the dawn, he had the rain, no longer pouring but coming down in gentle showers, actually pass.

"Cool," she congratulated him. "Now, we can move on."

For breakfast they both ate warm meat over the fire, along with some leaves and herbs for Minth, and an apple and berries for herself. Then, the song of the birds still clear and loud, direct sunlight finally all around, she shouldered her bags and they set off, following the stream upwards, as before. Minth crowed his joy, joining the calls of the birds.

Silmavalien sang too, a song that sprang to her lips at that moment, with a merry tune:

> Sing, birds and flowers;
> Risen at last is the sun.
> Let us sing, play, and run;
> How bright he is upon the waters!
>
> Let us all now sing
> Happily, rise on the wing;
> This is a happy day.
> Shout and sing to all the flowers!

After that, her song turned into beautiful syllables without any definite meaning.

S

Minth was still awkward. Often he tripped or slipped and sometimes fell. Once, he fell sliding towards the stream, with a terrified scream for help. Silmavalien yelped too, and barely managed to fling herself backwards, down upon the banks, between him and the stream. After that, she held and reassured him for a few minutes before he calmed down enough for them to continue, this time a little more carefully with him farther away from the stream and walking in front of her so she would be able to catch him more easily.

By high noon, he was exhausted. The terrain was rougher, with more boulders and little waterfalls to be climbed around. Their progress grew much slower, and Minth struggled so much that Silmavalien decided to look a suitable place to spend the night. Then she would spend the afternoon hunting for them, which might not be a bad thing.

It took a while for her to find suitable shelter, and when she did it was farther from the stream. On a slope – gentle for the mountainous terrain – she found a small clearing, almost entirely taken up by a huge sequoia, larger than any she had seen before. One giant branch, high above the ground, grew out from it, and two roots rose out from the tree in the drier patch under it, and formed a little sheltered hollow, just large for them to lie together.

There, Silmavalien left Minth and everything she did not need to hunt and gather. It was now late in the afternoon so she could have no more than a few hours to hunt before she had to head back. She wanted to make sure she was with him well before nightfall, lest some predator try to eat him, defenseless as he was.

As she wandered, Silmavalien was surprised at how many berries there were, in spite of the animal populations, which were not often thinned by hunters up here. She wondered what fearsome predators might roam these regions of the mountains that there were not so many deer and squirrels and other creatures that everything was stripped bare.

She wondered if the fearsome tales of the mountains were actually true.

In the depths of her heart, Silmavalien hoped for the one other – to her – apparent possibility, though it seemed unlikely. Still, before it happened to her, she would have thought her bond with Minth far more than unlikely.

As yet she had seen no dragons in the sky, but was it possible that these mountains were the hunting-grounds of dragons? If so, when might she and Minth meet them? That would explain the appearance of the two dragon eggs, as well as the legendary disappearance of all who wandered far and wide in the mountains. Some would undoubtedly bond to dragons, and have no wish to return, even were it possible to do so and live. Beyond that, the dragons would not want to hunted as demons, so they might kill or capture any wanderer in the mountains that they did not bond. It fit in perfectly with the stories, too, since everyone believed that dragons were demons.

The more she thought about it, the less unlikely it seemed. Against all the evidence in favor of dragons living in the mountains, only one thing puzzled her: she and Minth had not seen any dragons in the sky. It was possible, though, the dragons had eyesight even keener than that of hawks and eagles, and that they soared so high she would not notice them. Perhaps, they *had* seen dragons, circling high in the sky, where they would look like mere dots. Also, perhaps the dragons did not like to kill or capture intruders, so they tried not to be seen by them as long as they did not venture too far or stay long. That would explain why so many people could get away with wandering in the mountains a little, but if they got used to doing it all the time they never came back. It would also mean that every day that passed increased her chance of meeting the dragons.

While she was hunting that evening, Silmavalien kept glancing at the sky when she could, hoping to see a dragon. She tried not to get too hung up on the idea of dragons living in the mountains, lest she be disappointed, but she really could not help hoping it and even believing it. She felt Minth reveling with her in the awesome idea of entering the habitat of his own race. The idea was so appealing and, by now, seemed to her so natural and logical it was impossible to remain very skeptical, especially, with Minth encouraging the idea and adding his own highly emotional and inarticulate reasons. There just had to be. That was all there was to it.

She smiled, grinning at the possibility, then thought of Noren. How long did it take dragon eggs to hatch? What conditions did they need? Would he bond to the dragon? Had he? How was he? Did dragons need to bond? The thought of Dragonriders as well as dragons added to the appeal of the idea.

Finally, Minth had to remind Silmavalien to return 'home' before it got dark. She had been so caught up in her hunting, and more than that her wondering, that she had not noticed. Once again, she tried to remain cool and keep her head – otherwise, she really *would* be lost – and at the same time to hurry.

She berated herself for being so lax and distractable about something of such importance. Little baby Minth had saved them both!

That night she fell asleep, still dreaming about the wonderful prospect of encountering thriving dragons and Dragonriders. In her dreams, she met a whole flight of majestic, colorful dragons with noble Dragonriders, and even their children. Noren was there, and had a female dragon named Annagloria. In fact almost everyone from her village was there and bonded a dragon, and there were many other Dragonriderswho had been born in the mountains and raised among dragons and Dragonriders.

When she woke to the songs of the birds, Silmavalien wished fervently that her dream would come true – and soon.

She looked around for Minth. He had dragged a cloak with him, and lay atop one of the sequoia roots, watching the sunrise. He swung his head around to look at her, and she saw the same hope and dream in his eyes, which seemed more vibrant than ever.

She eagerly watched the sky for any sign of a dragon the whole time she was eating breakfast, but she could not see several of the specks in the sky well enough to identify them for certain. Minth, however, had keener eyesight, and announced all but two to be birds. The other two he was not certain about.

Both of them were dismayed, though it did not really change anything for them in the immediate future, even if it had been conclusive proof that there were no dragons in the mountains. It certainly did not rule out the chance of stray dragon eggs like his, or even a handful of dragons scattered here and there. Nonetheless, it was disappointing. They quickly packed up and began their trek upward and to the northwest, again following the stream.

There, they did find encouragement in their search for dragons. The mud beside the stream was covered in large paw-prints, such as they had never seen before. Apparently, some large beast had crossed the stream, much larger than wolf.

The two friends looked at each other, each with a gleam in their very-different eyes. Could it be a dragon? To be sure, the feet were not quite like Minth's, but what else could it be? She had heard that not all human feet were the same; every now and then there was even webbing between the toes like on ducks. Yes! They must have found the tracks of a dragon.

There *were* dragons in the mountains! Minth crowed loudly. It was an invitation to any dragon who might hear and an exclamation of joy to the world. Silmavalien smiled. They continued on.

20

The Old Woman

The stream poured down a series of little waterfalls and ran through little pools. All around were berries of many sorts and wild roses. They walked sometimes in the deep shadows of the woods and sometimes in open meadows, and all of it was beautiful, the more so because she had only to reach out her hand to eat the delicious fruit.

Silmavalien's eyes fell again on the fresh dragon paw-prints, and her heart leapt with joy. Not only must this beautiful place be the abode of dragons, but she and Minth were so close to others of his race.

Could it be true? and yet it had to be.

She took a step forward, and then froze with fear. Suddenly, she was not so sure. Perhaps, grown dragons were not as friendly and likely to bond as the hatchlings. Perhaps, there were no Dragonriders here. People who wandered far did not return because the dragons ate them. It might notice Minth too late to spare her life. That would be awful, not just for her, but for Minth. She had to turn back ... had to get away ... before it was too late. She spun round, panicked. She had made a horrible mistake. *Minth, forgive me!* she cried in her mind, afraid to make any noise.

Something roared, loud, close, and horrible. Branches snapped and broke as some large beast crashed through the trees. *"Help me!"* screamed Silmavalien, though there was no one to help her. Backwards she jumped into the cold, icy stream, fumbling for her bow and an arrow. She had to string it, and quickly! She had to protect Minth from ... whatever it was.

Silmavalien landed on her knees in soft mud in one of the pools. The cold water rose to her waist. She stood, knowing she must not get her bow wet. The adrenaline in her blood gave her the strength to quickly string it. She knocked an arrow. "Minth, back!"

Out of the trees flew a huge, furry, brown beast – not a dragon. It had long, awful claws, a deadly snarl on its lips and ferocity in its eyes. Huge, dreadful fangs were bared. Whatever it was, it would show them no mercy for invading its private territory.

Silmavalien wasted no time evaluating its strengths. She had known, the moment she heard its roar, that she would have to kill it, and fast. She released the arrow.

At the same time, Minth clumsily but hurriedly scrambled into the water, half-stumbling, half-slipping, half-running. Terrified as he was of the water, there was nowhere else to flee from the beast! He screamed, a terrible, wailing, ear-splitting sound. Floating on his wings, he desperately paddled as far into the pool as he could with his numbing limbs.

Even before her arrow struck the beast, Silmavalien had another on the string. Her first arrow struck the beast on the shoulder. It howled with pain, but kept on coming. Her second arrow struck the beast in the chest. It kept on coming. It was nearly to the pool's edge now. Minth's scream grew in terror and intensity.

"*NO!*" she screamed. Somehow, she shot again, hoping to get the beast through the eye – missed. The arrow bounced off the beast's skull into the water and floated downstream. Guilt for bringing them both to this in the foolish hope of finding dragons crushed her, wounding her far more than her arrows had wounded the beast. *Minth, I'm sorry. Forgive me!*

Then she heard a distant, "*NO!*" Somehow, she knew that it was no echo of her own cry or, if it was, it was an echo come to life. Desperate hope rose in her heart, but the memory that it was her hope of finding dragons that lead them to this was buried deep within her. She dared not hope wildly again.

She backed farther into the water around the edge. Grabbing Minth by the wing – it was the only part of him she could reach – she pulled him with her. The beast plunged into the water. She tried to run, but the water around her legs and her wet clothes weighed her down. She meant to get to the other side of the pool, and up, through a little gap in the rock that the beast would not fit through. It would have to go around. The next moment, she knew they would not make it. The animal was too near, too fast. They just screamed.

From the little waterfall above them sprang figure. In her terror, Silmavalien could not help staring at it in utter amazement, and wondering what it could be or be trying to do. Tatters of skin clothing hung from it and fluttered around it. As it fell, it held a bow and shot. Then, almost faster than the eye could see, it put away the bow and drew a sword.

She cringed as the arrow hissed by. Minth shivered violently and she drew him closer, protectively. The arrow sped through the air and struck the beast at the base of the neck. Next moment, the leaping figure fell upon the water, sword arm outstretched, and cut through the beast's neck. Silmavalien gasped in amazement. The sword was broken no more than a foot below the hilt, and its cliff-leaping wielder was an old woman.

She shoved Minth onto the shore, then reached out and grabbed the old woman's arm to pull her out of the water as well.

Her rescuer opened her eyes and grasped Silmavalien's hand in her own small, wrinkled one. "Y-you're the ne-new Dragonrider?" she gasped weakly, trying to force a smile.

"Well, I am a Dragonrider," replied Silmavalien. "We are in your debt. You saved my life and Minth's life at the risk of your own. Thank you."

"It was nothing," said the woman, her breath starting to return. "My life is of no consequence. For years now I have lived for a reason I did not know. I was going to die on those cliffs, anyways, but the knowledge of a dragon and Dragonrider in danger gave me the will and strength to do one more useful deed before I die. I know now why I did not die after Lelarina died. So I could save your lives."

"Then, you know of dragons?" asked Silmavalien. Minth shivered beside her and she put her arm around him to warm him. "Was Lelarina your dragon?"

The old woman closed her eyes. "Yes, I, Lexamarian, first bonded to her long ago in Treas. In that bond, we were able not only to see and feel as our partner died, to share our partner's life, but to see ourself in new ways. Losing Lelarina was like losing half my life. Her death made me physically ill. I did not know why or how I lived … Why am I telling you this? Do you really need to know what it is like lose one's dragon?"

Silmavalien gasped at the mention of Treas. Minth commented to her that Lexamarian and Lelarina's lives must have been much like theirs, and he hoped their lives would not end the same. "Treas?" she asked. "You came from Treas? I did, too. I'm Silmavalien."

"Ah," said the woman, then paused. "Silmavalien, as the only known Dragonrider, all I have is to be yours … care especially for the shards of the sword … when it is re-forged it will glow again with the light and fire of old and be wielded by a warrior among the Dragonriders … Do not lose it … Be careful, Silmavalien, Dragonrider … I will not be around … to save your lives … again. Make sure you are never found by anyone who is not … a Dragonrider or of the Ellenari. That is how

Lelarina died ... Take the Riders' Passage ... to the other side of the mountains. Take care ... that none of the dark creatures get you ... I don't have time to tell you all about them ... Do you have any questions, Silmavalien? Minth?"

The two thought together for a few moments. Then, Silmavalien asked, "Was that beast that attacked us a dark creature?"

"No," replied Lexamarian. "It was just the animal some call a bear. You can expect a dark creature to be much, much more dreadful."

Silmavalien cringed at the thought. "Then, how am I to protect myself? We could not hold our own, even against a mere bear!"

"For one thing," said Lexamarian, "hopefully, you won't have to until Minth is older and you both know more. The dark creatures won't do anything to you until they know about you ... which I doubt they do, yet. Try to stay away from places that feel wrong. If you want, I will tell you what I know about fighting them ... but you may not be ready."

Silmavalien's eyes fell on a long, horrible, ropey scar that wrapped itself around Lexamarian's arm, from her elbow to the palm of her hand. "Ouch!" she gasped. "How did you get that?" She could think not of any normal way to get such a scar.

"I was marked with it when I became a Dragonrider and would not burn Lelarina," replied Lexamarian. "It was a sign to be shunned, but to me it signified our bond. What? Do you not have one? We were all supposed to be witches and marked."

"No." Silmavalien shook her head.

"I am glad," Lexamarian said. "But why did you run away if Dragonriders are no longer persecuted?"

Because I had to hide Minth until he was strong enough to flee," she replied. "Dragonriders are burned alive if they are found out, not just scarred!"

"How did you – never mind," said Lexamarian. "If you are faced with a dark creature, don't fear *them*. It helps them. Bright sunlight hurts and terrifies them."

Silmavalien nodded. "Where can I go to find instruction, to learn to care for my dragon as best as I can, to ride, to ... ?"

"The Ellenari," said Lexamarian. "They wander on this side of the mountains, too ... but if you want to find them ... it is best to take the Riders' Passage ... to the other side of the mountains. Then, they will surely find you."

"Where is this Riders' Passage? How do I find it? What are the

Ellenari?"

Lexamarian was silent for a long time. Then, she said, slowly, "The Riders' Passage is ... the only safe passage from this side of the Greater Aravin Range to the other. It is ... looks like a cavern opening ... on top of a cliff ledge.... It is very bright ... within, and ... hard to find."

"Thank you," said Silmavalien, wondering what she could do with the information. None of it was enough or such that she could make anything of it. She wondered if Lexamarian were even sane. Her next words confirmed Silmavalien's fear.

"The way from the Riders' Passage is ... very dangerous. Do not attempt it without an Ellen to guard you.... At the bottom of that abyss is a Fire Shadow who ... destroys all who try to travel ... near the cliffs ... above the cleft.... When the broken sword is re-forged, his time will be over. The Dragonriders will live again.... Go to Dragonsong Forest... If you meet the snake-woman, be sure you neither fear nor are ... attracted to her.... Then, travel to the ... Vale of Aros Cor on the Island of Ellen ... and drink the waters of the stream of Nerya in the cavern of the Dragon Eggs."

Silmavalien looked into Lexamarian's eyes. "You are not making any sense," she said, firmly and quietly.

"You're right," said Lexamarian. "I ... can't think ... straight ... anymore. I am ... confused ... myself. Everything ... I've got ... I give to you. I am ... about to join Lelarina, at last. I can see her as I ... have not for ages. Her scales ... are so bright."

"Scales?" gasped Silmavalien. "Minth has no scales."

Lexamarian did not seem to hear her. "She shines more brightly than ... ever before. All her ... colors ... are fresh. It must be ... the light-one.... Oh, I come ... at last ... we are together ...."

Lexamarian went on for a long time, then trailed off. Silmavalien hugged Minth to her chest, warming him and talking to him to comfort him.

21
A Life's End

Silmavalien left Lexamarian to ramble to herself. She had to take care of her own things. Almost everything she carried had been soaked, so she poured it out of its bag and hung it up on tree limbs in the sun. Fortunately, she had been carrying the food sack over her shoulder, so that had not been soaked. With time, most other things would dry out nicely.

She took off most of her clothes so they would not re-soaked, then waded back into the water. She spent a long time pushing and shoving, trying to get the bear to shore, while Minth lay back, watching silently. She sensed his desire to lend a foot and help – if he could.

Finally, she got portions of the bear to the water's edge and just out of the water. It was all she could do, and fortunately all she needed. She collapsed on the ground, shaking from exertion, to catch her breath. Her sore muscles trembled violently. Her whole body ached.

Once she had regained her breath, she got her hunting knife and started to skin the bear. As she cut it up, she had to push more of it onto the shore and out of the water.

Minth watched for a while, then told Silmavalien that he wanted to come over, onto the same side of the water, and hee definitely did not want to try crossing the water by himself. It was too cold and he was too small.

Of course! she smiled, and crossed it again to carry him over, then went back to cutting up what had wanted to eat them but now they would eat. When Minth told her how hungry he was, she cut off a tough, lean chunk of meat and tossed it to him.

She wanted to use the fatty parts to get grease for taking care of his skin. That thought made her pause in her work for a moment. She had forgotten about that these last days. She would have to do it, that evening.

Fortunately, she did not have to go far to get sticks for a fire. She realized she would never be able to cook most of the meat fast enough using the bowl, so she used other sticks to move hot rocks closer or farther from the flames to cook on as well. Managing it so she did not burn the meat took a lot more attention, so she had to be careful not to get distracted cutting the meat.

Finally, Minth noticed the lengthening shadows, and let her know. Shocked by how she had lost track of time she glanced around, then cried out, "Oh no! I have to check on poor Lexamarian!"

Minth looked at her with glowing eyes before turning and ambling to the wood's edge, his over-sized tail scraping over the ground.

Silmavalien scurried through the brush to where Lexamarian lay by the stream bed. She was pale and still. Silmavalien knelt down and placed a hand on her brow. It was cool. No breath, no pulse, no warmth.

Tears pressed at the back of her eyes. She had hoped to get to know this woman who saved her and her dragon's lives as a friend. She had hoped to get to know the Dragonrider she had not dared hope to meet, and learn the true history of the Dragonriders and all about dragons and dragon-riding. That could not happen now. She felt Minth's disappointment and grief join her own. She glanced around. The light would not last much longer, and she had to find a place she could bury Lexamarian to give what gratitude and honor she could. She and Minth would find and do it *together.*

They headed a little ways upstream to a rugged rock outcropping just behind and above the falls. There, Silmavalien and Minth split up, though they were never far from each other, so that they could cover more ground. Each of them shared all they found with the other, and together they found a deep, narrow chasm in the granite. There was no way they would be able to seal it from all sides properly, but it was the best they could reasonably hope for. They headed back for Lexamarian's body.

The sun was just dropping below the western mountains and the land was bathed in soft shadows both like and unlike that of early morning. The light would soon be gone. Fortunately, Lexamarian's body was thin, frail, and light. Silmavalien took her ring and the shards of her sword and everything else in her pack. Then, she picked her up and carried her to the chasm.

Silmavalien let Lexamarian's body fall into the chasm with less delicacy and grace than she would have liked. But then, if she had been taught about the dragons and gods all wrong, might she also have been taught how to honor the dead all wrong? She let a tear fall into the chasm after her. "Goodbye, savior and friend," she whispered. "Goodbye, hope beyond hope and last old Dragonrider. Farewell …"

Then, she went a short ways into the woods with Minth to gather herbs and flowers with which to soften Lexamarian's resting place and scatter over her body, perfuming her entry into the afterlife. Minth carried several sprigs in his mouth while Silmavalien's arms overflowed with the burial perfume.

Minth dropped his sprigs into the darkness enveloping the old woman's body. Silmavalien opened her arms, allowing her bundle of herbs and grasses to fall into the same chasm. The air was filled with the fragrance of many herbs and grasses, all intermingled with one another. The sweet and sharp aromas of everything from thyme and parsley, rosemary, mint and other plants, filled their nostrils. Both dragon and rider bowed their heads.

Silmavalien and Minth went up around the chasm and crossed over to the other side. They set about dislodging, pushing and shoving, as large rocks as they could manage over to the chasm. When a fair number lay on its edge, Silmavalien worked on orienting and pushing them in, so that they would fall in and properly enclose the body of Lexamarian.

Then, they noticed how late and dark it was growing. There was no time to sing for Lexamarian, and Silmavalien did not even know what they should sing for her, so they just traveled back around the chasm, returning to their 'homeward' side. When they came to the spot where they had buried Lexamarian, Silmavalien knelt down beside it and kissed the stone lying on top of it. "Farewell, Dragonrider Saver and undared hope now lost. Rest in peace and honor. May your legacy be noble and great and your memory be sweet. Thank you." Minth waddled up to it and brushed his snout lightly against the stone also, paying a silent tribute in unspoken and inarticulate emotion. He squealed softly.

Then they turned away and headed for their camp through the deepening semi-darkness. Despite the fact that they hurried across the relatively short distance it was quite dark before they reached it. Silmavalien found it by its own firelight.

That night they ate voraciously, as they had not been able for many weeks – for Minth, never. It was a wonderful relief to be full and sated together, for their first time in their together-lives. They both felt well as never before. Well, whole, and one. Their wellbeing flowed into the other through their bond and back again, in a spiral of wellness.

Mingled with that was their sense of loss and sadness, as they each and together tried to keep all they could from the little they had from Lexamarian. Silmavalien twirled her ring on her own finger. The slender blue band glistened and shone in the dancing firelight. Wrought into its face was a curiously and amazingly intricate image – especially given its size. She examined it as closely as she could.

Above the picture was a crescent moon and a ten-rayed sun side by side. Seven perfect five-pointed stars completed the circle around the picture. At the bottom right of the circle ran a thick stream. On its nearer bank was shown the face of a young buck. On the other bank grew a large, somewhat gnarled tree. In its boughs was a squirrel. Over the stream a dove flew, bearing an olive branch. On the left, a huge-winged dragon flew in the sky. Though a tiny image, it imparted a sense of terror and strength, ferocity and wisdom. From its maw fire poured into the sky. In its claw it bore a stem of flowering basil. Below it stood a sword with wings below the hilt, its blade plunged halfway into the ground on the stream's bank.

In that light, her eyes could see no more, but the detail was amazing. She had never seen, or even heard, of anything that matched it. It greatly puzzled her – and through her, Minth, who also seemed to make something of it that she did not understand, and be puzzled by it in a way she did not understand.

Suddenly, she remembered she still had to oil Minth's skin.

This time, she was not sparing with the oil. She could get along from the bear, and he needed it. He was growing fast, and he had both scratched and sunburned himself. More of his skin than usual was cracking, flaking, and many places were covered with a pink rash. Fortunately, he felt good anyway, with all the food he had been eating!

That night they were cold, for most of her blankets and clothes had been soaked. She ended up carefully arranging the blankets to try to use the driest parts of them, and using the sacks as well, for warmth.

As they were settling in to sleep, cuddled as warm as they could get, she kissed Minth on the head, and he gently and affectionately nuzzled her face with his nose. The day had been disappointing and sad, yet somehow they had overcome that together and were contented.

Staring at the night sky between the trees, glittering with all its bright, twinkling stars, small, distant, and clear, Silmavalien whispered into the breeze, "Noren … Lexamarian … I wonder where you are and how you are. Please, be well, Noren."

Minth squirmed and cuddled closer to her, comforting and reassuring, and needy the same. Together they had to be all right … perhaps, Noren might hear and know.

22
Noren's Clue

He knew that every day that passed – more, every hour, every minute, every moment – took Silmavalien farther from him and closer to horror and death. (If she was not already dead, but that was a thought he could not let himself have.)

Yet so many days, more hours and minutes than ever he would be able to count had passed. Yet he could do nothing. Had done nothing. He must do *something!* What *could* he do? He must do something for her, to find her, even if he could foresee no other end to his quest than his own death. He just had to!

It had been a long, hard day for Noren, gathering and axing firewood for the winter. He was thoroughly exhausted. That night, he fell quickly into deep slumber, fully determined to spend the next day preparing for his journey and quest – and to set out the following day, no matter what.

At first his sleep was deep and dreamless, but after a few hours his desires and his fears came to torment him in nightmares, some more dreadful than any he had ever known before. Of most of these nightmares only a vague and cloudy yet strong sensation of horror and dread, death, darkness, and destruction remained in his memory. One clear image was left to him: the face of his beloved, Silmavalien. Her sweet, lovely dark eyes were filled with such fear and dread that it almost swallowed the beauty and enchantment of her strong character. Such pallor had come over her face that even her tan skin seemed white and colorless. Pain of unfathomed fear and worry, love and dread, was etched in every line of her features, features he had only known to be filled with beauty, love, sweetness, and determination, even though she could be a bit distractable, silly, and odd. He loved her and the image of her face, her eyes – windows into her soul – in such terror wounded him to the core.

A scream shattered the night, tearing Noren from his nightmare-infested slumber.

He sat up, flinging the covers away from him. The night was chilly. Deep silence seemed to cover the earth like a blanket. He held his breath and listened carefully, but he could hear no sound but the rhythmic beat of his heart, pounding like a drum in his chest, painfully and irritably loud. No other movement. No other sound. It as almost as if he was the only living creature.

The dim gray light of early dawn spilled through the window, and Noren noticed a piece of silvery white, near the edges of his straw bed. He reached for it and picked it up. It was a piece of paper. How long had it been there and he had not noticed it? He held it up. There was writing on it. Lighting his candle, he barely managed to read it:

Dear Noren, I love you. I long to be with you. Were that this moonlit night were indeed the eve of our marriage. May we one day be married and live our lives and die as one. This is indeed my prayer.

However, on this night I am forced to admit that cannot yet be. There is something I must accomplish and hastily. I will tell you one last hint: Both white ovals hold the secret of my mission. May it be yours as well. Keep your white oval and guard it carefully.

Farewell, love of my heart. May yours be a happy life of fulfillment
~Silmavalien.

Ah, it was indeed Silmavalien's handwriting! Noren had known the instant his eye had begun the painstaking task of turning the scribbling into articulate letters. What could all this mean?

His eye turned towards the shimmering white oval, wedged into a corner of his room, almost completely forgotten but for the nagging of his and Silmavalien's relatives, Krielasoriel and her Sons and Daughters of Queen Valiena, that he ought to take it to the priests, even to the oracle at the shrine in Delenois.

What secret could the white oval possibly hold, Noren wondered, that would be so pressing it could take Silmavalien in the dead of night without any prior warning, that she could send him only a vague note, *could not* tell him, her own beloved and betrothed, what it was or what had happened?

In this he did, however, find some comfort. His beloved had not been mysteriously abducted by an unknown and doubtless awful and dark enemy. She had left of her own will, whether deluded or not, on some quest she believed to be both noble and urgent.

He did not believe the old tales about gods and magic. But neither did he have any proof that they were not true. He had to take all sides into account. To him, at least, Silmavalien's disappearance, and its connection with the white oval, was important enough for him to seek out the answer to what that mysterious white oval might be – if the old stories were true. Even if it meant the long, arduous journey to Delenois.

Noren neatly folded up the wrinkled scrap of paper and tucked it into his nightshirt over his heart. Being the last thing he had from Silmavalien and his only clue to where, why, and how she had disappeared, it was an invaluable treasure.

Still exhausted, he fell back asleep. His dreams were no longer nightmares, for he had found a little contentment, at least for the time being. A hint that less evil than he had feared had befallen, and a clue about what to do now. Finally, something to do, and something possibly – even if unlikely – profitable.

When Noren woke again, sunlight streaming through the window, he felt refreshed and certainly excited. He rose and quickly dressed. His first thought was of telling his family what he had learned. His second was of his beloved's warning about keeping the white oval safe. What could she possibly have meant? What *did* she think the white oval was – or contained?

The first thing Noren did was to find his father and exclaim, "I have a farewell note that was left me by Silmavalien!"

His father looked confused. "What do you mean?" he asked. "That she sent you a note or a letter? In the middle of the night? Silmavalien hasn't been around in ages."

Noren already felt frustrated by his father's incomprehension. "No! I mean I've finally found the farewell – love note she must have left for me the night of her vanishing."

"What did she say, Son?" asked his father. "How do you know when?"

Noren recited the message from memory. It meant so much to him that that first and only reading had engraved itself in his memory, word for word. He could still see the letter in the candle light as he had earlier that morning. When he finished, his father held out his hand and asked, "May I see?"

Noren reached into his tunic and pulled out the precious scrap of paper. For a moment he stared at it. Just as precious nonetheless, the daylight revealed it to be about as dingy as paper could be. He unfolded it and placed it in his father's outstretched hand. His father only glanced at it before returning it to him. "Just as you said, Son," was his comment.

Noren carefully folded the paper back up and tucked it into his shirt just as before. His father asked, "So, Noren, what do you want to do now? I can just tell you're thinking of something."

Noren lost no time. "I want to take the white oval to Delenois to find out what the priests and oracles believe it to be – if they know. As soon as possible. I am tired of sitting and doing nothing while my beloved and proper wife wanders in peril – from I know not what."

"I understand," said his father thoughtfully. "When would you leave?"

"This very day, if I can," Noren replied, without a hint of hesitation. "However, I would dearly appreciate it if I could borrow a horse for the journey."

His father looked down thoughtfully. "I would, if I could. However, we will need all the horses to help us get firewood to last the winter."

"I am willing to wait a week or two, if I must – on the promise of a horse for the journey. Of course, I would gladly work during that time."

"We will consider it, Noren. I promise." With that his father strode away.

During a short break in his work that day, Krielasoriel came up behind him. "Noren," she said, in her sweet, clear, bird-like voice with its quiet and enchanting ring.

Noren turned about, instantly frustrated. "Yes, Kriela? What?"

"Oh, Noren, I did not mean to disturb you," she replied. "It's only, I am so grateful and overjoyed that the gods and their queens have pleased to guide you to the note left by Silmavalien and the path to the truth. It is what we have all been praying for, these weeks."

"Thank you very much," replied Noren sarcastically.

Kriela stepped back. "Noren, what is wrong?" she asked, sweetly. "I can tell that you are quite disturbed. Are you afraid for Silmavalien?"

"Yes," Noren snapped. It was true. Ever since she had disappeared he had been – and still was. "It's *better*, now." He muttered.

"What's that?" asked Kriela.

"Oh, nothing."

It was only the first of many interactions of its sort that he was forced to endure, and over the next week Noren worked hard and avoided contact with people, especially Kriela and the Sons and

Daughters of Queen Valiena – as they called themselves. He was finally preparing for his quest to discover what had taken away his beloved – and to bring her back and be reunited with her and married to her, if he could. He was absolutely certain that, no matter what had befallen her, she still loved him and would want to spend their lives together.

23

A Shred of Home

For the next several days Minth did almost nothing except to sleep. They were both comfortable, far more comfortable than they had been in weeks, perhaps months, and whenever he was not eating – or complaining of a bellyache from how much he had eaten – he was sleeping. It occurred to her one evening, sitting quietly and resting after a long day working on what was still left of the bear meat, that he might be catching up on all the sleeping he had not done while they fled. He would want to sleep a lot anyways, as a growing baby, and while he had slept a lot more than she did, his sleep in the bag might not have been very good.

As the days passed, he grew bigger and stronger, and when he was awake his thoughts were clearer and less muddled. He woke her every morning, crowing his greeting to the sunrise, and at night he snuggled up against affectionately. He seemed happy in a way he had never been before, and that made every bit of pain and exhaustion worth it. Lying, snuggled against one night after he had fallen asleep almost at once and she was not yet ready to fall asleep like that on the hard ground now that she was no longer sleep deprived, she wondered what their relationship would be like when he was a full-grown dragon and she was the same one. When it was *she* who cuddled under his wing and *he* who carried and protected – and probably hunted for – her.

Right now, the idea was hard to imagine, even though she knew it would happen if they survived long enough. His walking was a lot steadier, but he was still so clumsy and awkward, and when he tried to run he was not very fast and he always fell over within a couple steps. Flying was not even a thought at this point, though sometimes she would find herself watching the birds fly and perch in the trees with a longing that she knew came from him.

But though Minth continued to grow faster than ever, he did not seem to develop physically. His features did not grow more shapely or beautiful, and she saw no change in the awkward shape of his body which she was certain was the cause of half his clumsiness. Apart from his increasing size, he looked the same as he had the day they had so foolishly trusted their fanciful dreams and nearly fallen prey to disaster.

Perhaps it had been a fortunate mistake, she mused as she bit deep into a hunk of stewed meat and felt her senses confuse with Minth's as he also ate. It was, after all, why they now had plenty to eat, but she would not let herself forget how it ended. She could not hope for her mistakes to always turn out well, and the whole world was hostile. Even when Minth was full-grown, the world would be hopelessly dangerous, and it was even more so now.

But, for the moment, he felt safe, something she was so grateful for, and being able to sleep and eat enough was doing wonders for his health. Regular oiling with the abundant grease she had gotten from the bear had greatly improved the condition of his skin, though it was still thin and broken open easily if he scratched or fell, but for the most part it did not hurt him. He was getting playful and rambunctious like he had never had an opportunity to be in the village, but like every baby, human or animal, should get to be, and it warmed her heart to see him experiencing life the way he should have the moment he hatched. Yet while he played and pounced, he did not seem as energetic as she felt he should be. There seemed to be something wrong with him – or was she just worrying? After all, she really had no idea what young dragons needed.

At least, she decided, he seemed to getting stronger and healthier, and he definitely was not getting weaker. But, not only her mind and her soul, but her body was linked to his, and she could not dismiss the sense that something was not well.

But she would not let it taint their happiness. The joy and peace of their intimacy was enough to overcome every obstacle which opposed them and their bond, and she would not stand in its way. Not even death, she knew, could extinguish the fire of their bond – it could not always be the same, must always be a little different, yet it was always the same fire and nothing could ever put it out.

Every day, every hour that passed, she found herself loving him more, appreciating him more just the way he was. Though he remained clumsy and ugly, she saw even more than she already had just how cute he was, how perfect he was in its own way. The first love of their bond was continually growing, and she would always love him just the way he was, no matter what happened.

S

Once Silmavalien finished taking care of the products from the bear, getting all the oil she could, cooking the meat well, and laying out the

skin to dry, she had time for other things as well. She did not stop
hunting, both because she needed to hone her own skills which were not
yet enough for them and would be more and more insufficient as Minth
grew, until he could hunt for himself. But there was only so much that
she could carry, and so it was useless to hunt more than that.

That left her with time for other things. She experimented with
Lexamarian's bow and found it to be a superb weapon and also a work
of art, both wonderful crafted. It was double recurved and made of a
flexible, yet tough, spring wood which she did recognize. Graceful lines
and etchings of butter, flowers, and − above all − dragons had been
skillfully engraved into its polished surface. The pictures were
amazingly detailed and strikingly realistic, reminded her of the
engravings in the ring, and as a weapon the bow also balanced excellent
balance and symmetry.

The first fault − if twas a really a fault − that she noticed was the
effort required to string and the force of the snag when she unstrung it. It
was much longer than her own small hunting bow, and she knew that the
string would be harder. Not a bad thing if one had the strength for it,
since the arrow would fly faster and faster, but in reality it did not work
so well for her. Even if she was strong enough to use it comfortable, the
longer draw length was different and threw off her sense of time and
aim. It would take a great deal of practice to use well, and while it might
be best in the long run, she did not have the time for it now, especially
since it would need different arrows. But she kept the bow anyways,
since it was light and fit in easily with the rest of her bulky baggage.

𝓢

One day, Minth was climbing around on the rocks near the stream − too
near for Silmavalien's comfort, yet she could not really discourage it; if
Minth had recovered from the shock of falling in, she did not want to
plunge him back into that fear and force him to grow up to be a dragon
who was scared of his shadow. That was no way to live life, and she got
not take away from him the thrill of excitement that he was clearly
enjoying.

Then a sharp pain startled her, and her foot landed too heavily,
alerting the pack of quail she was stalking. But that did not matter. Was
Minth okay?

A closer touch to the connection between them told her he was
whining, but more or less unharmed. He had brought his talon down on

a pebble and broken one of his ivory claws. It was bleeding, and it *hurt!*

But it was not a serious injury, and she was not worried now. She took a few moments to mentally comfort him and then told him to be more careful and perhaps to stay away from the stream. Taking a nap in their temporary den might make him feel better.

Meanwhile she had to sneak up on those quail.

S

When she got back, Silmavalien gave Minth a kiss and a hug. Then she tossed one of the quail to the dragon and set about preparing the other. She had long ago given up on trying to make him eat his meat cooked, when he clearly preferred it raw. While she prepared the quail with hands so used to the task it took only a little attention, she watched Minth. Not only had he grown bigger, but he was plump now, even fat. His belly was fat enough it might even be contributing to his clumsiness. She smiled.

A feeling of contentment and homeliness settled in, as he ate and she worked beside him. His very presence was home to her, as hers was to him, even though was somewhat homesick and worried for Noren, and still a little tired. Autumn was an exhausting time of year, and even with their unexpected bounty, she was still working at least as hard as they would have been in the village.

A distant rumble of thought interrupted her quiet musings, and Silmavalien glanced up at the afternoon sky. Clouds were building along the mountains, and she saw lightning flashing underneath them. Still far away, but probably coming closer.

A gust of chill wind rattled the trees around her, the first touch of the storm, and then a larger, closer lightning flashed, bright enough she would have seen it even if she had not been looking.

Cold rain was probably not more than an hour or two away, maybe less. It was time to get everything she could under as much shelter as she could manage. Then build a fire under shelter if she could manage that as well to cook this quail.

24

Lost, Safe?

In the morning the clouds were already beginning to clear. Beams of golden sunlight came over the shoulder of the mountain and descended to the forest floor, and the birds who had not yet gone south for the winter were singing joyfully, not only for the new day but for the clearing of the clouds. Minth joined in with loud crows and the forest and mountains echoed with the joy and voice of a dragon.

S

Over the next several days that they stayed by the falls, the last of the blackberries ripened – more or like, got overripe, rotted, and fell off – and Silmavalien found that the wildlife immediately around their "camp" was becoming scarcer, or at least more careful. So, with a heavier pack, she and Minth set out again, still following the stream as it now lead up towards an eastern ridge. It was a laborious trek, uphill and heavily laden, but they reached the ridge by sundown.

Though both of them were tired and very hungry, Silmavalien took a moment to admire the view while there was still light to see by.

The stream wound away along the side of the sloping ridge, ever further into the towering mountains to the north which still rose so high above them! She wondered for again how they could ever get to the other side of the mountains, then decided that it was no use thinking about that right now.

She turned her mind again to the landscape. A deep, pleasant meadow-valley on the other side of the side drew her attention, but it was too far to make with what was left of the daylight. Instead she found a place to make camp in a little hollow between the stream and the ridge.

And this time, though Minth did not understand why, she did not allow either of them to eat to their heart's content.

The morning dawned bright and clear, and for the first time in a while Silmavalien woke early, but not to Minth's crowing. She felt very much refreshed, but he was still sleeping. She yawned and stretched, then hiked the short distance to a bare slap of granite atop the ridge and surveyed their surroundings again in the light of morning.

Northwards, and stretching towards both the west and the east, the Aravin mountains rose steeply up, at first cloaked heavily in evergreen forests, then patches of bare rock and great precipices, before fading into blue and gray in the distance, shrouded in cloud, capped in snow and ice. But eastwards was the beautiful valley-meadow she had seen yesterday evening, green, clear, and fresh in the morning light. It was less heavily forested than most of the mountains, but not any less green, and it looked just as much like paradise now as it had yesterday, except for a patch half way down the ridge, where a heap of gray ash marred the green loveliness. But when she turned her eyes from that scar, she saw what she had been looking for to confirm the decision she had already half-made to go that way: a little stream meandering down the meadow.

That decision made, she turned, just wanting to get a better feel for her surroundings and the lay of the lay of the land. Southwards the mountains descended less steeply, and eventually fell away into the distant green of the prairie steppes. She had not been so high and surveyed the world from a vantage point where she could see so far, beyond the home she had known all her life. It felt strange to think she was farther and higher into the mountains that she had ever before, and yet she could see all the way into land that was not mountain at all.

She stretched again, and took a long, deep breath of the chilly morning air, wondering where, in all that space, was her old village – and Noren.

Not that she wanted to go back. No, not at all. She was lost, but in a nice sort of way – the right way, at least for herself and Minth.

Beginning already to shiver from the cold of being out of her blankets so early, she climbed down from the rock and returned to Minth. Together they ate breakfast and drank what was left of the last night's water. Then, they set out up the ridge.

First, she took Minth to the granite slab, and helped him climb up, so he could see the same vision she had, with his own eyes. She knelt down beside him, and soon they found themselves gazing into each other's eyes, hers pools of dark liquid brown, his glowing minty orbs, united by love, and wonder, and excitement, and yearning. She felt more strongly than ever his yearning to soar like an eagle about the world.

Bending down further, she laced her arms loosely around his neck, and kissed him on the head between the ears, just to the side of his small pale comb. He returned the favor, licking and nuzzling her face.

Silmavalien stroked him a moment longer, then stood. It was

time to go on now.

They began the descent into the meadow from there, the tall, lush grass rustling as they passed through it. It felt like walking through the carpet of a Giant King, at least until the ground became bumpy and the descent steeper, but it was still too pleasant. It made them both want to stop and drink it all in, but they had to go on. They had not the time, and the "just a few seconds" would quickly come to mean endless hours. The minutes they had spent on the ridge viewing the world and then each other's eyes confirmed that.

But the colors, fresh and beautiful with the recent rain and soft and soothing in the overcast light, gave them plenty to delight their eyes upon without stopping. Everything was silent and still; a sort of hushing of life's goings-on, one that added to life and did not take from it, rested all around and lingered in the air. The day felt perfect in all by one respect – the cold wind that blew down from the northern peaks, chilled her even through her garments and feeling like a touch of frost on her bare skin.

She wondered how Minth handled as well as he did, given his small size, his weakness, and his thin skin, but even so it was not long before he began to shiver, so they stopped for her to put his sun-blanket on, despite the fact that there was scarcely any sunlight. Though made of a light material, the additional barrier against the wind would still keep him a little warmer. It did not help as much as Silmavalien hoped, but it did help. She wondered if she should make him a warmer blanket, or if it would get soaked through too easily and then take too long to dry, especially in the cold, wet weather that was coming, besides being too

heavy for him.

Her thoughts turned to Noren, as it took little attention to descend the relatively gentle slope. The realization that she was lost, that she would not know how to find the village if she had wanted to, brought a rush of homesickness and sorrow, longing for what was lost. She wanted to spend her life with Noren, to marry him and raise children with him. She knew that couldn't be. Even if Noren's egg hatched and they found each other, it could never be the way she wanted it to be. Sure, they could have children, but they would have to live and raise them alone, separate from everyone else, without play-mates or a village.

It made her so sad she felt a tear or two trickle down her face, but it also made her angry, angry at the people and traditions that made her unable to be a Dragonrider – be with Minth – and also marry Noren.

But then she found herself thinking about going back, almost wanting, almost considering it, a wild and disastrous desire that she knew was stimulated by the fact that it was now impossible and no longer real. She tried to fight it off, since it was not pleasant to think about, and it drowned her in homesickness and grief and other unpleasant feelings for which she had no name. Somehow, she felt trapped by the fact she could no longer do something she did not want to do.

Yet, on the other hand, it was a relief to be separated even from the possibility of returning to Treas. She could not go back and she was what the villagers considered to be high in the mountains, though their slopes towered far higher above her than she could possibly be above the village.

No one would dare come after her here, even if they did know, for they all feared the mountains just as they hated and feared the dragons and Dragonriders.

She was lost, yet, for that very reason, they were safe. Only one person perhaps, in all of Silrah, would follow her here – if he knew and could. Noren. She was not really afraid if he did, either. They trusted each other – she trusted him – too much for that.

Minth looked up at her with a puzzled look in his eyes as they walked, and finally she noticed the confusion in his thoughts.

To him, she, and she alone, was the reference point of *home*. He did not know any other friends, so he could not miss anyone. How could she be close enough to Noren to miss him, he wondered, if space could separate them and they did not live in each other's minds?

Yet, he sympathized with her in what he did not know.

It was strange how his confusion almost made sense to her, and she nearly wondered herself how it was that space separated her and Noren, that they were not bonded, too. But then she turned her mind to a more pressing issue.

Winter would be here soon, and they needed shelter. The farther they journeyed into the mountains and the more she thought about it, the more she knew that they simply could not climb the mountains, find a pass, and then climb down to the more temperate regions before the full force of winter struck. If it could even be done at all.

She remembered – or Minth remembered of something Lexamarian had said. Something about a Riders' Passage, an only safe route to the other side that did not require flying.

"The Riders' Passage is the only safe passage from this side of the Greater Aravin Range to the other. It looks like a cavern opening on top of a cliff ledge. It is very bright within; and hard to find."

How would she ever find it in time, if she ever found at all? The mountains were so long and so rough. It would be so easy to miss cavern openings, or even to never find the right cliff, the right valley, the right ridge. If Lexamarian had given her detailed instructions on where to look, then maybe she could have done it. But Lexamarian had been too addled in her mind, perhaps from having spent so long alone and being so close to death, to give clear instructions if she remembered them.

Perhaps, though they were lost in the mountains, they were not safe after all. Being burned alive was not the only way to die.

Minth looked up at her from where he trudged in the grass right beside her, underfoot except that the bond they shared kept them from tripping over one another. She felt the distress and turmoil in him. He had always looked to her for guidance. From the first few hours of his life outside the egg, he had learned to be in fear for his life. Then, at last! She had fled with him into the mountain-forests. That night, her fear had suffocated him as strongly as ever. Then, the fear was lifted. Such joy and freedom that it had almost overcome his fatigue – fatigue that still plagued him. Where *did* his partner get all her energy from?

Each time that fear had gripped Silmavalien, the dreadful panic and a terror of returning out of happy freedom back into fear had swept over him. He did not want to be afraid, but her reasoning was too sensible to dispute. They were not safe here – or below. He knew that she longed for reassurance and comfort, but he had none to offer. She was right, and he was powerless. If his partner and protector was scared, what could he do? How could he comfort her?

She knelt down and kissed him. Together, they affirmed their oneness, their togetherness. Simply being was a comfort to her. He did not need to do anything more, and she would try not to be afraid. In the village, she had needed him to be still and silent so no one would see him. Now, what she feared was not something like that. He did not need to worry about it, and she would try to be happy for him too, even though she had to do think about it because there were things she might be able to do about it.

It took only a moment to make him more comfortable. They continued walking, and she decided to put the issue out of her mind for the time. There was not much to be done about it at the moment, except explore cave opening that fit Lexamarian's description, and maybes one that didn't in case she was confused even about that. And with Silmavalien no longer fretting about it, Minth fully regained his ease.

Sometime in the late morning, they entered the lies of a small, dense firwood, that blocked most of the wind. Silmavalien wanted to linger where it was warmer, but abruptly they stepped out of the near-thicket.

The burnt patch was right before them. The long, green grass barely began at the edge of the trees before it stopped, only a few scraggly tufts poking up in a wide swath of white ash surrounding a mound of darker ash.

25

Ash and Eggs

Such a strange burn begged for an explanation. Minth, ever curious despite his chronic lethargy, encouraged her. She stepped out into the open, into the wind, and headed directly for the pile of ash, the little dragon beside her.

She soon realized that the heap was well larger than a horse.

They stopped right at the edge of the darker ash. Silmavalien scanned it, then stretched out her hand to touch it. It felt like cool ash, nothing remarkable about it.

Kneeling on the edges of it, she rested her hand on it and wondered, while Minth burrowed deeper, looking for protection against the cruel wind.

When she noticed what she doing, she smiled. "Great use for ash, huh?" she asked, amused.

He wiggled and squirmed. Her hand pressed deeper into the ash as she leaned on it, and then her fingers touched something hard.

She reached her hand farther in to grip it, then pulled it out and shook as much of the ash off as she could.

She started at it in amazement.

Fat, thin, smooth, and cool to the touch, it was shaped much like a triangle, but two of its sides were not straight, bent slightly, and the flat side was widest. Though somewhat singed, most of it was still a brilliant, clear, hard blue, sparkling even on that overcast day.

Since she knew now that at least some dragons had scales, though Minth did not, it took only a moment for her to think what it might be: a dragon scale.

As to what had caused this strange burn, that, too, now had an explanation: a dragon had died here.

She had no clue about the whys and particulars, but suddenly she felt sad, excited, and happy, all at the same time, without really knowing why. She threw the blue dragon scale aside, onto the white earth where she would be able to find it again, and burrowed into the heap alongside Minth. He squeaked at her with delight.

She soon found more of the glinting blue dragon scales, some singed more badly than others. They were all more or less the same shape, but they ranged in size from about the width off her outstretched hand to that of her thumbnail.

She and Minth were becoming extremely curious about whatever had happened and how the scales got so scattered, but he was tired and lay quietly in the ash while she worked, throwing every scale she found into a pile to the side. It was much warmer here than out in the open.

Then she felt something hard, larger than any of the scales, and much more strongly curved. She tried to wrap her fingers around it, but it was smooth and soft, and gave a little when she pressed on it. But she got her hand all around it and pulled it. Minth squealed when he saw it.

Dragon bones! As thick as Silmavalien's leg, it the cannon bone of an animal's lower foreleg. With some sense of reverence, she gently laid it near the dragon scales, then returned to searching the heap.

Almost at once, she touched another rounded object, though this time it was smooth and leathery. It was rather large, so she had to reach in and get both her hands around it to pull it out.

Holding it up she shook it, and the ash cascaded off, leaving a polished, smooth surface. She gasped, and Minth stared at it. She turned to him and whispered in an intensity of excitement "You're not alone!"

She had never forgotten anything about Minth's egg, and this one was very much like it. It looked a little larger, felt a little heavier, and was a little more elongated, yet it was clearly the same kind of thing. It felt firm yet soft in her hands and looked like perfectly polished leather except that it was shimmering white.

She sat down and cradled the dragon egg against her chest. Minth crawled out of the ash heap and lay next to her. He stretched his head out and gently nuzzled it. Both stared at it, dumbfounded with marvel, hope, longing, and joy.

But a shadow of fear woke Silmavalien's heart. Dragons breathed fire, but it could kill them, too. Otherwise, they couldn't be burned alive. What if the fire had harmed the dragon within, and he or she could not live?

She bowed her head and closed her eyes, as she sent up a silent prayer to any wise and gracious gods there may be that the dragon within this egg would be alive and healthy. Then, she kissed first the dragon egg and then Minth, before gently setting it down. She worked quickly to create a separate pile of ash to bury it in so she could find it again, with some vague idea in her mind that cold might hurt the baby dragon.

She had to find any other eggs that might be buried in the ash without spending too much time on it – she still had to hunt for herself and Minth, and any new baby dragons they might be blessed with. Minth helped her build the little mound, and then burrowed into it beside the egg. He would help to keep it warmer, too.

Silmavalien rushed back into her self-appointed task of digging through the ash, this time with a driving purpose and determination.

She found more and more dragon scales and bones, all of which she sorted into their respective piles. She did not know why she was doing so, but for some reason she was and she saw no clear reason not to – except, perhaps, saving a couple minutes.

She wished she could cart the ash she searched through away, so she would not have to search the same ash over and over again, because the mound was big enough as it was, and as tall as her. She wondered how she could possibly search all the ash in the amount of time she could spare for it? And what had guided her hand to the dragon egg so that she would not get bored of such an apparently useless task and walk away?

The sun came out from behind the clouds and warmed her pleasantly for a while but though she worked with a will, the time wore on and the work was dull. The magnitude of the task against the apparent insignificance of her progress discouraged her, and when she grew thirsty she considered moving on, at least for the day. She meant to stay in the meadow for a while, so she could come back later.

After all, perhaps some magic of the dragons had already guided her hand to the one dragon egg in the heap, and she was wasting precious time on nothing. When Minth offered no opinion to what she had not realized had been a question, she realized he had dozed off.

Another minute. One more, no more, she thought. Then she felt that smooth, leathery feel she knew so well against her hand again.

Thrills of excitement ran through Silmavalien, and she wasted no time getting the dragon egg out of the ash. Her excitement woke Minth, and he raised his head to watch her raise the dragon egg out of the ash.

All that differentiated the new egg from the others was that it was more of a squat, cone shape. The eggs seemed to differ much as birds' eggs did, and she wondered irrelevantly if there would be any color differences, or if all dragon eggs were the same stark white.

She ran to where Minth lay with the egg, and presented it to him to nuzzle and sniff, before burying in the ash on the other side of him. A few bounds took her back to her place in the main ash heap and she continued searching it, suddenly as fresh as when she began. Minth's encouragement and excited chirping kept that renewed excitement.

As Silmavalien worked, she wondered why she had found the second egg right as she was deciding to quit – as with the first. Then she remembered when the pre-hatchling dragon in the obsidian stone-egg had spoken to her, and the mystery surrounding that egg and protecting it. Did the same mystery hover over all dragons – or at least dragon eggs – with greater or less power? Did this, perhaps, hover over everyone and everything to some degree? Was it governed by some god, or were gods how people explained it?

With a sudden burst of homesickness, she realized that was a thought Noren would have.

This time, she did not tire so quickly. It did not even feel very long to her before recognized the feel of another dragon egg.

Minth, fully in tune with her, let out an exuberant squeak almost before she noticed herself. The sun came out from behind the clouds again while she carried the egg to Minth, and lit up the subtle variations of shade and color that she had not noticed before.

She titled the egg, and suddenly the pattern came into focus. Tendrils of pale brown spiderwebbed across the otherwise white surface of the egg. She gasped. Dragon eggs *were* variated in color – like and yet unlike the eggs of some birds!

She stared at it for a while, intrigued by the spiderweb patterns. Then, they remembered the shortage of time. She held it close again and knelt down next to Minth. The subtle shifting variations on the egg as the angles of its surface to the sunlight shifted, teasing her eye.

Again she showed it to Minth. He stretched out his talon to tilt it so he could see the shifting variations for himself. Then, she buried it with all of the other eggs around him. Impelled by curiosity, even though it was probably a waste of time, she dug up both the other eggs to see if they had the spiderweb pattern. Neither of them did.

Silmavalien returned to work, very excited about the prospect of so many dragon hatchlings. She had long since forgotten about keeping the old dragon scales and bones, as she dug through the ash, sending it spraying out behind her and splaying out heap. Now, she decided to work methodically from one end of the heap, so she would not search the same ash over and over again.

She was digging in the ash, almost burying herself in it, when the slope above her avalanched. She got a glimmer of white, just as she closed her eyes against the ash raining down all over her. She held her breath for a moment, waiting for Minth's squeak, then realized he had gone to sleep.

She shook the ash off her and opened her eyes. A shimmering white dome protruded from the slope of ash – *A dragon egg! Another one!*

Her joyful exuberance woke Minth, and she did the same with this dragon egg as with the three before it. Minth promptly went back to sleep, and she noticed how thirsty and tired she was becoming.

Then the sun came out from behind the clouds again, and she realized how much time had passed. It was not past noon.

When Silmavalien found another dragon egg, she carried to the egg-keeping heap at a more measured pace, no longer having the energy for running about. She rested with Minth for a couple minutes before returning to sift through the pile of ash in search of more dragon eggs. Almost at once she found another, which must have been right beside the one before it. This time, when she brought it to the others, Minth did not even stir, and she wished she could sleep like he was, then pushed away the thought. Dwelling on that desire would make it more difficult to do what she had to do.

For some reason, finding the dragon eggs went quicker, now. She kept going, thinking about how amazing it was to know that Minth – and the dragon in Noren's egg – were not the only ones left.

She desperately hoped all these eggs were alive.

The sixth dragon egg was larger than all the others and a rich hue of brown. Her excitement at finding a dragon egg which, very likely, enclosed a regular dragon, colored and scaled, a dragon without defects and problems, roused Minth from his slumber, more excited than she was. He nuzzled the egg with such care, curiosity, and expectation. Then:

A dragon is a dragon, no matter the health or power.

"Of course," she said, kissing him on the ears.

S

Within the next couple of hours Silmavalien found five more dragons egg, each one slightly different from all the rest, though all were plain white. She wondered why white dragons were so common and the others so rare, if indeed the color of the egg had to do with anything.

If there was any truth in the stories, it had not always been that way, and she knew it occasionally, but rarely, happened to other animals. One of the elders had once seen a pink-white wolf.

It was too late now to make it to the meadow and stream, particularly with all the eggs, so she decided they would have to make do with the water they had and make camp in the woods on the other side of the clearing. That took most of the daylight they had left, which left her just enough time to gather some deadwood for a fire.

26

Veine and Songeth

After dinner, Silmavalien sat with Minth sprawled across her lap, staring at the eleven dragon eggs, clustered together beside the fire. She was tired, too tired to lay down and go to sleep. Her gaze turned to the fire, and on Lexamarian's intricately detailed ring on her own finger.

Could she ... should she ... perhaps she could hatch one of the eggs.

In her exhausted and fire-mesmerized state, the thought did not seem odd or frightening. She fumbled for her knife, and when she had it in her hand, crawled over and grabbed one of the eggs. She thought it was the one with veins, but in this lighting it was hard to tell.

Carefully, carefully, she drove the point of the knife into the leathery dragon egg, while Minth lay watching her but not commenting. But she would know if he disapproved.

Now, she took the edges of the tear in her hands and tore it wider, inch by careful inch. The process was slow and painstaking but finally ... done!

Relaxing, she beheld the creature she had just hatched. Still partially covered in the clearish-milky membrane of the womb – or in this case, egg – lay a developed dragon, ugly as Minth, but not *as* ugly as Minth had been. The dragon was about the same size Minth had been at hatching, with a purple head and neck, and white shoulders and body. Veins of purple wove into the white and faded. The dragon stared at her with violet eyes.

Minth watched, excitement and joy pulsing through him, yet he remained relaxed and still. Something pulled Silmavalien, akin to the feelings around her bond to Minth, yet somehow wholly different. Softer, too, and not quite as deeply part of her.

She reached out, and touched the dragon's folded wing.

"I am Veine!"

The words sounded in her skull, but without being words. At least, they were not words in any language, either one she knew or one she did not know. Joy flooded through her with the words, the joy of hatching, of seeing the world for the first time, of living, of knowing she was loved. Of seeing the one who loved her. Echoes of the intensity of her bond with Minth bounded through it, and she drew both dragons into her arms. "I love you, Minth. I love you, Veine."

Veine nuzzled her hand, completing the connection between them. Then compelled by hunger, she turned around and licked the membrane off of herself, then gnawed on her leathery egg-shell. Silmavalien watched her intently as she lay in the largely intact shell, and her tired mind slowly put things together. Compared to the size of their eggs, she was much larger than Minth. There had not been enough room in the egg for her to hatch herself, and that was why she needed Silmavalien to do for her.

Then Silmavalien noticed how different she looked from Minth. Her whole body was built differently. Her small wings were more curved and swept out at the shoulders. Her forelegs were shaped more like a wolf's, and she had paws instead of talons. She was more slender and proportionate as well, and her tail, though far too large, was not so large as Minth's had been.

When Veine was done eating her egg and had curled up out of the way with Minth, Silmavalien took the knife again and another dragon egg. She hatched this one the same way she had done Veine's, but even more slowly, too aware of how disastrous it could be if her tired hands slipped with the knife.

It was almost a surprise, certainly a relief, when Silmavalien realized the tear in the egg was now easily large enough for a baby dragon to squeeze through. She slipped the egg off of the dragon, and the skin of her hands brushed against the dragon's skin, she felt the familiar but-always-new tingle of energy. She was too tired now for it to be the excitement it might have been, and it did not disrupt her motions. It simply flooded her with a quiet happiness that the dragons – and in particular *this* dragon – lived.

His name was Songeth, and when he stood free of the egg shell, she saw that he was larger even than Veine, with a bulkier tail but a reasonably proportionate head and neck. His stubby wings were straight like Minth's but flared from his shoulder like Veine's, and his legs and paws were shaped like Veine's, but stout like Minth's. He had a comb like Minth, but larger, and similar wing-like ears.

Then she noticed a prick of blood on his wing as he turned to eat another part of his egg-shell. Guilt poured over her and she resolved to be more careful. She did not want to hurt the next dragon worse.

Lightly, she stroked Songeth's wing. *I'm sorry.*

Then Minth moved in her mind and comforted her. Yes, she was right. She needed to be careful. But it was okay. She was saving – had saved – the lives of these dragons who had grown so long in their eggs that they were trapped and could not hatch themselves. Her thoughts mingled with hers so that she could not tell what came first from her and first from him, but his comfort wrapped around her. Then Veine and Songeth joined the conversation as well and offered their own reassurance. It was also less articulate and rational than Minth's, but a flow of gratitude and love, a desire – and need – for her happiness surrounded her. They were so happy to be free of their eggs!

As they spoke to her, insistently making sure she understood, she realized their thoughts *would* be clearer and more articulate than Minth's, but right now they were still hatchlings and they had not shared her mind for as long.

Closing her eyes, she drank in the love. She was so grateful to be surrounded by such loving, gentle creatures, so intimately close to her. Especially Minth, but also Veine and Songeth, and each for their sakes and in their own special, unique way.

Silmavalien took a sip of water, while Songeth – who seemed to strongest as well as largest – dragged his egg-shell to where Veine was still gnawing on hers next to Minth, and lay down next to them for warmth and companionship.

Silmavalien sat down between the dragons. Then she stroked each of them and they nuzzled and licked her hands. She pulled a cloak and blanket over them to keep them warmer without having to get closer than they liked to the drying heat of the fire, and donned a cloak for herself.

27

Tears of Dragons

Driven by an urgency she did not try to understand, Silmavalien hatched the next dragon. When it was time for her to slip the hatchling out of the egg, she felt neither warmth nor the familiar tingle of energy. She took a long moment to breathe. It might not mean there was anything wrong with the baby. She might have just not chosen to bond with Silmavalien.

She finished slipping the egg, and took the white hatchling in her arms and cradled her against her chest. Still there was no tingle of energy, but not only that, there was no motion or warmth in the small form.

The other three dragons crawled over to watch and snuggled up against her. She stroked the limp dragon's head as it dawned on her why the dragon – somehow, she knew this dragon was a she-dragon named Dinora – was acting so strange, so ill. Dinora had died or was nearly dead.

At that moment, the three dragons began to wail, though whether they grieved through some knowledge of their own, or because of her own thoughts, she could not tell. Three piercing tones, ascending and descending, communicated tragedy and sorrow in a way no bard's tale or singer's song ever had. It hurt her heart, and her ears together. The unique tones of each of the dragons broadened still further. Minth's voice was squeaky and scratchy, and it rubbed her heart raw. Veine's was smooth and soft, overflowing with both sadness and consolation. Songeth's was the widest of range, a song in itself weaving Minth's and Veine's wailing into a single river.

Tears trickled from her eyes as she listened. Finally, Silmavalien said, "Enough."

Carefully she laid Dinora aside, and tossed her egg to the living hatchlings. Since both Veine and Songeth were still occupied with their own egg-shells, Minth took it. Then she picked up another egg, but before she started she took a moment to send a fervent prayer, to whom she did not know, that this dragon – and all the others – might live.

Dread, tinge with anger, swept over her when again she felt neither warmth, nor movement, nor the tingle of energy as she slipped the over-sized dragon out of his or her egg. She did not even know the dragon's name. Unwilling to gave up hope, she felt for the dragon's breath and, in several different spots she had found to work on Minth, for his or her pulse.

Nothing.

Silmavalien looked up at the stars and yelled inarticulately, disturbing her dragons. Why! Why did these dragons have to die! She wanted to know each and every one of them! Each of them was as special as Minth, though only he could be so close to her.

She dropped her head and her eyes fell on the glinting silver of her ring. She twirled it around her finger, absentmindedly. This was unfair! Life was unfair! Not just not fair. *Unfair!* Why! She screamed in her mind, Minth with her. In that cry she remembered and placed all the pain, danger, and fear – both her own and Minth's – of living in the village with a dragon and then the constant danger and hardship of surviving alone in the wild with a helpless baby – now three – to care for.

"There is more to life than this … Than this world."

The dragons heard it too, but though their eyes searched the shadows, she could not that they could tell the direction with their ears, the speaker with theirs, or the soul with their minds. Already not one of them could remember what the voice sounded like, whether deep or soft, high, low, or hard. Only Silmavalien felt that it was quiet and masculine.

"Who are you?" each of them asked in their own way.

There was no answer, and Silmavalien grabbed her knife and another dragon egg, desperately hoping that this one lived. Her dragons cuddled up together again and returned to egg-eating, and she took a moment to drape blanket and cloak over them again.

It happened again as it had happened before. Until the last moment she resisted the possibility that this dragon, too, had died.

Then she bowed her head in defeat and despair. She felt she had neither the hope nor the strength to continue on. She was too tired and she could not bear the thought of hatching yet another dragon, only to find that he or she was dead. Yet something made her pick herself up and take again the knife and a dragon egg. Perhaps, it was the hope and desire within her dragon friends. Somehow, she could not fail them, especially not Minth, even if it meant failing herself. So, she hatched another dragon, hopefully – if she could dare hope – alive, and maybe dead.

A soft tingle of energy ran through her hand into her blood, and with rivers of joy. Minth, Veine, and Songeth shared and multiplied the joy, nearly squirming out of the blanket with it.

The dragon himself yawned and stretched, ever so glad to be free from the confines of his egg.

Silmavalien smiled, congratulating him. She took a moment to rest her hands, which were beginning to cramp, and noted how he was different from all the rest, uniquely himself even in his physical form.

Wydth was the longest of them, but he was neither the most slender nor the stoutest. His feet were taloned like a bird's his forelegs were those of a wolf, in a different combination of traits than she had seen yet. His 'winged' ears were on top of his head and where Songeth's and Minth's combs were, a row of tiny, evenly-spaced spikes, pure white and almost transparent, began on his head. He wriggled up against her thigh, and she stroked him for a minute as he set about licking the membrane off himself. Then, he lay down next to the other dragons to eat his egg, and she lifted the corner of cloak and blanket to cover him.

She took a moment to watch them with a tired smile on her face, wishing she had the energy to get excited about each one of them, and about all the ways they were different. But grief had sapped what energy she might have had for that.

Nonetheless, she felt much more hopeful as she hatched the dragon. Wydth had lifted a little of her weariness.

This egg happened to be the rich brown one, and when the time came to slip the dragon out, she was dismissed to feel no sign of life. What she did feel was hard and sharp – not too sharp – edges. Slowly, she realized what they were: scales. This dragon actually had scales, like the dragons in the false stories. Why was he or she dead?

She lifted the egg away to reveal a dragon who was a deep blue, beautiful and lovely like the evening sky, cloudless and viewed from a mountain. The color was clearer than any blue she could hold in her memory, marred only by a few scales that were dulled and blackened. Damaged by the fire?

Gently she laid the blue dragon with the other dead dragons. Half the dragons she had seen were dead. *Half.*

She gave the egg to her little dragons, but no one claimed right away, and she went on to tackle another egg. Saddened as she was, she was glad she had explored the ash and hatched the eggs with her knife for the sake of those dragons who were alive – including Minth. For all of them, she hoped the four who remained were alive, yet she wondered how she would ever be able to care for and get enough food for the ones she already had.

But she had to try.

This dragon, too, was dead. She sat gazing on him or her, lying in her lap. Each and every dragon, whether he or she died unhatched or not, was a dragon, special and unique. Why must they die – all of them, sooner or later? What *did* death mean?

She remembered the voice that said, "There is more to life than this … Than this world." But what could it mean? That there was an afterlife? Where had all the false tales of dragons and Dragonriders come from? What and whom could she trust?

Certainly not some mysterious voice that would not explain himself.

Silmavalien shook herself out of these thoughts and laid the new dead dragon with the others.

Before she hatched the next egg, she prayed, "If you can hear me, please bless us all. Please let these dragons live. If you are loving and good, PLEASE REVEAL YOURSELF TO US!"

There was no answer. Perhaps, she hoped, he was considering her pleas – *if* he even existed. Silmavalien, however, did not wait. If he could hear her ahead of time to influence whether the dragons were alive or dead, then he had plenty of time to consider her request – ahead of time. She hatched the ninth dragon egg.

He or she, too, was dead. Despair nearly choked Silmavalien's will to continue. It seemed to her that there was either no god or he did not love or care about her or the dragons. She wanted to crawl into a hole and hide there from the pain and despair of her life.

Yet something made her go on. She did not know why, but she reached for one of the two remaining eggs to hatch it. She did not even hope that the dragon within was alive. She had despaired of all hope and purpose. For the first time since she had found Minth's egg she felt completely alone.

Again, the dragon was dead and Silmavalien gently laid him or her with the other dead dragons. It did not sting her now. She no longer had hope left to die. Instead, she just went on to hatching the last of the dragons.

The cold, tingling energy ran through her arm. Despairing and exhausted, she did not even notice it, but the dragon within was determined to wake her to his joy in existence and freedom. *"I am Coroneth!"*

She extended her hand to touch him, glad that she could not break his joy with her despair and purposelessness. Perhaps, it was love. Somehow, deep and true, she knew that Love alone mattered; there is a

Love who will triumph and reign. Who is.

In fact, she did not have any choice about knowing. Bonding had left its imprint on her soul for eternity. When she had bonded Minth, she experienced in herself the amazing power of love and met a world of love beyond. Even in despair, she knew the song of her dream was the most real and the most lasting thing in her life. Nothing could take away that knowledge that Love was greater, even if she forgot it for a moment.

But Coroneth reminded her with his own bond and his own soul, and after a moment's struggle not to live, not to hope and be disappointed, his joy and love coursed through her, completing its spiral and flowing back into him and her again, and all of them together. From her heart, she bent down to kiss his neck and stroke his wings.

Then she sat back. She was done hatching the eggs. There was not another disappointment to face. She rested on her hands, and examined Coroneth.

Unlike the others, he had a small, bony knob on his tail, which he swung back and forth as he licked off his wings. Like Veine he had no visible ears, but he had a comb like Wydth. She did not think he was as stout as Wydth but he was close, and on him the bulky tail seemed a little less oversized, instead reminding her of a lizard.

She was so glad she had gone through all the dead dragons' eggs so she could meet Coroneth and, more, so she could help him not die in his egg, like so many others had.

28
Song in the Morning

That morning, Silmavalien woke very late not to the chorus of birds but to a strange song the like of which she had never heard. It was accompanied by the distinct voices of four croaking dragons. But whose was the singing?

Immediately she knew. Songeth was singing. She should have realized that was his name, but she had had no idea that dragons could sing when only a four hours old. Minth's own development did not exactly suggest that.

She sat up and rubbed the sleep from her eyes. The day was bright around her, and five dragons greeted her with joy. Songeth even stopped singing to squeak good morning with the rest of them. The others waddled over to her, barely able to crawl along the ground because their bellies were so full of egg. Veine lay down quietly on one side of her, and Coroneth and Wydth crawled up on the other. Minth wiggled into her lap and affectionately snuggled up against her and licked her arm, complaining quietly of his aching stomach. All of their stomachs hurt, and they hurt whenever they moved.

Silmavalien stroked their wings and necks, murmuring soothingly to them, the way she had murmured to babies she watched for their mothers sometimes, or the way she had heard mothers murmur to their babies. She almost choked on a laugh when she realized how many dragon eggs they had eaten … just how much volume of food they had stuffed into their bellies. It was no wonder they hurt now.

She just hoped that so much dragon egg would not harm them, whether the newly-hatched ones or the older Minth. She did not think it was likely, since mother's milk did not harm older children, either in humans or in animals, and somehow dragon egg-shell *felt* like mother's milk to her, as if it was sort of the same thing. So it ought not to hurt young dragon, or older ones.

And, if it was good food for them, then apart from their stomachaches, this was a good thing. Free food was never bad, and they were as full as they could be, so it would be a little while before they were very hungry, though Minth caught the edges of her thoughts and made sure she understood that being too full was *much* preferable to being too hungry.

She shook her head gently, wondering how she was going to hunt for five growing dragons with her rather meager hunting skills. But she would manage as well as she could, even if that meant everyone went hungry.

But it was time for other thoughts. It was time to celebrate their hatchings, and the bonds she had with all of them. She had not done that last night, and she had never done that properly for Minth, so it would be for him too.

Calling Songeth to her as well, Silmavalien sang a song that came to her as she opened her mouth.

> Above us rise the mountains tall
> Where swift of wing eagles nest
> When below us earth does fall
> We'll soar in blissful rest
>
> Upon wings of gold the sun flies
> Earth below in peace doth sleep
> Out of night we will arise
> Enter the highest keep
>
> Silver stars weave blessed trails
> That we follow as we fly
> In spring o'er rainbow vales
> Where earth fades from the eye
>
> We'll sing and sing and sing again
> We'll fly, rejoice, evermore
> We that are as of one kind
> All this shadow ne'ermore
>
> We'll live in blessed daylight
> And with those who have been lost
> Where everything is sweet-bright
> There no more has love cost.

She did not know where the song came from, but it filled her with the peace and strength she needed to face what she needed to, and reminded her of the peace and strength she already knew. Maybe it came from the same place the dream-song when she bonded Minth came from, from the Love that was the heart of their bond.

The other dragons joined in their song, punctuating every line and almost every word with shrill squeaks. Their exuberance and gladness rang in the bright, morning air with a joyful noise. Songeth sang, and within a few lines Silmavalien found herself found his tune. Dragon-syllables, which she knew she could never utter, hang in the air, floating from his clear, mellow voice.

When the song came to its completion, she spent a few minutes individually stroking each of the dragons. She already knew Minth's favorite spots to be patted or scratched, and she took the time to find where the others liked to be stroked as well. Then she got a small, cold breakfast for herself and split the last of the water she had them.

While she ate, she listened to their thoughts while a deep contentment filtered through her. They were constantly chattering like little children, despite their stomachaches, and she felt a new joy in Minth, as if some core desire, some void in his being, had been filled. There was a crispness, like the morning air in spring, to his joy, and she identified that as the source of her own contentment.

The presence of other dragons around them enriched their bond.

The song they had just sang still flowed in her heart, and she considered how it hummed with such absolute opposite to the despair and uselessness and doubt of the night before. Confusion smothered her as she tried and failed to understand. At Minth's quiet urging – not an urging really, but a thread of thought she felt from him even though she was not sure he even meant to send it towards her – she dismissed it. She did not need to understand, and it was already late into the morning and she had done nothing other than spend time with the dragons.

29

Requiem of Dragons

She told the dragons to stay where they were, not that it mattered much. They could hardly move, and they did not want to move any more than had to, with the current state of their stomachs.

She needed to find a good place, not too far away, to bury the dead dragons. In the face of that grim task, the dragons chatter kept her from drifting into the grief and despair of the previous night, and she listened to them discuss birds and butterflies, and worms while she searched for her burial grounds. It amused her to hear Minth telling them about all the things he had encountered and heard, and some of their responses amused her even further.

Soon she found a glade in which stood an ancient ring of huge, weathered stones, with sequoias standing over them. The ring itself was nearly filled thigh-deep with the needles of sequoias and a loose dirt that came from the needles of years long past. Here was the place.

She returned to the dragons. Their were still far too fat, bloated, and not-so-good-feeling, so she had to carry them, one by one, which took a lot of time.

With each of the dead dragons, Silmavalien climbed into the rock ring, while her five friends remained below. She dug a separate grave for each of the seven dead dragons in the loose dirt and up against the rock of the ring. When the holes were ready, she went down to gather herbs to bury them in the proper way, with the fruits of the season. She returned with her arms full of a bundle of the Cure of the Dusk – a fern whose scent helped with nausea – as well as a little mint, rosemary, wilted wild rose, and anything else she could find. She covered their bodies with the herbs before burying them, and then ritually scattered what was left over their graves.

Then she climbed down out of the rocks, to where she had left the dragons, and sang, as she had not been able to sing for Lexamarian. But somehow, she felt closer to these dragons, and it was more important to do everything right for her. Or maybe Songeth was here now, and he could find a song when she could not.

Her voice rose softly, slowly, with trailing, sorrowful, near-wailing, notes, as the words flowed into her mind.

Sweet, sweet vales, fair and sweet
Ever filled in memories
Thought of sorrow and of joy together meet
Where lives freeze

Dragons called to arise
Still lie in slumber too deep
For words of any that live beneath earth's skies
To wake here

We find all here are lost
In this land beneath the sun
None the falling night and shadows of the past
Can outrun

Beyond the storm what wait
All of earth to grasp e'ermore?
Unlooked for light? Else a dark, haunting fate
All t'swallow

Finally, she broke off, to listen only. Songeth was singing a tune of such sorrow and loneliness she could not meddle with it. Until now she had followed his notes, but now his tune has passed beyond her, so she listened, her silence giving more meaning to his song than her voice could ever do. The other dragons still crowed along, but their noise seemed fitting and right, still woven into his tune in perfect harmony as the song echoed and re-echoed across the mountains.

She let Songeth's song drop into her mind, without putting words to it, some sense telling her this was at least part of why she had to stop now. His words, if they were words, were something else, and hers would have only diminished them, made their meaning and power less. To define his song would be to ruin it.

So she just listened, feeling his sorrow and loss – but no sense of death as she had one, which surprised her at first, though that might be another reason why she had to stop. Yet Minth could still crow with him, and she knew Minth had some understanding of death. He had learned it long ago, from her terror and warnings in the village, when he learned fear within his first few hours outside the egg. But though linked to her, and though they spoke mind-to-mind with him, the others did not share his sense of death. The urgency of her need for him to understand fear, and to know what he feared, had been necessary, and it was not there for them.

Gladly.

They had never known captivity and prison, never felt the imprisonment she and Minth had shared together. A prison it had been to both of them, for him to be unable to go outside, to feel the breeze and the sun, sniff the grass, and crow aloud, and a prison it had been to her, to have to keep him secret and to share in his imprisonment.

And that was why, and how, Minth had come to share her sense of death, while the others only felt the sorrow of something lost.

Songeth's song faded away into echoes, and they waited for the last of the echoes to fade. Then Silmavalien started carrying the dragons back to their camp, one by one. They followed slowly until she came back for them, Minth last.

Finally, they were all there. She picked up all her things, telling the dragons they would have to walk the rest of the way with her. Carrying their food and shelters and tools was enough for her.

As she stepped back out of the shadows of the wood, she looked up at the sky. A feeling of dread tingled in her heart. It was well past noon, and she hoped that, despite the dragons' slow pace, they would still be able to reach the stream and find a good place to spend the night before it got too dark.

Having drank the last of their water in the morning, all of them were very thirsty by the time they heard the stream. Its free, joyous bubbling only made them thirstier, and when Silmavalien finally saw the stream, the desire to stoop down and drink from it right there was almost more than she could bear.

But she dared not. She could not take the risk, small though it might be, of the water making her sick before she boiled it, not with so many lives depending on her. But the dragons were thirsty, too, so even though her temples throbbed from thirst, she knelt by the stream and called to them one by one. Minth had shared with all of them how he had fallen into the cold, fast water and almost been washed away, so they understood not to get close to the stream unless she called them.

One by one they came to her, and she held each one tightly while he or she drank, enduring the mixed pleasure and agony, agony of watching someone else drink while she longed to do so herself, and pleasure of feeling their thirst satisfied.

Finally, they had all drank to their heart's content, and she led them along, looking for a good place to spend the night. Darkness was falling, and they made do with a small hollow, nestled under a cedar tree that grew a fair ways up the bank of the stream. She left the bags and the dragons there, telling them to stay safe, and went to gather some sticks for a fire, careful not to stray far in the falling darkness.

She only managed to get a small fire. Once she kindled it, she wasted no time in getting the metal bowl and bringing water from the stream to a boil. While she waited, she stroked each of the dragons and tried to pay attention to them and distract herself from her growing thirst. But at least the water was cool enough to drink – though still hot – and she gulped it all down, then went back to the stream for more water to re-fill the water-skin.

After dinner, she sang the Dragon Song with another verse that spoke to the growing bond between her and many more dragons:

We will dance together
In joy like never before
Now with another and another
All together One forevermore
In One who draws us more and more.

Once the water-skin was filled with the boiled water, she took her blankets and lay down with the dragons in the hollow. In moments they were all asleep, and though the night was cold they stayed fairly warm, tucked together under several blankets. The embers of the dying fire were between them and the night, and the great cedars stood as a shield against the warmth-stealing night-sky and the chill wind flowing down the valley.

30

The Pine Cone Collector

The next days were going to be hard. Taking care of one dragon had been difficult enough. Taking care of five seemed impossible. They were all so ravenous. After breakfast there was far less left than Silmavalien had hoped, and she left to hunt immediately.

She had hardly left the dragons when she stopped, staring at a pine cone that hung from a branch above her head, just out of the reach where she might be able to jump for it. Food. Delicious, rich food.

But hard to get. She turned her mind back to the hunt, leaving a corner free to contemplate how she might get to the pine nuts.

She returned late in the afternoon with far less to show for the day that she would have wished. There seemed no way she could ever feed them all. True, she was much better at hunting than she had been, but still, she had only five rabbits! Together, the dragons could eat that in a single meal, and they were going to grow!

After she skinned the rabbits, she tossed three to the dragons raw, trusting them to divide the food in a reasonable way, and buried the other two in the hot ashes to cook over the night.

That was breakfast the following morning, and everyone was still hungry, but it could not be helped, and she was not going to let them completely devour their stores. She could not help thinking about how soon the dragons might possibly be able to start hunting for themselves. She had thought of a way she might be able to get pine cones, but it would take some time to put together. She went out to hunt again, reminding the dragons to stay put, and trying to silence the worry in her heart that said they were very much like prey. She hoped the fact they were very much predators, and must smell like predators, would keep other predators away with the fear the mother dragon might be close.

That day, she was far less picky about what she picked out to hunt, taking anything she saw. That meant that, in addition to four rabbits, she also brought home four small squirrels, and looking at them she wished so much they were the larger gray ones that were common a bit below the old village.

More than that, she wished she was a better shot. She missed her target more than once and had to waste a lot of time searching for her arrows. She could make new arrows, but that would cost a lot of time too, and she was not very good at it yet. She could not make arrows the equal of the ones she had.

After dinner, Silmavalien sat down against the cedar, with Minth in her lap watching her braid together strands of yarn, the first step in her plan for a tool to get the pine cones. The newer hatchlings had gone to sleep immediately after eating, but Minth was not that sleepy yet, and he kept her company until she got too tired to braid well and went to sleep.

The next day, though she still brought her bow and game pouch, Silmavalien's focus was on looking for a long stick, not too slender but also not too thick, and relatively straight, to form the backbone of her new tool. It took her a long time to find something suitable, and in the end she used a young fallen pine. It was not quite free from its anchor in the ground yet, so she carefully used her knife to help pry the fibers apart, a task that took a long time since she could not risk breaking the knife.

She dragged it away triumphant, struggling with its length, since it was much longer than she was tall, but that was the whole point. She needed it to be long to reach up into the tree tops.

But her triumph was for more than the young tree. She had only gotten a few squirrels and rabbits, but her game pouch was stuffed full with herbs and bulbs. She had found lots of onions, a delicacy she loved though she was not going to share them with the dragons since they were not good for most animal, but she had lots of herbs for the dragons as well, and the thought of the delicious meal she would cook for herself gave her plenty of energy for wrangling the tree back.

That energy flowed over into the dragons, and they started out to meet her once she was near. Squeaking and squawking, flapping their wings and thumping their tails, they accompanied her back, and sometimes she had to remind them to stay away from the tree, since it would only slow her down and make it harder if she had to worry about hitting them with it.

After she made dinner, she used her knife to carve a hole in the narrow tip of the pine tree. The next day, she spent less time hunting, and returned a little after noon so that she would have plenty of time to finish the pine nut collector. This time, the younger dragons were not all asleep, so they too got to watch her braid yarn, attentive glowing eyes following the deft motions of her fingers and the wiggly ends of the yarn, with curiosity and some confusion. No matter how many times she explained what she was doing or why, they did not understand.

When she had braided all the yarn, she made a loop to thread through the hole in the pine tree, tying it off with a slip knot. Now a long rope of braided yarn hung down the length of a stick, and a loop that she could pull loose or taut hung from the other end of the stick. It was a little unwieldy to hold the stick up, but she was certain with practice she would get good at it. Already, she could flick the stick, caught the loop to fly loose, the way it would need to catch the pine cone.

She laughed, and put the cone collector down. It was finished. It was perfect!

Hopefully, it worked.

The dragons squealed and Songeth chirruped, joining her laugh. They rushed over – stumbling and falling over each other's tails with almost every step – not that the dangerous stick was on the ground, and she knelt down to hug of each of them. The young ones already felt so much bigger, and she was amazed at how quickly they were growing, despite the fact they were almost always hungry.

Why was it that they and Minth wanted to eat a similar amount, but they grew much more quickly *and* had more energy? Her sense that there was something a little bit wrong with poor Minth returned to her.

The oldest little dragon looked up at her with his minty eyes, and corrected her. No, he was not a poor dragon. He was with her and he was satisfied to be with her. He was a happy little dragon. He stretched up his neck and licked her face. She kissed him on the forehead and stroked his shoulders in return.

Then they went to sleep.

S

It was drizzling again in the morning. Sensing that it would soon be raining harder, Silmavalien hunted around the hollow and found a large cedar tree that would keep more of the water away. She took the dragons and her bags there, and told them to stay dry. With the bearskin shawl over her shoulders in case it poured, both quiver and knife belted on underneath it to keep them dry, and dragging the pine cone collector, she left. When she found game to stalk, she would have to leave it, but she wanted to get some pine cones first.

As she had suspected, it was still not easy, but it did not take her long to get better at wielding the pole. She had already got six, and she had successfully knocked a seventh off its branch, but it had caught in another branch on the way down. So she hiked up her clothes and scrabbled into the tree. It took a few minutes to climb her way through the spiral of branches to where the pine cone had caught. A few moments later, it was in her pouch, and she was looking around, considering the best way to climb down, when she glimpsed motion in a tree across the small clearing.

Habit took over. Supported against the limbs of the tree, it took only a moment for her to get her bow out of its quiver and string it, and then an arrow was on the string a moment latter.

The leaves were still quivering, showing her where to look, and then the squirrel ran onto a barren branch to reach the next tree. Her arrow flee true, and it tumbled from the branch onto the ground.

She finished climbing down the tree and picked up the squirrel. A moment later, a change in the tempo of the rain, a hazier and thicker sound told her that the drizzle had changed to pour somewhere close. As she stood, it drew nearer.

Between the branches of the trees and the bearskin shawl, she stayed much drier than she could have and it was not a miserable day. But since the heavy clouds meant darkness would fall sooner and suddenly, she made sure to return to the dragons with plenty of time to spare. As she struggled to get a good fire going without a large, dry space, she wondered how they would survive the winter. She knew enough about snow to know it was going to make it much harder both to gather and to hunt.

When she woke at first light the next morning, it was still raining heavily, but by the time she and the dragons had eaten, she could see a bright radiance in the east which must be the sun. She wondered if the rain was going to pass soon, or if it was just a small area where the clouds were thinner.

When she stepped out of the little shelter in the roots of the cedar tree, she saw there were rivulets flowing through the hollow everywhere that had not been there – had certainly not been that large – even yesterday evening. She went out to hunt, leaping the larger rivulets that she could not step across, and found that the morning was the best time to hunt rabbit.

By the time she came back in the early afternoon, the rivulets were even larger, though the rain had definitely slackened off. She struggled to jump some of them, since while they were not fast and deep enough to be dangerous, they were cold enough to hurt and wet enough to damage leather.

On her way back, she noticed clear deer tracks. It occurred to her that hunting deer might be the key, and she wondered if hunting deer was something she ought to try. She knew she probably still was not ready and that it would require a lot of effort, but she had to feed the dragons somehow.

Shortly after she reached the dragons, the sun came out, even though it was still raining. All of them held their breath in awe as if slipped out from behind the heavier clouds, and washed the rain-fresh colors of the whole with its rich red hue. From east to west the clouds flamed with color, dark and bright, purples and brilliant pinks and golds.

Songeth burst into brilliant, soaring song that seemed as if it would fill the whole world with inexpressible delight.

31
A Life for a Life

When Silmavalien woke the next morning she knew by the gentle tap-tinkle-tap that it was no longer pouring. Songeth was singing jubilantly, joyfully proclaiming the rain was lightening and would soon cease. She got up.

The rivulet which flowed through the hollow was much larger than the previous night but still easy enough to cross. This time, she left her pine cone collector against the cedar.

The thoughts of yesterday had resolved over the night into a determination to try to take down a deer, despite the nerves twisting her stomach. She found a pile of fresh deer manure, and was able to guess at the direction the deer had gone. The nerves twisting her stomach unraveled in the excitement, and she very carefully followed the trail, her senses alert for any sign the deer were near. She tried to calm the excitement and relax, knowing the more casual she felt, the less fear she would send ahead of her.

But as time went on, and she neither heard nor saw the deer, she relaxed naturally, though she was still careful and stepped lightly, avoiding making sound as much as she could.

Then, out of the corner of her eye, she glimpsed a silver-gray creature, grazing. Almost reflexively, she brought up her bow, drew the string back, and released. Swift and sure, almost too swift for the eye to follow, flew the arrow.

The deer screamed. Silmavalien cringed. The moment when she had watched the deer in the glade came back to her. The agony in the animal's voice made her feel a traitor, and for a moment she regretted shooting her.

Then, she remembered Minth and Veine, Wydth and Coroneth and Songeth. To her, the lives of these dragons were more important. She had made no pact with the deer. She was a huntress, from a people of hunters.

The whole herd of deer, suddenly unmistakable and they bounded and fled, recalled Silmavalien. She sprang downhill after them, keeping them in sight, the one she had shot still among them.

In what felt like moments, the stream lay before them. Over it leapt the deer, beautiful and graceful. She almost faltered again, when the one she wounded leapt, blood staining her coat, the cruel arrow wedged in her flesh.

Then she recovered and ran on, too distracted to think much about it as she made the leap, barely clearing the water. On she ran, after the deer, but they gained on her. She glimpsed them for a while through the light underbrush of the conifer woods, then realized it was hopeless to keep them in sight. Pacing herself, she hoped she would be able to follow their tracks.

Again and again, she crossed smaller streams and found the tracks again each time. The rain was intermittent now, and she was getting hot and thirsty. The day wore on, and as she started to get a headache, she realized she would have to take the chance of getting sick, and drink. Either that, or give up and leave the wounded deer out there, which was an unthinkable option. That commitment was part of the challenge of hunting deer.

The next time she came across a large rivulet she stopped to drink, and found she was able to continue the pursuit with renewed energy. She struggled up one of the little ridges that broke up the valley and finally caught the glimpse of a deer.

The doe she had injured raced between the trees up the other side of the smaller valley between ridges – what other could it be? The sight encouraged her and yet discouraged her at once. She knew she had not lost the deer, but there was so much distance – up and down! – still between her and her prey.

She tried to regain what energy she could down the slope, but it was not really a rest, since she still had to control her descent. Even excitement could not make her feel fleet as she took the run up the ridge, following the now-vanished doe.

This was becoming more than a little tedious, but she struggled onward. She felt Minth's presence move in beside her, and a moment later the others joined him. They had sensed her strength flagging, and they sent her their encouragement and their love.

Finally, she came upon her prey, lying down, in a glade. When the doe saw her, she struggled to her feet and tried to flee, but it was clear that the wound was taking its toll. Silmavalien raced forward, half in a burst of energy, half in determination, and fell upon the deer, her knife in hand. The doe crumpled under her.

In a few moments, the animal was dead, and confusion overwhelmed her in a downpour of emotions. The killing of a rabbit, squirrel, or bird had never affected her in a such a manner. Perhaps, it was this doe's agonized scream, and fight for life, and that of her herd with her, that made the difference. But why?

Or maybe it was the recent experience with the dead dragons.

She knelt down by the doe, and stoked the soft, smooth, shiny, silky silver-gray coat. "I'm sorry," she whispered, and then, "but I do not think I would take it back, if I could. I will honor your life. But why must it be? Why a life for a life, pain for satisfaction, loss for gain?" She felt a tear trickle down her cheek.

Her eyes fell again on the ring that she wore, and she saw a new picture in its complex engravings: a deer browsing in thick foliage, and a dove bearing an olive branch. She looked up towards the white, drizzling sky and a Voice spoke to her, as if from nowhere.

"This is the law of the universe. And has been perverted."

"Why do you speak to me, now and then, but never reveal yourself?" she demanded.

"I will," came the Voice, and she knew he would answer no more.

She also knew that she could not possibly get 'home' before nightfall, which was almost upon them, and she could not travel after dark or she would almost certainly get lost.

She reminded the dragons to stay where they were, since she could feel their disappointment and hunger raging through her, and then searched the area where she had caught the deer for sticks she could coax a fire from. It would not hurt to begin cooking the deer, and she needed a fire to keep predators and scavengers away.

After she roasted a good deal of venison, ate as much as she could, and built up the fire again so that it would last, Silmavalien went to sleep as close to the flames as she could bear their heat.

Early in the morning, as soon as it was light, she got up. The passing rainstorm could just be seen in the east, through gaps in the ridges there, and overhead, the sky was clear blue strewn with milky white. The ground was very soaked, and unfortunately, Silmavalien had to cross many rivulets burdened by the doe. Fortunately, they were starting to get smaller, but many of them were still far too large for her to step across with her burden. More than once she had to take her boots off to avoid ruining them in the water.

The day wore on, and exhaustion caught up with her. It was well into the afternoon by the time she reached the stream, and the little hollow was beyond it. Baffled as to how she could get both herself and the meat across it, she sat down the banks to recover some energy and think about it.

An idea came to her. First, she ate from the roasted venison in her pouch. Then, she took her knife and continued cutting up the meat. She threw the chunks across the stream, where the dragons devoured them whole-heartedly.

After the dragons had had a good-sized meal and were all sated, she took another chunk in her pouch, ran at the stream, and just managed to leap it. She drank heartily, and then re-kindled the fire and got some of the venison stewing, before leaping the stream again to continue taking care of the deer.

When she threw the skin over, the dragons helpfully arranged it flat, the skin-side up, just beyond the edge of the stream for her. Then she told them that they had enough food for now, and they did not want to both have their stomachs hurt now *and* be hungry later, and finished cutting up the deer and hurling it across, on the skin. By the time she was done, it was dark, and this time when she crossed the stream, she did so barefoot, with her boots tucked into her pouch.

That was certainly a good decision, since she landed in the edge of the stream. The water was shallow, but still enough to ruin her boots. She stepped out of it and took a deep, bracing breath. Her work for the night was not yet over. She needed to cook the meat and store it before it became too much of a temptation for her small friends to resist.

Fortunately, Minth snuggled up against her to keep her company. The other dragons also took turns keeping her company, and keeping her awake. They were such great friends, she thought with tired gratitude.

32

Up the Meadow

The last glow had faded from the west when Minth left Silmavalien. A short while later he returned with a shred of rabbit-skin. Suddenly she remembered, as though from a dream, but Minth's memories were not a dream.

He was very hungry, and his Silmavalien would not be back any time soon. She was sleeping. Minth walked away from the tree in the hollow. It was drizzling lightly. Quite pleasant, actually. His minty eyes dimly lit the way. After about ten paces he stopped and sat down. His tail twitched. He swung his neck around, to look behind him.

Out of the darkness Veine's brilliant eyes gleamed the purest rainbow shade in the blue of excitement. She knew what he was about, only a hatchling still. He could not count the days, but he knew he must be much older, and he had not known this when he was as young as she was now.

Arranged behind her were the eyes of the other three, varying shades of blue. They all knew what he was about, and they were happy for him.

Minth continued to creep forward. Excitement and anticipation caused his heart to beat faster than usual, and his muscles tensed. He sought out a patch of grass, and lay down, to wait for his prey.

Silently, he watched the rabbit, waiting for the moment to pounce. It became clear to him that the rabbit was drawn towards the light of his eyes – towards danger and death. The tension in his muscles became as discomfort, and as he struggled to be perfectly still, tremors racked him.

The browsing rabbit came closer and closer, and his muscles hurt and trembled more.

Suddenly, he realized the rabbit was less than the length of his tail away. Confused emotions and impulses washed over him. He shut his lantern-eyes and sprang, jaws wide open, claws un-sheathed. He felt them tear into something. Then, he dropped his neck, and bit into the living, quivering ball of fear and fur.

The taste of fresh, hot blood filled his moth. The rabbit screamed and yelled, in pain. No! It should be dead. Not living. Not in pain. Not in fear. Not what Silmavalien feared for them. Dead. Food.

He released, and in another quick, jerky movement, bit down. The rabbit quite struggling. He opened his eyes.

Minth lay half over the rabbit, which he had between his claws and in his teeth. He really enjoyed the fresh, warm meat, but he did not care for the hair and skin. He got up and did his best to tear off the bulk of the skin. Then he attacked his meal with energy and wolfed it down. All the while, thrills of fulfillment raced through him.

Songeth sang for him, punctuating the stillness and quite of the night. Then, Veine gently reminded him.

"Minth, are you going to share that with us, please?"

"Yes," *Minth grudgingly replied.* "But it is my kill, you know."

He returned his attention to the rabbit, and when he had devoured most of it, he stood aside and walked partway back to the hollow. He invited his friends to come out, and each take a bite, to ease their hunger.

Silmavalien's mind raced with thoughts as he shared his memory. When she had heard it all, she asked first, "Now, why didn't you wake me up with all of this, Minth?"

He nuzzled her arm. His thoughts flowed together with hers. She had been too tired and worn out to wake up unless they really tried. He loved her too much to wake her just for his pleasure. She could be with him in it later.

She bent down, and kissed him. "You know what," she whispered, "I really appreciate your love and consideration." He nodded, and she felt his little self burst with happiness at her appreciation.

She waited for him to enjoy that, then continued, "But why didn't you share with your friends? That was not very friendly of you. And when did I not give you – especially more than one of you together – more than I took for myself? What, Minth, were you thinking?"

Her criticism stung him, and she felt his disappointment when he realized that he had not been a good friend. He snuggled up against her and into her. He was sorry. Really, sorry. She put his arm over him in acceptance, and all his friends came up around them and offered their forgiveness.

Then she noticed the sores developing on their skin. A shock of guilt raced through her. She had neglected to care for them. She put Minth out of her lap and jumped up to get the oil to rub into their skin.

And, how had she forgotten she needed to get the oil out of the venison, too?

S

When Silmavalien finally went to sleep, it was very late, and she woke late into the day. She ate quickly, and then packed up, since she still had an urge to get farther into the mountains and away from the village, and she also wanted to find some better shelter before it rained again – or snowed.

The pine cone collector continued to prove a hassle to drag, but it also proved its worth, as she got several more of the cones full of rich nuts that did a very good job filling her belly. She also shot two rabbits without losing an arrow, and decided that she was getting better at this.

That night, she found a sheltered little clearing under fir trees, just off the bank of the stream. It was not the shelter she would like, but hopefully it would not rain again just yet and she could find something better in a few days. After building the fire, she remembered to oil the dragons, except for Veine and Wydth. Their skins were both different, and so far they had not seemed to need it. Veine's skin was soft, but it stayed smooth and moist, and Wydth's skin felt thicker and tougher. She had not noticed right after hatching, but it was obvious now.

She hoped the others would be able to find some plant to rub into their skin that would help or start to produce their own skin oils as they matured. It would be tedious to make enough grease and keep them oiled once they were big, though she would gladly do that, in return for having them able to take care of themselves and even hunt for her.

It would not do to think on that too much.

The next day the sky was still clear and the wind felt clear, and she decided to trust that the weather would hold and go hunting. It was her best day for hunting yet, though she only got pine cone, but Minth's experience was disappointing. No matter how hard he tried, he could not repeat his kill of the rabbit, and was only able to catch insects, though he did do a fair job of that. He got not only ants, whose bits interestingly did not irritate his otherwise fragile skin, but moths and even flies. The younger ones watched him and copied his example, and were soon hunting bugs themselves.

The next day they traveled again, and Silmavalien's hunting luck held. Though she did not get as much as when she dedicated the day to hunting, she got more pine cones. She noted with surprise that Veine –

the lightest, slimmest, and smallest of the dragons – was already the best at moving about. Well, not quite, but she was not far behind even Minth.

S

The routine of travel-one-day-hunt-the-next-day continued as they journeyed up the meadow-valley. Somehow, it seemed suitable, and the weather held. She lost an arrow more than once when hunting on travel day, and looking for it reduced the distance they could cover, but that was not really a problem now.

She still entertained the hope of the Riders' Passage, so highly recommended by Lexamarian. Silmavalien was not entirely sure she had been in her mind, but if she had not been, that did not mean that there was no truth to anything she had said. Perhaps there was significant truth to all of it, and she was only confused, to a greater or lesser degree... or, perhaps not. Silmavalien did not know what to think, but she could hope.... And she did not want to see if they could survive the entire winter in the only elevations that were safe.

Despite Minth's repeated attempts to try, Veine was the next to successfully hunt something larger than a squirrel. Like Minth had, she shared her delight and her pride in her cunning and patience with Silmavalien afterwards. Her story was very different from Minth's: she had watched the squirrel until she knew his favorite tree, and then she had snuck and waited patiently by its base for her moment. She did not manage an instant kill anymore than Minth had, but it seemed not to disturb her.

The next day, they made camp at a place where another stream joined the one they had been following, and here Silmavalien hunted her second deer. Though it was still a challenge, it was a quite different experience, since she came across a large herd almost by accident, and watched them from the hill for a while, before choosing her target. The deer did not move as constantly or as jittery as the smaller animals, so she had time to aim carefully and really follow some of Noren's instructions.

He had not really been instructing. He did not expect her to hunt deer any time soon, if ever, though they had vaguely planned to go hunting together sometime after they married. But he had talked to her a lot about what he had learned and was learning, and about what he did: what he did well, where he had failed, how he was improving. So she dived into that, and then swallowed back the rush of homesickness and longing for him – worry, too, and sadness – that came over her, and shot her arrow, aiming for the place he had described as best.

A few moments later, she knew she had not got it quite right, since the deer did not drop dead the way it was supposed to, but it was not like last time either and died quickly, without her having to chase it far. And since she was much closer to the camp, she was able to drag it back before nightfall, and she did not have to get it across a stream either. She was even able to go out again and get another rabbit, without even risking losing an arrow.

The next morning, she noticed that the birds no longer sang, but she did not feel it as a loss every previous winter of her life. Songeth's singing was more beautiful than ever, and she was happy waking up to his singing, with no accompaniment but for the crowing of the other dragons. It was not like birdsong, but it was even more beautiful.

S

A few days later, they moved on again. This time, they mostly climbed uphill, as the valley was growing steeper and rising into the mountains.

During their trek up the side of the valley, it rained again, and this time it was colder. Silmavalien tried to remember when she usually saw the snowline above the village, so she could guess when it was likely to snow, though she supposed it could be anytime, since according to those older than herself, it usually snowed in the village.

The dragons but none of them succeeded again. Minth and Veine both got close to their prey but never touched it, often frustrating themselves. Silmavalien was not disappointed in them, but she was disappointed, since she had hoped they would be able to help contribute to their meals with more than a few insects, and those were becoming much harder to find too, as the winter rolled in.

She wondered vaguely if they would do better at learning if she could bring them live prey, the way she had seen cats do with their young, but she dismissed the thought. It was not feasible.

33

The Light of the Ring

It was raining heavily while Silmavalien trudged up an especially steep slope. The dragons trailed behind her, only Minth quite on her heels. A thicket of conifer trees sheltered them from the worst of the pouring rain, and the soft lighting was dim.

Suddenly she stood in the open. The dragons were still struggling to make the ascent, but they were easily within sight even in the darkness under the trees. She held her bow ready, under her new deerskin cloak to keep it dry.

The rain was much heavier, here, and the light, though still soft, much brighter. It could not have been much later than noon she guessed, earlier than she had feared. Across a short distance of steep, rocky, open space there was a high cliff of aged granite. Directly in front of her, the yawning black mouth of a large cavern opened in it, a perfect place to shelter from the storm. The stream she had been followed bubbled out of the ground not far from its opening.

She turned and took a step back into the shelter of the trees, to wait for the dragons to catch up. Once they had all caught their breath, they began the climb up the almost cliff-like ascent of rock to the mouth of the cavern.

Finally she stepped into the darkness of the cavern, and suddenly it was not dark. In fact, it was much brighter than outside!

The cavern was filled with light, at least as bright as unclouded noon. She gasped, and raised her hand to shield her eyes. Then she realized the source of the unearthly light.

The figures etched in her ring glowed so bright that she could not look at the ring, but in one brief glance, she saw that each figure glowed the color most appropriate to it.

And the dragon glowed purest white, white hot. White like Minth and the others.

What was this ring? Etched with skill and detail beyond any human craft, there were times when she looked at it and useful ideas came into her mind or voices from beyond earth spoke, as if through it. And now it shone and gave off radiance of its own, like the noon sun!

But she did not control it. Someone else did, perhaps the one who had now spoken to her several times. Had Lexamarian known what it was capable of, or *who worked through it?*

What did it all mean? She wanted to look at the source of the light, but she could not. The ring was too bright. Instead, she looked at the cavern walls, which reflected the light back at her.

Her first glance around the walls revealed nothing but the shifting, confusing riot of color that overawed it. It looked a dancing rainbow that was constantly re-arranging its colors. The walls glittered and shone as if studded with every kind of gem. The patterns were so complex and intricate that she wanted to gaze upon each one for minutes, but they would not let her. They were in constant moment, never the same for a blink of an eye, always flowing sinuously into a new form. She just wanted it to stay still for her to see it.

Then she realized what was causing the light to shift, or part of it. With every pulse in her body, her finger twitched. It was so little it usually did not matter, but even the slight change had huge effects on the way the light reflected off the cavern walls, even if she did not really understand why.

But she wanted to see the light patterns stop moving, so now she had realized that, she bent down to the floor, which shimmered with the same brilliance, and began to twist the ring off her finger.

The moment it was loose upon her skin, it went dark. All the bright colors faded, and by contrast with their brilliant the soft, overcast daylight that came in through the opening was like pitch blackness. Fear filled her heart so rapidly she almost panicked, but not before she shoved the ring back on, as quickly as possible.

Instantly, the light from the ring flared high, and she knew at once that it was different from before, though not how it was different.

She did not have time to consider it, because in the same instant she heard the *twang* of a bow-string being released, and then the *whizz* of the arrow speeding through the air.

A thrill of icy cold fear tingled through her, chilling her blood, and a long, black arrow arched past her head.

As if in a moment of silence, quicker than a thought, the words of Lexamarian came back to her, as if spoken within her mind.

"Do not be afraid.... Fear helps them."

She drew herself together, grabbing her bow and an arrow. She held up her bow and knocked the arrow. Then she drew the string to her nose. She held it there, while her eyes sought her target. Unemotional, cold feeling filled her. She was fighting a being of comparable intelligence and skills. She was both hunter and hunted. She tried to focus and pretend she was hunting.

Fortunately, the light of the ring was now a brilliant warm light, that did not cast reflections, and in a moment Minth pointed her prey out to her, showing her where he felt a darkened thought.

Together, they probed the mind to know what hunted them. It was ugly and repelling, dark, and enclosed in a fortress of hate and fear, of shame and bitterness. Hatred, fear, shame, and bitterness so strong that she feared it would poison her own heart. It was an intensity of fear and bitterness that left room for nothing else, and in that moment she resolved that she would never nurture bitterness, lest it devour her like this.

But to fear and shame she knew no remedy. Who could overcome? Who could remain?

The dark thing crouched in a crevice, terrified and half-blinded by the noon-bright light that shone from her finger and thronged by more living dragons than could remain. Now, Silmavalien saw it.

Where should she aim the arrow? She knew how to hunt beasts, but she had learned nothing of the weak places of a human-like skeleton. She stood there, still as a statue, intuitively assessing her options, and then a straight line connected her eye, her arrow, and the heart of what had to be an orc.

Twang-whizz.

The sounds of the twanging string and the flight of the arrow echoed in that wide cavern. A moment later, the ugliest, more frightful and unearthly howl rang through the cavern, shrieking as if it would freeze the air. Silmavalien shuddered, and then arrows descended upon her and the dragons.

She had never seen more than one arrow in the air at a time, and panic seized her. She dropped her bow and threw up her arms cowering. A moment later something shoved the panic aside. She recovered herself and stooped to pick up her bow, as Songeth's voice rang out in the air.

> Dearest light and dearest thrill,
> Rise, conquer the rising chill.
> Find the Land Beyond Fear,
> Remain there even here.

Upon you shines a bright light
That their overwhelming fright
Cannot touch you, for near
Is the light even here.

Shines the light from and around,
Gift from the skies beyond;
True even in the fear,
Trust the light even here.

Words to the song flowed through her mind in a flash, while she knocked an arrow. Not one but three creatures that must be orcs by the description had come towards them out of the crevice, while she had panicked.

Hastily she released the arrow, and it flew wide.

She knocked a third arrow, while the orcs rushed towards her and the dragons. Their advance halted as she held up the bow, and this time she took a moment to be careful with her arm.

The arrow struck the orc's chest, but it had no effect. It pulled it out of its armor and came on with the others.

Dreadful fear gathered within her, then dispersed. Suddenly, fear could not touch her. It was at once totally incomprehensible and ridiculous. She knocked another arrow and stood steady, waiting for the perfect moment while the orcs flew towards her.

Twang-zip. Time seemed to slow, and nearly halt.

She had released the arrow, and it had pierced through the eye. One had fallen, two more rushed upon her. Feeling like all the world was slowed, herself included, she thrust her bow into the quiver and drew her hunting knife, then threw herself between the nearest orc and dragon.

As it rushed upon her, she got one perfect glimpse of the creature and its crushing size. Stiff blond hair stuck out around its dark face and huge, block-like ears protruded from its head. Its body was as thick around as two men, its legs and arms enormous, and her head would not have come up to its shoulder. But more terrifying were the small yellow eyes in its shadowed, contorted face, the yellow fangs that protruded from its thin black lips and made her think of poison. Its face wrinkled with hate and fury, and as it flew upon her, the expression of terror, and horror, and all ugliness seemed to fly upon with it.

It came down upon her and almost crushed her, but she stepped back was thrown aside by its fall, the knife knocked out of her hand.

Somehow, she was not killed when it fell towards her again, flailing with its sword. For a few moments they both thrashed, seemingly blindly.

The ring blinded them.

She thrust the hand that bore it in his face, and out of the corner of her eye she glimpsed light glinting off white steal. White, not the black of the orc's blade. She reached for the knife, grasping it by the blade, and hardly felt the cut into her palm. The orc grasped her leg just as she got her ring-hand on the hilt, and the whole blade glowed white-hot.

She twisted, jabbing the knife which nearly blinded her, too, into its shoulder.

A howl of pain tore at her ears, and the hand on her thigh tightened, bruising.

A glimpse of the second orc caught her attention. The dragons were still in dire dangers. She yanked back the knife and slashed furiously, then struggled to her feet with a strength and speed that was not hers. Immediately she threw herself against the second orc, knife first. The terrified squeals of five frightened dragons and the orcs' howls of anguish mingled in an eerie combination.

The orc half-stumbled and turned to face her, with a wide slash of his broad, dark sword, just like his companions. She twisted out of its path and lunged again. Her knife tore through him and she landed hard behind him.

Scrambled to her feet, just in time to see the orc she had wounded earlier rushing at Minth, who cringed and fainted. She fell upon it, knife-point first in a killing strike, just as it fell on Minth, but she had no time to do anything about it. Through their own eyes, she saw the other orc rushing at the younger dragons.

If it had not been already wounded, there would have been no chance – unless some other power acted again. But her slash had crippled it, and the dragons scattered as it rushed them. It threw its sword, barely missing Veine's tail, and then Silmavalien was upon it.

This one died, too.

She rushed to Minth, and struggled to haul the orc's body off him and assure herself that he was okay. She could feel the life in him through their bond, but he was unconscious and she did not know how hurt he might be.

But he seemed okay and was breathing deeply.

The other four gathered around her as she knelt beside him. She bowed her head.

"Great mighty and mysterious One, knowing yet unknown, seeing yet unseen," she whispered, "we thank you for delivering us. We thank you for this ring through which you work, and for your light. We thank you for caring about us and being with us, mere mortals. We thank you for your words of encouragement and purpose along the way. We thank you for one another. We ask that you would continue to be with us, continue to encourage us, guide us, continue to protect and deliver us, provide for us, and, most of all, that you would keep us together. Thank you for hearing us!"

Minth being unharmed after the orc fell on him like that, sword still in its uninjured arm, was miracle enough. She could not doubt that her victory had come from someone else, through the Light of the Ring. And doubtless that one was the same one who had spoken to her several times before and promised to reveal himself to her, sometime. Even if she did not like not being told more, she could not question such a one. She could only think him for caring about her, when no one did – except maybe Noren – and whom no one else knew anything about. She did know why he did it, she did not know what could cause him to forget about her, and she wanted to stay in his good graces, so she made one last plea.

"Please tell us what you require of us, and show us how to please you?" she asked.

No answer came then, but that did not mean he would not tell her what he wanted another time.

34

Living in the Cave

Silmavalien changed out of her torn and bloodied clothes, and then took them out to scrub in the stream. She was soon soaked through and it was hand-numbing, but the ring keep its hand warmer, and she could not afford to let her clothes be ruined if she could help it. They were all the clothes she would get, and while she knew skins could be made into garments, she would like to keep the clothes she had.

After she had washed most of the blood out of them – they would be stained, but not stiff now – she laid them out of the floor to dry, and made a mental note to sew them again before she used them. Then she looked around the cave floor for her bow, which she found just as Minth was waking up from his faint. He was sore from being fallen on, but miraculously that was the worst of it.

She took a few minutes to cuddle and reassure all the dragons, and then she got back up to look for her arrows, in case any of them were still whole. Wydth, Coroneth, Veine, and Songeth followed along, looking for the arrows with their paws and noses. She let them look for the arrows, and kept her eyes on the shadowed places and the walls, scanning for anything that might conceal another 'surprise,' but she tried to hide what she was doing from the dragons, since she did not want to scare them, least of all Minth. She felt him tense a little, but she was partially successful.

Once they found all the arrows, she took Minth and laid him against the wall near the opening, in an area she already had well-checked, swaddled in a pile of blankets and sacks. Then she continued to explore the farther sections of the cave, followed by the younger four, who wanted to help her. They did not seem phased by the terror of the recent fight, and she wondered if it was only because they had been raised differently than Minth so far, or if their personalities were that different as well.

In the back portions of the cave, but not nearly as far as the true back wall, they discovered a strange formation. A substance that seemed to be to rock as snow is to ice, airy and bubbly but hard, boiled out of the granite walls. Its colors shifted through soft tones of gray through misty blues, faded purples, shadowy green, and washed-out reds, with the grays predominant and the blues next in line, as if it were a rainbow that had lost in light. Once she got up to it, she saw holes everywhere, about the size and shape of dragon eggs, and something about it reminded her of a wasphive. Had this cave once been the home of gigantic wasps? Could insects come as big as dragons, and how dangerous would they be?

Perhaps, they were another danger of the mountains, one she had no idea how to handle, but it did not look as if they might still be around her. She decided not to worry about it just yet.

She walked around the edge of the formation, since it looked like treacherous footing and would have been difficult to climb up to. It curved back towards a niche in the wall, and just as it was made to meet the niche, a second, lower level of the bubbly rock extended from the wall, this time at eye-level.

A glint of brown and white – the first white that she had seen in this rock stuff – caught her, just where it met the wall. Veine squeaked next to her, and she felt Minth pay attention through her eyes.

Suddenly, they all realized what it was. A dragon nest. And dragon eggs! At least two.

She had to climb up to get them down, and soon she stood, balancing precariously on the rocky bubbles, she could see over the next level. She put a hand on the cave wall to stabilize herself, and looked over it carefully, but she did not see any more eggs. She could not help a stab of disappointment, along with a wave of relief. It was so joyous to meet new dragons, to have new hatchlings, but at the same time she already had more than she could care for.

And she definitely did not want to see more dead hatchlings.

While the dragons watched her intently, she hobbled towards the two eggs, and knelt down on the bumpy rock. She placed her hands on the eggs. A white one. And a brown one! Like the egg the dead blue dragon had come from.

Looking up, she prayed that both of these dragons would live. Then she slipped her cloak off and spread it across the holes that might have once held eggs. She gently lifted the brown egg onto the cloak and wrapped the cloak around it. Holding both ends of the cloak with one hand, she climbed down again, and left the egg on the ground with the dragons, who all nosed it, while she went back up for the white one.

Then she brought both the egg back to where she had left Minth, the four younger trailing along behind her. It was getting dark outside, and while Silmavalien was no longer exactly comfortable in the cave after that fight with the orcs, it was far too late to find another place to spend the night in the rain. But she did go out to gather some wood, and then built the fire just within the cave opening, to one side. She was unable to bury the orc's bodies, and she did not want to drag them away lest they attract other nightmare creatures to hunt the orc-slayer, so she dragged them into the fire to burn.

After eating, she curled up with Minth and fell asleep instantly, despite the stench of burning orc.

S

She slipped away early in the morning and opened her eyes. The fire had died down, her ring was no longer shining, and no sparkle of light pierced the blackness. Sharp terror burned through her, then just as quickly washed away in a flood of joy she recognized as coming from the dragons.

The whole was being born, and she was part of it.

She turned her head to see seven pairs of glowing eyes. The eggs had hatched!

She sat up and opened her arms. All the dragons crowded around her and piled on top of each other, but they let the two newest hatchlings through, to rub against her chest. *Tiela and Airrock.* She knew their names, as they rubbed their faces against her hand, Tiela's face rough and scaled, Airrock's smooth like the other dragons.

A song seemed to ring out of the darkness, and she joined it, singing along with Songeth.

> Borne on wings as old as time
> My choice, my love, as chosen me
> Our souls made one, our hearts must climb
> Evermore one we must be
> You are my great desire, to ever see
>
> Closer and closer we draw together
> Ever since the day of your birth
> My soul's desire is to know you ever
> To soar with you above all earth
> To share in your, unknown heretofore, mirth
>
> Dear, you are my closest heart

With you alone I find life complete
Without you, empty is my part
With you I'm freed, no more bound by feet
With you I'm freed and truly fleet

Come bright wings, be my light
Carry me to the world I've never seen
Show me what it is to see, shine bright
Lift away from me the dusty screen
So I can see the world beyond me

Sweet sweet heart of mine
Together away we shall fly
To lands more fair and fine
Than any we have yet come by
Amidst the beauty and wonder of that sky

All I desire is with you to be
Yet I find to me no power
To reach out, I to you, you to me
Desperate and helpless, call out to the Higher
All then perfected, outside and the Inner

In joy we are ever-bound now
In this gift we are truly now together
One another truly now to love and know
This is for us life's very fire
And the water, pure and clear, living ever

It is so glorious and lovely
To as one soar together there
In bliss beyond what can be
In those heavens, fairest fair
With healing and life ever in the air

We will dance together
In joy like never before
Now with another and another
Altogether one forevermore

In one who draws us more and more

We have been given victory
Over all the might of blackness
Because he loves us in unity
Fearless we walk through darkness
As he turns it to brightness

Somehow the song seemed far more complete now, and when its last notes faded into silence, she shooed the dragons off the blankets they were lying on top of, and then they all cuddled underneath with her.

S

Light poured through the opening. Rain drummed on the ground outside.
Tiela's scales glimmered and shone, varying shades of the loveliest teal color Silmavalien could imagine. The light sparkled white on her scales white, so that it looked like she was studded with diamonds, or indwelt by stars. But for all the glory of her scales, she too was ugly and disproportionate. For all the glory of her scales, Tiela was ugly, for she, too, was disproportionate. But her pastel eyes shone blue with happiness as she nudged Silmavalien awake.
Silmavalien sat up and greeted her, gathering her chunky body into her arms. Then she turned to Airrock, who clambered over Tiela into her lap. Her eyes glowed bright blue and purple as she reached up to nuzzle Silmavalien's chin, and her skin shone with a silvery sheen.
Silmavalien kissed her nose, then shooed both the babies out of her lap in order to get breakfast ready.
After that, she wanted to leave the cave, but between the downpour and the two new hatchlings they could not travel. She dared not even leave to hunt, because she could not take the risk that there had been more orcs and they might show up when she was away and could not protect the dragons. How she longed for the day when they would be stronger than her!
But thinking about the possibility of more orcs made them all uneasy, and so did thinking about the food they were eating up without getting more, so she tried

not to. They were immediate issues, but worrying about them would do no good and it would only taint present joy. So she shoved all these worries out of her mind, and played with the dragons, like she had played with toddlers before.

When they had all used up some of their energy, she sat down and told them stories, she sang them songs and told them stories, some of them traditional stories of the village, some of them stories she made up, often as she went.

"There used to be a little fairy," she told the dragons, "who lived in the trees and the flowers. I have forgotten her name, but it was very beautiful. She was pretty, too, and always dressed in leaves and flowers. Deer came to kiss her face and nibble her hair, and also her clothes. She had hair like the clouds, and eyes like the sunshine. Her best friend was a water fairy, whose name I do remember. It was Sprinka. They would sit together in the sun on some bank, rejoicing and laughing, singing and soaking in the sweet-warm-light..."

So Silmavalien went on, and the dragons listened to her stories and her attempts to make jokes, some of which they understood, some of which they did not understand, though she did not understand what was the difference. Finally she dozed off, and the rain had not yet slackened.

So they ate, and then talked for a bit in their different ways, and as she lay down again with seven dragons snuggling against her body, she wished it could be like this always. It was good to have a break. Good to have a day to just get to know her dragons and be with them, without any concerns. These moments were needed to live.

As she drifted into dreamland, her last thought was how cozy this cave was.

S

The rain was still pouring in the morning, but it was no longer constant, and splashes of sun shone through it, making everything sparkle with light. She decided she needed to hunt, and it was not likely that there were more orcs when none had showed up yet. But it did not hurt to be careful, and she made sure she never strayed far out of sight from the cavern opening, and then only for a few minutes at a time. That meant she had to be more careful about where she shot as well, in case she missed.

There were lots of animals out, trying to forage in the sunshine, and even with these constraints, she had a relatively easy time. This method of hunting was quite convenient, too, because she could go back to the cave and drop her kills off for the dragons to eat, instead of having to carry them with her.

Twice during the day, she thought she heard something that might have been an orc in the bushes, only to find that it was a false alarm and they had all been frightened for nothing. She hunted a fair amount, and did not lose a single arrow, and she wondered if the ring helped with that, too. Late in the afternoon, she decided she had gotten enough, and spent what was left of the light gathering wood. Even soaking wet as it was, it was easier to light on dry ground, and that night everyone ate as much as they wanted.

While she cooked the rabbits, she looked out and noticed that it had not been raining for a while. It was the longest lull yet. Perhaps, the storm would pass by morning.

Or it might be going as hard as ever again.

35

Return to Fear

Silmavalien woke late in the morning, and the first thing she did was remember to thank the Lord of Light – as she had decided to call whoever made the ring glow – for anything he had done for them and ask for his blessing.

It was not raining and the light was brighter than it had been. When she went to the mouth of the cave to check the sky it was blue, with only a few tattered clouds in it. Yes! They could look for a new place to live today, though she felt a touch of regret. She liked living in the cave. It felt more like a house, a home, than anything else.

But she did not really want to stay long in a place orcs had gathered. She would never be comfortable here, but maybe they could find another cave.

She carried Tiela to the mouth of the cave, and then had to go back for Airrock, who could not follow quickly enough. She leaned against the wall and tried to think. She needed a way to carry both of them, since it would be far too slow to carry one a few paces, then put her down and get the next, and repeat again. Her bags were too full with meat, and pine cones, and other food, for her to fit even one dragon in them, like she had fit Minth, and she needed to keep stocked on the food for when it snowed and she could not hunt.

Finally, she got an idea. She pulled one of her cloth cloaks out of a bag, and bunched the ends together, then tied them in a knot she hoped she would be able to undo. She laid it on the ground and helped Airrock climb into it, then lifted the knot over her head, and stood. She could carry Tiela in her arms, like this. She would be slow, and she would not be able to hunt, but it would not be as slow as carrying the dragons one by one, and not as hard on her back as having to constantly pick everything up and put it down would be, either.

They walked along the stream, looking for a place they could ford. Tiela and Airrock took turns riding in the sling or her arms, depending on which one was tired, and which one wanted to look around at the world with curiosity, and hear from her – and the other dragons – all about everything. She dragged the pine cone collector along behind her, tied to her hips, and the older dragons pushed and pulled and helped to free it when it got stuck.

When they found a good place to ford the stream, Silmavalien crossed it with one dragon at a time. Tiela was in the sling at the time, so she crossed with her first, stepping carefully from stone to stone, barefoot. Her feet were numb by the time she crossed it, but she knew every angle of the stones now. She put Tiela down and scratched under her chin, telling her to stay put and be calm. She would be back, and then she returned for Airrock.

Minth decided he wanted to be brave and spare her from having to carry him, as well. He knew he was much heavier and harder to carry, and he wanted to be as helpful as he could, so he insisted on walking beside her – upstream so that he was safe from being carried away, while she took Airrock. Before they were half-way across he was chilled to the bone, so he huddled with the hatchlings for warmth while she made a quick trip across for her bags and then spread a cloak over the dragons.

Veine and her hatching-brothers wanted to follow Minth's example and be helpful, so she took them across by twos as well, carrying one while the other walked against her legs. They got just as cold as Minth, so she found a patch of sun for them to warm up in.

There was just enough daylight left for Silmavalien to find a nearby place to spend the night and collect some firewood.

The next morning, it was clear that she needed to go hunting again. She had got nothing at all that day, and the seven growing dragons went through her stores as if they did not get exist. She stood next to one of the boulders under an ancient fir tree and looked out at the dark tangle of woods reaching into the sky, clad in a myriad different shades of green. It was beautiful, but terrifying too, now.

Now that she knew that the monsters of the mountains were real, and were not just things like bears, but included dragon-killing orcs. She could not expect orcs to stay away because dragons smelled like predators and there might be a ferocious parent near to protect them. Instead, orcs would be drawn to the dragons as helpless creatures for them to terrorize and slaughter, for them to envelop in the horror that was their nightmare existence. That meant she meant to leave them.

Yet starvation would kill them all just as surely as nightmare creatures could, which meant she had to hunt, and she could hope to get enough food if she stayed so close she could guard them from every side. She felt thrust right back into the fear and danger and difficulty of her position in the village, with no good choices, and she felt Minth pulled into that with her, though the other six did not seem affected.

Yet. And perhaps they would always be less so, because whatever choice she made would not involve imposing on them the kind of unnatural silence Minth had suffered.

But she did not want to make Minth suffer either. She did not want this situation at all. She dug her fingers into the moss that coated the boulder, tearing it, and wished desperately for an answer.

"In the cavern, how were you protected?"

The voice, like a thought, seemed to follow naturally out of her own mind, her own search for something that would make this right, for anything in her previous experience that could help her. Yet she knew beyond all doubt that it came from the Lord of the Light, their Protector in the cavern.

Still, compelled by the fear she had let herself be sucked into and the thought-patterns she had used to survive in the village, she argued. *That was through the ring,* her thoughts protested. *And it worked only while I touched the ring. Could your power work without the ring? Would you do so?*

"You have not known me. Yet you question me?"

Yes, because I do not know you. Since when are we supposed to trust and believe what we do not know and cannot understand?

No voice came in reply. Only a deep, troubling sense of displeasure. A sense that she had missed something, was deliberately missing something obvious.

She longed to say, *I'm sorry, please forgive me,* but she could not. She could not take back her doubt of the unknown. She could not step out into what she could not see. However she might wish it were otherwise, she could not do what pleased her Protector. She could only hope that he was merciful and understood her predicament, understood that she could not. Because she could not trust him, and even if he accepted her shortcoming, she must live with the fear she could not step out of.

Yet she was not the same person she had been. Every bond had become part of her, but most of all her growing relationship with Minth had changed, and all the things she had enjoyed, and suffered, and done because it. She no longer depended on others for her life, except that she owed it to a Protector she could not depend on. Instead, she was the care-taker, provider, and protector, too. A shadow fell on the new love and life she knew, even as she knew what she must do.

She bade the dear dragons farewell and safety for the day and left, her heart heavy with fear. In the evening she returned with a load of kills and pine nuts, bountiful but within the range of normal, and looked over the dragons' skin. Airrock's skin did not show any sign of needing it, so at least while she had new mouths to feed, she did not have more skins to oil.

She woke the next morning to Songeth greeting the new day with all song, all six of the other dragons accompanying him with squeaks and even what sounded like chirps, but there was little joy in it for her now. Overnight, her life had become incomplete, and what she longed to do and be was impossible.

She felt the dragons sorrow for her as one by one they noticed that the unhappiness of the previous day had not gone for her at all, and though the fact they cared ought to comfort her, it only made her sadder. She could not be enough for them, and for the first time in her life not really wanting their company, yet incapable of truly escaping it – something she wanted even less, if she really thought what what that meant – she left to go hunting. Their pain over her pain haunted her.

By evening she had an amazing armful of pine nuts and a small, young buck. Why, she asked herself as she returned laden with a bounty, did she get all this now? Now, when she had just displeased her Protector. Now, when it was the wrong time. The right time would be when traveling and only hunting once in days, not when she get enough food for them all without luck.

They would have to stock up when they could, both in their bags and in their bellies, which would make them both heavier but also more prepared.

Silmavalien was working on cooking the meat and extracting the oils from the fat, when suddenly she shivered.

Yes, we're cold, too. Colder.

The collective thought came from all the dragons together, and when she turned back to the fire, she saw it stirring in the cold wind flowing down from the mountains, cold enough to steal the heat even where she worked. She glanced up at the sky, and there, against the stars, she could see what might be a storm front moving in.

Was this one cold enough to snow?

She moved closer to the fire to work, but even when she could get no closer without risking burning her clothes, and the heat on her skin was fierce, she was still cold. The dragons curled into the deepest shelter between the boulders, and she covered them with all the blankets she had, then sat between them and the fire while she worked late into the night and kept the fire going.

At last, she was done for the night. She stretched, loosening sore and cramped muscles, and a single white fluttered down and landed on her nose.

She held out an arm against the firelight, as she watched another glittering speck flutter down, not dropping like rain but fluttering like a butterfly or a leaf on the wind. It came to light on her sleeve, white for a moment.

Snow. It was snowing.

She built up the fire some more, glad she had set it in a sheltered spot on a lip of rock where it would not find itself sitting in melted snow, and then snuggled under the covers with the dragons, the bearskin on top. They did not exactly have the best shelter, and the bear fur would shed snow and water best of anything she had.

She woke several times throughout the morning to shake the snow off them and keep the fire going, and before it was noon the ground was covered in a sheet of snow as thick as she remembered people describing snowfalls in the village. And it was only just beginning. It was not snowing just this moment, but the clouds looked heavy with more of the stuff. How deep would it get?

She hoped that the Protector's ring would – and could – shed warmth on them, as it had light, without burning her finger. Feeling still the shame of her failure, she knelt and prayed, "Lord, please hear me and have mercy on me in my failing. Please grant us warmth through this ring to survive the winter. If you can work without the ring please turn this meadow to late springtime, so that I may know I can trust Your power anywhere and in any way."

Then she left the covers to warm up food over the fire while it was not snowing. Then she worked to make a sort of tent that would keep the dragons warmer, and left to see if she could hunt anything in the snow. She was careful not to go far, in case it snowed more. She did not want to get stuck.

The rabbits and squirrels were out, and she got a few of each, before it started snowing again, forcing her to return, even though she was sure it was still early in the evening and she had at least an hour until dark.

Contrary to her prediction, it hardly snowed that night, and it was warmer than it had been for weeks. She woke in the morning to the

usual mist, but by it burned away quickly, and above it the sky was clear
and the sun was bright. The dragons were already moving about as well
as they could in the snow and squeaking with delight, and she could tell
the day was going to be the warmest in a long time, too. She sang as she
made ready to leave to hunt:

> The fire flies with passing brightness
> The sun is shining high and clear
> The sky is blue and oh-so-bright
> Banishing the snowy coldness
> The sun on the snow is dazzling white...

That evening she returned with a reasonable catch, making her
way through the slushy snow while Minth groused in her mind about his
inability to hunt successfully, joined by Wydth and his siblings, who
were mostly following his lead. She could feel a lot less frustration in
their complaints, but she reminded Minth that he was still very much a
baby, and she had practiced longer than he had been alive before she got
her first kill.

After that, they all begged to be told about the rattlesnake several
times, and Songeth proceeded to sing about it, which made her laugh.
He wanted her to sing it with him, but she could not stop laughing.

36

Action of the Lord of Light

The next morning was as warm as the last, and Silmavalien decided it was time to move on. Their current shelter was not the best, but it was not the worst either, and Airrock and Tiela were now able to keep a reasonable pace.

That day, her luck hunting was horrible. She only got three rabbits, and she lost an arrow twice, something that had not happened in a long time. Between finding the arrows – with which the dragons were quite helpful – and those same dragons' slow pace, they could not travel very far, and the best place she found to make camp was a small rock near the stream.

Again the night remained fairly warm, and the dawn was misty but the morning bright, but her fear returned full force to haunt her as she went out hunting. She could not trust that the dragons were safe, she could not be comfortable leaving them. She could not stay with them and let them starve. There was no solution to these two, and fear quickly turned to resentment.

Why did the Lord of the Light have to do this to her? Why did he have to put her in a situation where if she would trust him it would be well, but she could not trust him?

And yet, he took care of her.

Once she had gone a fair distance it all overwhelmed her, and she fell at the foot of a huge sequoia tree in an agony of lost contentment. "Lord of Light," she begged, "reveal yourself to me that I may know why you've cared for me and trust you! What is it you want from me?"

Soft and quiet but firm and almost terrible in its simplicity came the reply. It seemed to be the whisper of her own soul, born of both doom and desire. "Let go of your fear."

"I cannot!" she replied in desperate anguish. "I cannot give myself, even less my dragons, to the unknown! That is what trusting you, Unknown One, means."

"You saw my power in the cave. You have heard my voice from all around you and from within yourself. You have received help through that ring you bear. Why do you doubt that you and the dragons are mine?"

The words struck at her soul.

"No, I do not!" she yelled defiantly. "But, if we are all yours, did you not make us? If you made us, why did you make us so we cannot do what you want?"

There was compassion in the voice that came in the silence following her anger. "Silmavalien, if you did not fight me, you would be able. It is you who hold onto your own fear, with your thoughts, your excuses, your choices. I did not make you so."

The conversation tore at her soul, and she was silent in her darkness for a long time. Then she cried, "I implore you, lift the shadow from me! At the very least, do not make it grow deeper!"

"Do you want to know the truth – or not?" The voice was quieter and smaller than before, and Silmavalien did not respond. After lying there for a few more minutes she got up and looked around for something to hunt. She did not have any time to waste. She had already wasted far too much. She had eight mouths to feed.

She barely made it back before dark with a good catch of both rabbits and squirrels.

S

The warm weather held for a while. Silmavalien alternated hunting and traveling, and she made time to play with the dragons and sing to them. Songeth especially loved her singing and he learned every song she sang and sang it back to her in his dragon language, more artfully than she could ever sing. Minth loved to snuggle in her lap and lie right next to her or play chase and catch one. Once, she jumped a log, chasing him, so they had a jumping contest, which she naturally won, but it did not matter. It was play, and they were one and shared everything.

The meadow-valley grew steeper. The snow melted everywhere there was direct sunlight but remained in the shade. She supplemented the meat she caught with roots she dug up.

One day she saw a strange print in a long patch of snow when she was hunting. About as thick as it was long it resembled a widened human footprint, but for marks at the tips of the toes like claws. Immediately, it seemed likely to her what it was: an orc.

An idea formed in her mind. Could she hunt and kill it? Perhaps, if there were only one, but the nightmare monsters were said to be exceedingly cunning. If she tracked the orc, would it not either elude her or ambush her in the shadows of a thicket, where she found it difficult to both see and move?

Yet if she left it, it would be a danger to her and the dragons, and it might ambush them when she was not around.

The ring! Could it be the answer? She knew that the Lord of Light could provide her the light she needed – and victory over the orc – if he wanted. If he still cared about her. He certainly cared about her enough to speak to her, and he hated the deeds of the orcs.

Silmavalien knelt right beyond the snow in the soft pine-needle dust. She took off her ring and cupped it in her hands, then prayed over it, "O Lord of Light, please guide me to do your will. Please help me to hunt and kill this evil orc and enemy of your dragons. Have mercy on me and help me despite my inadequacy. Thank you."

Silmavalien put the ring back on her finger and stood, her resolve firm. She loosened her knife in its scabbard and took her bow and an arrow in hand, then followed the track of the orc with as great care and speed as she could manage at once. If she could not move quickly she would never catch up to it and get a chance to kill it. If she was not very careful it would ambush her instead. She had to balance the two.

She would have liked to run to make time in the open places where ambush would be unlikely, but there the snow was melted and the track was harder to follow. As the day wore on the folly of her decision dawned on her, but by then it was too late to make it back to camp before nightfall, so she went on. She paused for a minute to ask the Lord of Light for His protection for the dragons, and ask him again for his blessing and guidance for herself.

The shadows grew quickly longer. A ridge of the mountains cast the whole land in shadow and the thickets were dark. She knew that it was about now that she would see the orcs, so she became very cautious.

Firelight gleamed through a thicket of trees up ahead, and she wondered for a moment if she had lost the track and wandered back towards her camp-site. No, that could not be. It was too far from the stream. She did not hear water. She had not left a fire going and the dragons could not have kindled one.

The smell of roasting meat wafted towards her. Even if the dragons could kindle a fire, there was no meat to be cooked nor could they possibly get it started. And they assured they had not killed a fire. Whose was the fire? Did orcs use fire? Were they not supposed to? What did she really know about them?

Carefully, Silmavalien crept forward. Soon she saw a huge lumpy creature near the fire. She knocked an arrow, but froze with her finger on the string just as she was about to release it. Fear surged through her, and she could not let go.

Brilliant light flared around her but left her seeing the dimness better than before. Two arrows whizzed through the air – hers and an orc's.

The orc's arrow embedded itself in a tree just behind her and to her left. Her own resulted in a short scream.

A shadow materialized out of the trees, looming over her. She slipped her bow into its quiver and drew her knife. Leapt to the right – now towards the fire – froze there, poised to strike at any moment, any direction.

The flying orc crashed into the tree trunk where she had been a moment before. Warmth flowed through her, momentarily protecting her against the cold nightmare fear. She lunged at the orc in an extended stab.

Flew over the fallen orc and landed against a redwood. Her breath came in gasps and her heart pounded. She fought to remain standing. It was all she could do.

The orc she had struck slowly rose, a black shadow among shadows. She stabbed him again and he fell. Turned and saw that she was surrounded by far too many of the shadow-brutes to fight alone. Hope died in her heart. What had she come to this for? To die, thereby killing her beloved dragons?

Out of the darkness flowed a voice of shadow. It seeped into her soul and mind, and moments took forever. "You have been deceived by the apparent care of the Lord of Light. When you try to do what you have every reason to think would please him, he lets you be slain and leaves your loved ones to starve. There is no mercy. There is no hope. The nightmare will reign forever."

She sank to the soft, white earth in despairing defeat. Minth's fear, Veine's, the others too, washed over her. Airrock's voice rang a defiant note – *fight!* – but she could not listen to it.

Expecting to die at any moment she sent them a last, *I love you. I'm sorry.*

She did not die. An arrow whizzed through the air but the sound of it was unlike anything she had heard before. It told of a flight incomparably swifter and truer.

The spell was broken. A second arrow followed the first before it even struck its target. She opened her eyes and saw that three of the orcs had fallen. The others scattered but were quickly downed by shining arrows so swift they left a trail of light in the air.

Reality broke over her like the dawn. The Lord of Light had saved her again – in a way strange and new, but always with light. She knelt there, the ring cupped once more in her hands, to thank Him. As she began to pray the ring shimmered, illumining only itself.

"Thank you, O Lord of Light, for once again saving me, helpless doubting person that I am. I'm sorry for mistrusting you. I hope that I will not mistrust you again, like I have this day. Thank you, thank you, thank you!"

With the last "thank you" the ring burst into brilliant light, illumining the woods around her and becoming too bright to look at. She put it back on her finger and jumped to her feet with a last jubilant "Thank you!"

Joy and thanksgiving instantly flowed between her and the dragons and back again.

Made bold by the light of the ring, she went into the orcs' camp. The meat seemed to be raw venison thrown onto a pan to roast. Nothing wrong with that, but she decided to pray to the Lord of the Light that it would be clean for her and then touch it with her ring of light in case He choose to work through the ring. Then she searched the orcs' bags.

Under the cape of the orc she had shot she found two white dragon eggs. In the tents and around the fire were strewn what looked like the shriveled shreds of more dragon eggs. She tried not to imagine what the orcs had done.

When the huge venison roast was done cooking she took it off the fire to cool in the night breeze, and then stuffed it in her pouch. Wrapped tightly in her cloak for the night was cold and the ring was not making it warmer, she tried to return to her camp by its light. It was not liked daylight though, so her sense of direction was skewed and she headed to the stream and walked down it until she found a familiar place. From there, she easily found the camp.

The dragons greeted her with excitement and relief, and she hugged each of them individually, then gave them the rabbits and squirrels she had shot. She felt asleep as she got the fire going and without eating her own dinner, her last thought: *I hope these eggs take as long to hatch as Minth's or, better yet, Noren's.*

37

More Snow

After that the days and nights grew slowly colder. Then came a night when the stream – which was much smaller than it had been when she first started following it – froze over on the top, and she had to break the ice to get water in the morning.

That morning, she climbed up towards a small ridge to search the land and think about where would be best to hunt. Half-way up the ridge, the forest opened around her, giving her a good look at the sky.

A huge rampart of dark clouds towered above the tree tops, twisting into fantastic and intimidating shapes. She thought back a moment. They could not have been there just a handful of minutes earlier. Her view from their camp-site was good enough for that.

Even as she watched, they built still higher, dark beneath, but there was a different tone to the darkness than she had ever seen in a storm cloud before. She could not quite put her finger on it, but she knew it was different, yet vaguely familiar.

She could not stand there staring at it. She had to get back. But just as she turned, she realized what it was.

It looked a little like the snow-clouds. It was much darker than the snow-clouds had been, but the texture of the darkness was similar.

She moved quickly, imagining what a deluge of snow would be like. A cold wind swept past her, driving her yet faster, and then there were snowflakes swirling around her. Soon, the snow was thick enough she could see her footprints in it. She wondered in fear if this was a blizzard. If blizzards were another part of the stories that were true. But whether it was a nightmare creature taking on a shape, this time of weather instead of flesh, or whether it was to snow as a deluge is to rain, did not matter right now.

What mattered was how they were going to survive this, since they had not found another cave, and they were certainly not housed in one right now, and even if they had a cave, they could be buried in it. And the ground was already thick with snow ....

She reached the camp and worked in a hurry, the dragons helping her to drag everything up a slope that was sheltered by a warm, south-facing rock that jutted over it. She had not put everything here to begin with because she was not certain how stable the boulder was, but in the present circumstances it was a risk that would have to be taken, since they would certainly be buried or frozen otherwise.

Somehow, decisions like these did not bother her, and there was still peace in her heart as she cuddled up with the dragons under every cover they had, the bearskin on top again. She did not sleep much though, since the snow blew in under the overhang in flurries, and she had to get up often to shakes inches of it off the bearskin cover and down the hill. Several times, she sat staring into the darkness afterwards – it was not really dark, but an eerie world of half-light, as the snow covering everything shimmered with the little bit of light that filtered through the clouds, but it might as well have been darkness for all her ability to see anything. She always lit a fire to keep the wild animals away. Even the smoke after it was mostly dead should deter them a little. Would they want to be out in this snow and wind, or would they be taking shelter too?

By mid-morning, the snow was falling lightly, but it was so fluffy that she could barely walk on it, though the dragons managed a little better. It took her all day to find some wood that she could reach, and then drag it back for a fire, and she was chilled to the bone with bits of snow that had slipped in every opening in her clothes and melted against her skin.

She relished the thought of hot food.

S

Over the next days, the snow slowly became easier to walk on, though it did not melt. Silmavalien found it hard hunting for the eight of them, so even when she did not find good shelter, she spent more of her time hunting and less traveling. She left off from following the stream so closely since the snow made a ready source of water if she could find enough wood to get any sort of fire going. That meant for a great deal more choice in where she camped, and they usually stayed in caves in the cliffs or hills. She hoped, almost desperately to find the Riders' Passage, but she did not see any caves on top of ledges, at least that were within her reach.

She wondered sometimes if Lexamarian had left off the all-important fact it would take a dragon to reach the Riders' Passage in her description, but she tried not to think about it.

One night, after a successful day hunting, Silmavalien could not sleep. She sat up awake, sitting next to the sleep dragons with the bearskin drawn up around her shoulders, watching the sky. The winter stars twinkled overhead with an intensity she did not think she had ever seen before, and blue Zeluin flared most brightly of all, a brilliant flame in the dark canopy of the northern skies, a bit above the mountains.

She felt the dragons' minds stir in their dreams, and then a squeak in the silence. It was so silent, the squeak so sudden – had she only imagined it.

It came again. From her bags. She slipped out of the covers, heedless of the cold, and rushed to them, digging through them. How had she forgotten about the dragon eggs!

A white head poked out between two folds of cloth, and she reached out to touch the dragon. His name rang, as clear and hard and cold as that northern star in her mind. *"Jareth!"* Her heart skipped a beat and went on pounding with a wild, untamed excitement, and the intensity of the stars burning of the sky above seemed to match the fire in her and Jareth's hearts. They twinkled, flaring and dimming again, as if all the whole world was part of one dragon bond.

S

Soon after Jareth's hatching, a cold, heavy rain fell for a night and a day and half a night again, but it washed away most of the nasty snow, and Silmavalien was glad to see the brown and green of the world again.

She took to hunting deer more often and deliberately, forcing her to spend nights, often more than once in a row, away from her dragons. It was not something either she or Minth liked, but they were needing more food and they had all been getting skinny and hungry, and she did not doubt that it would snow again. The mountains above the village saw snow many times in a year, so she had to find a way to hunt enough to get them through that.

Fortunately, hunting deer worked, and they were able to eat comfortably again, though no one got as much as they wanted. Sometimes, for a moment, she wished it was just her and Minth. At this point, she could have taken care of just the two of them with ease.

The ninth dragon hatched during one of those deer-hunting journeys, when she was miles away and unable to return that night, even if she did abandon her skill.

The ninth dragon hatched during one of those deer-hunting journeys, when Silmavalien was miles away and could not have returned that night, even if she did abandon the meat. Airrock's joyous cry pulled her into itself, as the young silver dragon called her friends who were out trying to hunt – with some success. They greeted Daurth and snuggled around him in a ring to keep him warm, and she heard them telling him all about their mother, and how she was far, far away, hunting big things, bigger than them, for them to eat, but she would be back soon.

Silmavalien smiled, amused. Mother? She laughed, imagining herself as a dragon dam, fierce, and powerful, and protective of her young. But then, it was not that preposterous. She cared for them, snuggled with them under the blankets, and rubbed the fat-slave on them when they needed it. And, like a dragon, she was a huntress.

No, their picture of her, even with its hidden wings, was not so far off.

And she was so grateful for this life. In that moment, she decided she regretted nothing. This was the best life. Her dragon hatchlings were the best friends and children she could hope for.

S

When she returned and met Daurth, she finally realized what was different about her bond with him, Jareth and the others, and her bond with Minth. Her bond with Minth was the most soul-changing, but the others were not inferior, but other. They were her children, she the mother. With a sense of both loss and relief she understood: they would grow up, and she and they would always love each other, but they would not need her in the same way that she needed Minth and he needed her, as parts of each other's souls.

38

Out of the Storm

A few days after Daurth hatched, they were traveling up the gorge, looking for a ravine they could use to get out of the canyon. Somehow, traveling back towards the village was not Silmavalien was comfortable doing.

Plus, she still wanted to find the Riders' Passage if she could.

Suddenly, she saw dark clouds sweeping across the sky above and gathering. She watched them grow larger as she tried to think of where to look for shelter.

Though richly forested and rocky, she did not know of any good places to shelter out a snowstorm that they could reach quickly. But perhaps she could find a cave in the cliffs.

Striving uphill slowed them down. She carried Daurth in her arms, and she had to stop to help the others sometimes, Jareth most often. The ground was all rocky and steep, and soon dark clouds covered the sky from end to end. A cold wind blew down the gorge, and she could not help becoming afraid. Her fear and the dragons fed on each other.

The glint of the ring caught her eye when she glanced down, climbing up a particularly rough place and trying to make sure she did not trip and Daurth. She knelt down right there, putting him down for a moment, and all the dragons gathered around, knowing what she was doing.

She took off her ring and cupped in her hands, then prayed:

"O Lord of the Light, thank you again for all that you've done for us. Please save us again. Thank you."

The dragons chirruped their union with her words.

She put the ring back on and rose. She should have done this far earlier, but she got out the cloak she had used for a sling before, and tied it up again to carry Daurth more securely. Then they continued their uphill hike toward the only hope of shelter. Snowflakes were soon fluttering down and settling on her arm, even though the conifers, both young and old, that grew thickly even in most of the rocky places overhung their way and kept most of the snow off.

Her hope froze as they toiled up and the wind grew harsher. The dragons were shivering, and their limbs were growing numb, causing them to stumble. Their progress slowed still further, as wind howled in the trees and down the walls of the gorge. The snow felt harder, and still they had not found shelter.

This could be very bad.

She half-forced, half-encouraged them on. The poor dragons struggled, and she helped as much as she could, but she was already carrying the one who could not walk by himself. Sometimes she would carry one of the others for a stretch, but the climb was taxing her too. Nonetheless, she was stronger and surer of foot, and she ended up carrying another dragon in addition to Daurth once again.

She dared not think what would happen if they did not find a cave, though she would not give up until she died.

The snow fell still harder. Soon, they could hardly see twenty paces ahead. Then even less. She was getting cold, too, now. The wind stole their warmth relentlessly, and she wondered if it was time to give up on looking for a cave and do what she could in the trees. The dragons were freezing.

But she was not ready to give up just yet. The ground ahead of them, even steeper. She cursed it, then realized what it probably meant.

They were almost to the cliffs!

A moment later, she glimpsed what looked like rock wall through the swirling snow. She left the dragons at the edge of where they could climb, mentally promising she *would* return – no time or energy for anything more – and clambered over the rocks, sometimes walked across them, stepping across foot wide gaps, or squeezing through narrow corridors between boulders. Nothing offered much shelter so far, but perhaps she could find something that would be better than nothing.

Then she looked up. A black maw opened in the cliff above, obscured by the falling snow and half-hidden by a ledge of rock. If she had looked up a few feet further back, or forward, she might not have seen it.

She was not sure *how* she would get the dragons up there, but she hurried back to get them. She had taken long enough, and now that they weren't moving they were freezing even more.

She had to lift all dragons, one by one, over many of the rocks and gaps. It took painstakingly long, but their spirits had all risen. They were excited and hopeful for reasons of their own that she did not understand, but she did not argue with them or try to understand. She had no energy for that. All of her attention was spent on making sure she took the same path and remembered where to look up for the cave.

Even if the snow just thickened a little, she might not be able to find it. But if she knew when it was directly above her, maybe she could still manage.

But when she reached the spot, she could still glimpse the black maw. She laid her bags down and took Daurth in the sling. She hardly felt his weight, and just had to be careful not to drop him.

She felt his anxiety build as she looked up at the cliff and tried to plan her route to the ledge, and she reminded him he was a dragon. He was born to fly, and she would not drop or fall. He need not fear.

It was only a little over twice her height to the ledge, but it was fairly vertical, and for a moment thinking about it made her slightly dizzy. She shoved that aside and reached on tiptoes to catch a lip of rock. She tested it, to make sure it was not about to break, then placed her foot in another nook.

She pulled herself up and got her other foot steady on a ridge of the rock. Daurth's sling slung away from her body, but it remained right side up, folded over and closed, and she was satisfied. But she could not hold her current position for anything, and she stretched with her hand for another crevice.

A few moves later, she found a true ledge where she could rest for a moment and catch her much-needed rest, before planning the next steps. Those steps were strenuous, and she was thankful that she was small and Daurth was still tiny. She did not know how much weight she could trust to the ledges, and she would have to think about how she did this with the larger dragons, like Minth or Coroneth.

Not right now. First she had to climb this.

She found a foot ledge where she could lean against the cliff and took another breather. Then she discovered the difficult part would not be getting her head twelve feet off the ground, but getting her feet there.

She lifted Daurth out of the sling and put him on the ledge. She took a moment to make sure he firmly understood: stay away from the ledge and *be careful.*

Then she made her way down the cliff, which turned out to be far harder, and more frightening and unnerving. She had to see how high she was, and the swirling snow did not help. It only made her feel further from the ground, not closer to it.

She closed her eyes for a moment to steady herself. This was not so bad. She would not be afraid. She had been much higher in trees. She hoped to be incomparably higher one day, flying on dragonback.

But she had climbed many trees before, learning when she was young and going higher gradually, as she wanted to. Not like this.

Once she got to the bottom, she decided to take them in order of size, the lightest first, if only so she could get more experience before she had to get the larger ones up there. But she also thought that, if a hold *did* break, hopefully it would be with the last one and she would be able to get the next hold as it broke.

If that happened, she could figure out how they would get back down while they waited out the storm in peace afterwards.

She knelt down and directed Jareth to climb into the sling. As with Daurth, it swung away from her at the start, but not as much. If it swung away less with the heavier dragons, that was a good sign.

When she got to the first resting place, she got him out of the sling and managed to lift him onto a ledge. Then she climbed up the precarious stretch, so it was not so precarious, and hung onto the cliff, while she directed him to climb back into the sling, showing him what to do with nudges in his mind. She hoped that the rest of the dragons were watching, mind-listening, and learning. Then, she finished the climb.

Daurth was happy to have a friend on the 'cold ledge' and She climbed back down. It was not so difficult or unnerving this time, but the thought, *Eight more times!* was appalling. She would be so tired and the last runs would be the hardest.

There was one good thing, though. Going down would be easier each time.

This time when she stood to look up at the cliff, with Airrock in the sling, the snow was falling thicker. She could no longer see the ledge. She ought to be able to do this by now without being able to see it, but she had to fight down another surge of discouragement.

Airrock complained about being cramped when she lifted onto the small ledge, and Silmavalien told her to shut up so she could climb. She had no patience or energy now to deal with this. When she finished the climb, she took another moment to regain her breath, and impress upon the dragons the importance of following her warnings not to play or tumble off the edge. Airrock struck her as likely to be … thoughtless.

The next dragon was Tiela, who really did feel cramped on the little ledge, but did not complain. Silmavalien wondered how the larger dragons would do.

But they would find a way. They had to.

Tiela had the good sense to sit on the other side of the ledge, away from the others, and Silmavalien was not worried about her, but the snow was now falling so thickly she could only see a few feet in front of her face. The little ball of dragons at the bottom of the cliff was constant- ly stirring to keep from being buried in the snow, but they were all happy and they excitedly urged her to go on. The next one was always eager, waiting in place to climb into the sling

But they presented different challenges, some of them more so than others. Veine wanted to chatter about her experience, and Silmavalien had to tell her more than once to be quiet so she could focus on her climbing. But she did mind her turn on the small ledge at all, and crouched with her four paws together, like a cat about to pounce, taking up less than half the space she could have. She went to lie down with Tiela, and Silmavalien thanked her for showing the way for the larger dragons to get up.

Next was Minth's turn, since some of Veine's hatching-brothers were now larger than them, even if not by much yet. Silmavalien wasn't really sure which one of him and Songeth was the larger. Some days it was clearly him, some days it was clearly Songeth, and today she was not sure, but she decided to take him first. She had been worried he would not enjoy swinging in the sling while she climbed, but he loved that experience, though he found being alone on the small ledge frightening. So frightening his nerve failed when it was time for him to step back into the sling. She tried to get the sling as close to him as possible and encourage him. She could only hold like for so long ....

When they got to the top, she pulled herself onto the ledge for the first time and hugged him close to tell him how much she loved him, and how great he was. He nuzzled her in return, then crawled over to be with Tiela and Veine. She climbed down, hoping that none of the remaining dragons would freak out like Minth. She had only barely manged with him.

Songeth, as she had expected, did not have any trouble. He was too good at remaining calm and unruffled, except when it came to his excitement over songs, and if something did bother him, he always sang it away. Wydth she was not too worried about either, and she was not really worried about Coroneth either ... except that he might disregard her warnings, and she had noticed if he thought he should do something a certain way, he did not listen to anyone else, even when the other dragons clearly had more experience than he did. She had noticed that dynamic when he tried to hunt, and so he absolutely had to go last, even though Wydth was slightly larger. She did not trust him to behave himself and stay away from the cliff edge for long.

He complained about how unfair it was she did not trust him the whole time she took Wydth up, but somehow she managed to shut him out pretty well, and while Wydth was heavy, she knew the climb well now.

Taking Coroneth was uneventful, and finally she went down the last time to get the luggage. She almost chuckled on her way down, when Coroneth proved her concerns about his ability to behave, and pushed himself and Songeth into the cave.

The last time up one of the foot-ledges as she pushed off it, but it did not matter for the moment. Everyone was safely above it, and she could figure it out later.

Coroneth and Songeth squeaked at her as she climbed up onto the ledge. They could not get out! It was too steep and the pebbles kept sliding out of underneath them! But she could manage! She could climb up so many things they could not!

"All right," said Silmavalien, and the other dragons – led by Airrock – stepped into the opening and cascaded down the slope, showing more pebbles on Coroneth and Songeth who squawked in indignation.

She shook her head at their behavior, and Minth looked up at her, waiting. Together they began the descent, moving carefully and paying attention to where they put their feet. But then her footing gave way, too, and they fell to the bottom together amidst more pebbles.

From at least as far above them as they had climbed to get up here, a dim shaft of light fell into the darkness of the cave, shining on the floating motes of dust they had disturbed.

The good thing: they were out of the storm.

39

Travels Among the Stars

Silmavalien looked up. She was standing on pebbles, and a steep rise, covered in more loose pebbles, led up to the open ledge. They were well-sheltered, and even though only a little light reached them, the visibility was much better than it had been in the snow-storm.

She attempted to crawl-scramble her way up, taking it slowly and carefully, and taking a step back to consider it every time she slid back down. Half an hour later, she gave up. All it had gotten her was scrapes and bruises. She sank down in the midst of the dragons.

"So little ones," she asked out loud, though everyone knew she did not need to, "Do any of you have any ideas?"

No one did.

Minth crawled into her lap, squirming under her arms. In the process, he caused her hand to turn, changing the angle at which the ring caught the light. It glinted. She stroked Minth and scratched his head, thinking as she did so. *Lexamarian. Could anything she said help us now? She gave us so much that has been useful. Could anything she told us be put to use now?*

Minth answered without being asked. An image formed in her mind, as he reminded her of the images Lexamarian's words had formed in her mind. *"The ... the Riders' Passage!"* they exclaimed together.

Had they found it at last?

If so ...

Somehow, that was troubling. She had no idea how long or far it would take them ... only that it would be on the other side of the Greater Aravin Mountains. She did not know if they had enough food to make it, even rationed. She did not think they would be able to climb back out to hunt, and more trying would only tire them.

It seemed they had only one choice: to go on, *through* the Passage. She could not help but realize that she would have to scarcely eat, since she could go without food for much longer than the growing hatchlings without it hurting her. She shouldered her luggage and spoke to the dragons, telling they that they would travel farther into the cave, into the mountain, in the hope of finding the opening to the other side. Their eyes gleamed at her, like ten pairs of little lanterns, lighting up the ground right around them.

Suddenly it struck her. Lexamarian had said that the Riders' Passage would be bright within. This was certainly not bright. Could this still be the right thing?

She turned, to see the little bit of light still shining through the opening, when one of the dragons noticed a different kind of soft light on the walls – which, apparently, turned several paces ahead.

The light had to be coming from somewhere. And, Silmavalien remembered, Lexamarian had not said it would be *right away*. And the light did not look like firelight.

That had been her first fear: orcs. But there was no scent of smoke, and it did not look like firelight. She stepped forward, the dragons with her.

They walked along the wall to the left for perhaps twenty paces before they reached a place where light fell directly on the walls. They had turned a while ago, and when she looked back Silmavalien could no longer see the light that came in from the snowy day, but she looked another direction she could see what looked like a rift in the rock, where stones had pulled apart, through which a diffused radiance spilled.

They walked up to the rift, which was tall and narrow, and opened a few feet above the level on which they currently stood. She scrambled up the rock ahead of the dragons, and in a moment she knelt on the higher ground of an entirely different cave.

She ignored it for the moment, and bent down to half-pull half-lift Minth into this brighter cave. He stepped further in, and she did the same for each of the dragons.

Only then did she turn about and examine her new surroundings.

They were in a high, vaulted cavern. The left wall was only a few paces away, but to their right it was much farther off, though it would not be far to walk. Farther in that direction the lights dwindled once more to a diffused brilliance. Everywhere else the walls were visible and distinct. When she looked behind her, into the cave they had just left, the rock was of the same kind as the rest of the cliffs of the gorge – a weathered, red-toned stone. But the floor at her feet, and as best as she could tell the rest of the walls and roof, was a pale green rock with very distinct and delineated strata. Throughout it were set somethings that glowed and sparkled. She could see those nearest to her well enough to tell that they were many-faceted and the light was a little mottled and variated. They came in almost every color imaginable, pure and bright.

Never before, thought Silmavalien, had she seen such color, so pure, clear, and not merely bright, but actually glowing its own tones.

It was like stepping through a portal from the mountains familiar to her into another region entirely.

Fascinated, she stepped towards a pink-purple glowstone a couple paces away, embedded in the pale green rock at her feet. It was about the size of her hand and its thousand facets were all smaller than a fingernail. She touched it, ran her hand over it, and invited each of the dragons to see it too.

"Curious, isn't it?" she asked. It seemed to be something that was neither gem nor rock yet somehow both.

Glowstone would do for lack of a better name.

She led them along the wall to the left. She ran her hand along the wall to feel the glowstones of many colors, sizes, and shapes, marveling at the feel. The light seemed so clear, and there was no dust underfoot, no dirt collected in the nooks or coating the walls. Though she was tired from the hike up the slope from the gorge, and then all those times up and down and down the cliff, the cleanness of the light and color was mentally stirring and almost energizing, and the temperature in the caves was pleasant.

As she contemplated the glowstones studding the Passage all about her, above her, and under her feet, it came to her that they were very like stars. The stars of the places under the earth. She repeated it to herself, this time out loud. It sounded nice. She liked it.

Perhaps, she thought, *the stars in the skies above are very like these stars in the places under the earth – glowstones studding the halls of heaven and the dome of the sky. How beautiful .... Stars above and stars below.*

This idea so fascinated her that she decided to look for a glowstone she could get out of the surrounding rock. She wanted to keep a star, or a portion of a star, that she could hold in her hand and have forever near. The more she thought about it the more it appealed to her until it became a near obsession. She kept her eyes peeled for any glowstones that she might be able to pry out of the floor or walls, and some of the dragons kept an eye for her. Veine seemed to particularly like the idea.

On and on they walked until they were very tired. All except for Daurth, whom she still carried in the sling.

With no change in the light or the temperature, she had no way to guess the time, but at last, they had to halt, although she dreaded traveling, and sleeping, and traveling again in the changeless light of the Passage. In heaven people were said to live among the stars, and she had often wished that she could live among the stars above the earth.

Now, she felt that such thoughts were folly, spoiling the delights that one had in hoping after delights beyond one's reach which might turn out not to be delights after all. But whatever she thought about that, she had to stop, and the dragons needed a rest, too. Their stomachs were all growling and crunching. She gave each of them a slab of venison and had a couple of pine nuts herself. Then, she warned them they had better not try to get more meat out of her bags, and made sure they all understood how serious it was.

She pulled out a couple of blankets and laid them on the hard ground to soften it, and they all snuggled together, more comfortable than they had been for many nights, with fewer blankets.

Breakfast was just as meager when they woke. They had had a 'good night's sleep,' but Silmavalien did not think she could exactly call it a morning now. She packed the blankets up and held the sling open for Daurth. Then she led them onward, still running her hand along the wall. On and on they walked, and her own stomach felt very empty and growly. The dragons were even worse, but she made them all continue onward. She no longer found pleasure in thinking about glowstones and stars, above and below, but she still looked for a glowstone she could take. If ever she got out of here, having her own permanent light would be very nice.

When at last the dragons were too sleepy, tired, and hungry, and she was feeling pretty faint and awful herself, Silmavalien stopped. She laid down the blanket on which they slept, and after they all ate their rationed dinner, she realized what was even more important, but they had even less of.

Water!

How could she have been so stupid? She should have that much, much sooner. She should have thought of that the very first time they had eaten in here, but she had gotten too used to the fact that water was easy to get, and food was not.

But she could not think of anything to do about it. Ration the water. Hope that the Passage led them out on the other side before they died of thirst, or that they crossed the path of a drinkable underground stream.

But none of this was a reason to neglect the dragons' other needs, and she sat down to oil the skin of those who needed it before sleeping. She spent some time cuddling Wydth, Veine, Tiela, and Airrock so they would not feel left out.

When she woke, the last thing Silmavalien wanted was to get up. Nothing seemed more pleasant than just lying there ... and nothing more distasteful than trudging on again, through an endless, unchanging cavern.

But she knew that if she did not rise she might never rise, and she could not give up, yet.

Later that day – if it was day – she found a piece of mint-colored glowstone she could pull out of the rock. She stopped to look at it for a minute, comparing its color to Minth's eyes. It was amusing how close the two shades were. She dropped into the bottom of her quiver, and they went on.

For the most part, the cavern floor was level and smooth. At times, but sometimes it would climb up, run on for a while, and then descend again. The steepness of the uphills and downhills varied, but it was always manageable even for the weaker dragons. When the rock was not level it was usually a little rough, rough enough that it was not slippery, but not so rough it was hard to walk. Sometimes the Passage curved, and sometimes the glowstones were more clustered, or more of one color.

After what must have been many days, if day and night existed amidst these stars, she finally ceased to feel hungry. All of them were always thirsty and uncomfortable, and still there was no sign of daylight ahead. Then, the water ran out. Still, Silmavalien made them go on, though they only grew more uncomfortable. What else was there for them to do? They could no longer go back.

At least, there was a glimmer of hope this way. She was not going to give up until they were all dead.

40

The Pool of Liquid Light

Silmavalien stared in muddled confusion. Her head pounded.

The Passage had widened around them, and it seemed that they hung alone among the stars in the sky – no, it was the stars in the earth. Tiny points of many colored light gleamed at them from all around – above and below, to both sides and far ahead. It looked so like the night sky except none of the stars or constellations were familiar. She wondered what the regions of day would be like under the earth. What was the sun?

Down below them and ahead was a large patch of milky, misty light. She continued forward, the dragons at her side and trailing behind her, moving through exhaustion as through deep water or a dream.

Almost at once they began to go down ... towards the milky light.

On and on, down and down, they went, for far longer and farther than they had ever gone either up or down in this long cave. At last, they stood on the banks of a large pool of water. The air was delightfully cool and moist on their dry skin. Silmavalien stuck out her sticky, dry tongue to feel it. It felt nice.

The water itself half-shone half-glowed with an inner light. It looked strange and unearthly, but Silmavalien knew why and what caused it to shine and glow so. The light of the glowstones, buried – who knew how deep? – beneath the water's surface, shone upwards through the still water. And the water was still, so still, still as if it had never stirred and would never stir.

Despite the confusing and mingled light coming through the water, it looked so delightful to Silmavalien. But dare she drink it?

Blizzards, at least, were real, whether or not they were creations of the nightmare. What of the tales of the waters of Nour? The waters whose source, a well deep within the mountains, had been touched by a dreadful demoness, the mistress of poison and of creeping, slimy things, who defiled whatever she touched. The tales did not all say the same thing what happened to someone who drank – or bathed in – the waters of Nour, but they all agreed that it was bad. One would go insane, perhaps even become a vampire, or one might only fall deathly ill. Death was all but certain, but in some stories the light-flowers in the Hidden

Vale were the cure. Whatever it was might happen if one bathed in the waters, or it might happen only if one drank them.

So, dare she drink?

Silmavalien reached out to touch the water with the hand that bore the ring of light. It felt so cool and delicious about her fingertips. So sweet. The water so attracted her … *tantalized* her.

Still, she debated with herself, even against the agony of thirst. Could such evil lie so still amid the unwavering light of these stars? Even less, could such evil lie, so quiet and still, unpurged, over the stars beneath and with their light shining through? Could it be? Dare she trust the unknown power of light?

The Lord of Light. Could he – would he – how would he – let her and these dragons know, whom he had intervened to save, twice with obvious, visible actions, and uncounted times through soft nudges to her thoughts?

Her eyes turned from the water to the ring, which glinted and shone through a thin sheet of illuminated water. Absorbed in her thoughts, she had allowed her hand to sink just below the water's surface. She heard again words that Lexamarian had spoken. "… Drink from the spring of Nerya in the Hall of the Eggs…"

Silmavalien glanced around.

Whether this was some Hall of the Eggs or not, she could not tell, nor could she see any connection between those words and this

place, but nonetheless they seemed to have some connection ... and it was when she glanced at the ring of light that she had seen it.

Silmavalien bent down and cupped her hands under the water. Her first sip refreshed her dry mouth, and the water quickly relieved her burning headache. When she had drank her will – which was a surprisingly small amount – she invited the dragons to come forward. She put an arm each over the first two of the dragons so that they would not slip while they lapped.

Not only was their thirst immediately sated and their headaches quickly relieved, but by the time they were done their gnawing hunger was also gone.

She helped them up and away from the water's edge, and the next two walked down with her, until all of them had drank their fill. They felt good again, for the first time since they had fallen into this Riders' Passage, realm of the stars below.

When they were all refreshed, Silmavalien took out the water skins and filled them with the water through which light had shone, the water from the pool of healing and light. She stood for a moment gazing into the depths of the pool, luminescent at a distance, but at the edges she could see the light from the individual glowstones beneath.

It looked like liquid light.

S

Silmavalien and the dragons walked around the banks of the pool, until it narrowed into a small rivulet of water flowing through the rocks. The ripples, illuminated sometimes by glowstones beneath, sometimes dark, were lovely, and the first thing she had found in this realm that changed and seemed alive, apart from herself and the dragons.

They came to a place where the rivulet flowed into a crack between a glowstone boulder and the pale green rock. Ahead of them, the rock led up again. They had come to the far end of the depression that held the lake of liquid light. There, they drank again straight from the waters, and then climbed up and continued as, straight and level as far as Silmavalien.

When they were all very tired and thirsty and hungry again, they stopped. A sip of the light-water refreshed them, even though it no longer glowed, but it though it lessened the dragons' hunger, this time it left them still feeling empty. So Silmavalien gave each of the dragons a small slab of meat and had a handful – quite literally – of raisins.

Then they went to sleep, as usual, between two blankets.

When Silmavalien woke, a sip of the water roused her so thoroughly that she did have to through the struggle of *knowing* she had to get up and *wanting* nothing more than to never move again. She could only thank the Lord of the Light for the blessings of the light-water, and yet she felt guilty about her lack of trust, even now. Would she ever be free from this awareness of inadequacy? She wanted more than temporary relief, but was this what it felt like to live in the care of a god?

The time wore on and on. She tried to trust the Lord of the Light to lead them out into the fresh, free, bright daylight again, and yet even now she found she could not really trust him. She tried, but failed. She doubted still. She could never be good enough, and the feelings of guilt and hopelessness at her own inadequacy tore at her. She wanted to despair and give up on even trying to trust him, even though she knew now he deserved that trust.

Yet did she really know it? If she really knew it, then she would trust, right?

Then, they ran out of food. The light-water still eased the worst of their hunger, but it could not satisfy the need for solid food. Even Silmavalien began to feel hunger and weakness again, and the dragons struggled to go on.

Then the light-water got low.

That did it. It was too much and Silmavalien gave up even trying to trust the Lord of the Light. There was not a glimmer of hope left in her that they would wander out of the Passage and find water before they died of thirst. She simply could not trust him completely under these circumstances. How could she even be expected to? she told herself.

But giving up, even if only in her mind, did not make her feel better. She felt worse in more ways than one, and even while she drank of the light-water, she felt the whisper of the nightmare in her heart grow and darken her soul.

41

Dragon Eyes

Noren rode around the curve in the road and, without the thicket obscuring his view, he finally saw the city of Delenois. Weaving gently back and forth through the plains, the road headed towards a tall gate set in a tall wall and framed with lanterns. With its houses of many stories, castle, and guard towers, the city rose beyond the wall, a black silhouette against the brilliant colors of the sunset.

It was still a handful of miles off, and he was not going to reach it by sunset. If he went on any farther he would be among the farms, with their fields and farmhouses, that covered the plains around the city.

Instead, he rode off into the edges of the thicket and dismounted the horse, a young bay bare mare named Evena who he had on loan from Krielasoriel's family for a very generous price. He untacked her, rubbed her down, and picketed her where she could graze. By this time the light was all gone, but he built a small fire just beyond the canopy of the trees from nearby deadwood. It seemed that, for whatever reason, not very many people camped and made a fire here. Maybe most of them timed it so they could get into the city before dark.

Tomorrow he would buy a loaf of fresh warm bread in the city, he thought as he ate his dried food. A city! He would see and walk into a big city. He would taste the food city people ate. Only a couple of the grandpas and grandmas of Treas had done that. Most of the time, they traded what they needed through the steady trickle of bards that came and went between the villages and the city, and sometimes they would go down to another village. But never the city! And never Delenois, the City of the Oracle.

As Noren spread his blankets out to lie down, other thoughts took over. *So now I shall know what took my beloved Silmavalien away – at last! If not tomorrow, then I am sure the priests will be able to tell me what this white oval may be, the next day.*

A wave of uncertainty and fear swept through him, almost choking him. It was just a whim of the human mind before the unknown, before choice and determination. Just a silly trick. He lay down, settled deeply into his blankets, and slept.

N

Noren started, instantly waking from sleep. He rose on one elbow. That was not a mouse's squeak. What was here?

Had he heard something like it once before?

Evena tossed her head in the air, then settled back to grazing. The narrow white stripe on her face gleamed in the surrounding darkness. Noren waited, tense and alert, ready to snatch up his hunting knife. Gradually, his muscles released the tension and the quiet stillness of the night with its soft, barely audible lullaby reached out to envelope him again.

Suddenly, discordantly, another squeak shattered the stillness. It … it came from one of his saddlebags. Just an arm's reach away.

What could be in that bag that would make such a sound or attract something that made such sounds. He mentally ran through its contents. Two changes of clothes. His blankets when he was not using them.

The white oval! What could be in it?

Noren loosed the tie that held the saddlebag closed. Then he grabbed it by the folds in the bottom and dumped the contents onto the grass, next to his blankets.

The white oval shimmered in the faint light of the new moon. Several dark lines that had not been there before ran its length. It squeaked again, a shrill, piercing shriek, and then split in half!

There, sitting in the middle of its split egg was the strangest creature that Noren had ever seen.

It had four stumpy legs, a short, thick neck, and a tail, body, and head too big for it. Its body was strangely humped, but then he realized those two short wings crumpled over its back. Its tail was not just too large for its legs and neck but for its body and head as well.

But its eyes were a beautiful, bright rainbow blue.

His heart thumped. Once. Twice. Something about this ugly, helpless, beautiful, bright-eyed creature called to him. Noren reached out to touch it, ah, her.

As suddenly as a bolt of lightning, or a shriek in the night, fire flowed through his veins, through his soul. It left him shaking, a tingling cold skittering through him.

Elninya crawled up to him where he lay sprawled on the ground and nuzzled her face. Life and feeling flowed back into his veins and he turned his head to look at her. Unspeakable joy shone in her eyes which were now a purpler blue, and it sparked and flooded through him, too. He sat up, scooped her in his arms, and kissed her. The love and happiness in her eyes made him want to melt, and then her gaze drew him into another world.

A wind, a flame, the widest sky! Soaring through a sky too wide to ever reach the end, a fire within, borne upon the wind but not confined to that wind ... Images and sensations neither of them had ever known before swept through Noren and Elninya together. Wonder, love, and happiness rendered them speechless, able only to enjoy the other in new yet long-awaited unity, and they gazed into one another's strange faces, the one in the arms of the other, as if time itself was no more. Noren felt that he would burst with the unbearable energy of the love and joy of the wondrous unity he did not understand, but could never live without now that he had experienced. "Elninya ... Elninya ... Elninya ..." he murmured, when he had a voice again.

The splendor of the bond softened into gentle companionship and a quieter wonder, leaving Noren tired. Elninya, too, he thought. He took her with him and crawled under the covers. He fell asleep with her in his arms, and the strange bond followed him into sleep and dreams, wrapping him more tightly in a companionship he could never again escape.

𝒩

When Noren sat up in the light of morning and saw the marvelous – if ugly and clumsy – creature at his side, he incredulously asked her, "You're not a dragon, are you?"

Elninya stared at him quizzically. The word meant nothing to her and neither did the pictures in his mind.

Suddenly, the meaning of what had happened, what he now was, dawned on him.

Terror, and a thrilling sense of being part of something great and noble and perilous ran through him, and he tried to dig through them down to the reality of this new existence.

He would have to hide Elninya, or people would kill both of them. He could not let that happen. He was about to tackle the problem of how to make a living *and* take care of Elninya among hostile people, when he realized what happened to Silmavalien. His world tumbled again.

The dragon egg she found had hatched for her. That explained the state of her room when he searched it after her mysterious disappearance. She had been keeping – or rather, hiding – a dragon in it. The eve before they were to be married had crept up on her. She realized she could not marry him without revealing her dragon to him. Fear that he would betray her and the little dragon – as if he would ever do such a thing! – had overwhelmed her. She packed up and got everything that belonged to her and, almost certainly, stole some food too, and fled. Yet, she had not wanted to abandon him either. That explained the strange note she had dropped on him through the window that awful night.

Now Noren felt hurt as he had never been hurt before. It had been pain and trial enough to believe his love kidnapped by some despicable evil creature whom he could not hope to hunt and bring to bay in the normal ways of a man and a hunter. It had been unthinkable heartache to know nothing that he could do ... But now, to know that all those sleeplessness and all that anguish had been for nothing ... Had been for lack of trust on the part of his love ... It was pain and heartache anew and redoubled. It ruined the joy he should have had at finally knowing what had happened to his love and discovering a clue to help him find her.

Yet, he still wanted to find her. He still loved her. And she, at least, *had* loved him.

So, where might she have gone?

His earlier thoughts about his own survival forgotten, Noren considered that. One by one, he eliminated possibilities. He knew she could not have disappeared into the forests of the Greater Aravin Mountains around Treas. Her hunting skills were nowhere near good enough and, besides, it had been harvest, with winter coming on. There was no way she could survive that, and no way she could have thought she might.

That meant she would have to deal with hiding a growing dragon and making a living for herself in the hostile kingdom. So, where would she go?

At the end, Noren concluded that the most likely place for Silmavalien to live would be a city – large or small – on the edge of the wilderness, perhaps mountains. She would hide the dragon, as she had at Treas, until he or she was big enough and strong enough to survive in the wild, or at least live outside. Then, she would sneak him or her out in the middle of the night. She would probably live on the outskirts of the city, preferably outside the wall. That way, the dragon could fly just over the wall in some hidden place, and she could meet him or her by first light.

Perhaps she is here, in Delenois, thought Noren, knowing that it was unlikely. *I wonder how developed her dragon is by now. And how big.* He looked down at Elninya, who had crawled into his lap.

He stroked her and she hummed, sweetly and softly. It was a strange hum, for though definitely a hum it was relatively high-toned. He liked it. Then he noticed her eyes. They were now a light green, clear, pure, and bright, a color he had only seen in rainbows. He wondered absently what the different colors meant and why dragons had glowing eyes that changed color.

Little Elninya knew as little about the 'mystery of dragon eyes' as he did, but to her it was no mystery. It – she – just *was* that way.

Hunger.

Hunger that was not his own.

Elninya! She was hungry. He gently put her down on his dewy blankets and got a thin slab of dried meat, tore it up, and gave it to her. She devoured it all while he ate half a piece of dry bread. She looked at him with pleading green eyes. The color was a little deeper now and more on the blue side. She wanted more.

"You are such a little creature," Noren asked Elninya. "How can you possibly want to eat so much?"

She just looked at him, hungry and expecting more. He dug around in his food satchel until he found another slab of poorly cooked – more like, half over-cooked – rabbit to give her. Again he tore it into small chunks, and again she devoured it after barely chewing each piece.

This time she did not look up at him with hunger in her beautiful eyes. Instead, she looked at him with brightened, bluer eyes and, urged by an impulse coming from her, Noren scooped her up and laid her in his lap. He stroked her with one hand while he finished eating with the other. When he wanted to drink after the meal he needed two hands, but she continued to nuzzle his arm, gently so he did not spill his water all over himself. She was too young and helpless, an infant who could not be expected to be aware of such things on her own, yet she seemed to glean them from his mind without effort.

Noren kissed her on the top of her head when he was done drinking. The sun had not yet risen and all the land was bathed in the gray twilight before light and shadows come. There was only the fuzzy deeper darkness of the thicket behind him between him and the dawn.

He could not afford to allow Elninya to be seen, and it was now light enough for that to happen. He slung all his bags and blankets over his shoulder and picked her up. He took them deeper into the thicket, but left Evena where she was, just where he could still see her – or a portion of her – if he looked in the right direction. Then, stroking the dragon in his lap, he considered what to do now.

42

Light and Shadow

They drained the last of the light-water, and it left them hungrier than before, though Silmavalien knew thirst would soon chase hunger away again.

She felt very weak, and she was glad she did not have to carry a dragon. She did not trust herself not to drop one, even in the corridors of the caves. The dragons were all as weak as she was, and she wondered when it was time to give up. Even if they did find the daylight, were they strong enough to survive, or should they spend their last days cuddled together and let death take them that way, unresisting?

She could not bring herself to give in, or maybe it was one of the dragons. She knew she felt someone's scolding thought when she considered it. So she put one foot in front of the other, on and on, for what felt like an eon, before she saw a different kind of light on the pale green rock.

She dared not hope – perhaps it was only the light of a very large flow-stone boulder of single color, yellow-white – but they trudged on, around a sharp bend.

Silmavalien nearly leapt for joy. It was still a long way, at least in her present state, but she saw the mouth. She wanted to run towards it but neither she nor the dragons had the strength or the energy.

The glowstones continued to sparkle and shine in the cavern walls right up to the mouth, where in poured the daylight. Beyond she could see conifers of various kinds, with green ferns all over the ground and then, between the tree trunks, the sky, clear and bright and blue! The outdoor world and its sky, which she had not seen for so long.

They started towards the day, and her excitement waned as she remembered it was not over yet. With what strength she had left she still had to bring back water and hunt enough food to fill ten empty stomachs. How could she ever do it?

They reached the cave mouth, and walked out on a rock floor that slowly sloped down into pine-needle covered earth. She walked out and felt the breeze on her face. It must have been weeks or more since she had felt the stirring of fresh air against her skin, and for a moment she forgot the hunger and the weakness in its pleasure.

Then she looked around, and tears filled her eyes.

The little dragons were so thin. She could see every rib and every bump of their spines, and the light of their eyes was so dim she could not tell it was there in the daylight. She knelt, and Minth came to her, stumbling as he had not done since they had fled the village. He climbed in her lap and she put her arms around him, hugged him tight, and kissed him. She sat there with him in her arms, and the love between them drowned the pain in the fire of their bond.

Finally, she asked him to get out of her lap. She stood, held out her arms and examined herself. She was thin, herself, thinner than anyone she had ever seen, even the dying. She hoped she would still be able to draw her bow.

Then, like a whisper in her thoughts, she realized what she ought to have done the moment she had seen the daylight in the Riders' Passage.

She knelt down on the green rock, beside a glow stone, facing the sun, which hung half-way up in the eastern sky. "O Lord of the Light," she prayed softly, "thank you for leading us into the day. Please forgive me for not remembering to thank you at once. Please provide food and water for us or make me able to get it. Thank you for what you've given and for hearing me."

She walked off the rock and into the trees, Minth walking by her side, the other dragons trailing behind them. The land was mostly level, but instead of seeing more trees ahead as she walked on, the trees in front of her thinned, showing more and more of the sky. She walked more carefully, and then asked Minth to stay back, while she dropped down on hands and knees to look over the edge.

The land fell away in steep drop-offs and sheer cliffs. For a precipice it was not *too* vertical, but still far too steep for her to have a hope of climbing it, even when she was in her best shape. As far as she could see in every direction the cliffs continued, striped with narrow strips of zig-zagging green forest, and mottled with striations of many colored rock – sometimes blue-black, sometimes bright, but mostly light, pale shades of green, red, pink, or brown, and sometimes white or gray.

It was strangely beautiful, soft and pastel, yet hard and earthy.

She dared to look straight down, and there at the foot of the precipice, what looked hundreds of feet below, was more green forest. Still mostly conifer woods. But it, too, was a narrow strip before it fell away in another cliff.

She scanned the cliffs again. Far off a bright, double rainbow gleamed across it, and when she looked closer, she saw the spray of a waterfall, spun every which way in the winds until it could hold a rainbow.

Silmavalien looked down again, looking for what was at the bottom of the cliffs, and then she crawled backwards, away from the edge. She was beginning to want to lean further out from the cliff.

She turned and looked around. Above them, it looked much the same as below – cliffs and terraces of forest rising ever upwards. A stream, perhaps the same as she had seen below, flew airborne down the face of the precipice immediately above them, and she wondered what the pools it fell into were like. She would look for the nearest one as soon as she took the dragons back to the cave and spread out a few blankets on the rock, one in the sun and one in the shadow for them to lie on.

After that, she left into the direction of the stream. Minth was unwilling to be parted from her, so she decided he could come with her as long as the rock was still easily visible. After that, he had to go back. She could not have him wasting his energy, or slowing her down, or getting hurt, trying to follow her when they were all starving.

He was still complaining weakly in her mind – she was certain her own protests sounded as weak to him as he sounded to her – when she stopped short and almost stumbled.

A dark chasm opened in the earth a few paces ahead of them, and she remembered something else Lexamarian had said. Something about only taking the Riders' Passage with an Ellen to guide one.

Inarticulate terror poured over her. Then …

Standing on the brink of the chasm was a Shadow. Unlike any other shadow she had ever seen, this Shadow had substance. It raised two shadowy wings to envelop her and Minth in darkness, and though its face was formless shadow like the rest of it, there was something utterly terrifying about it. Its only features were twin fires that had to be its eyes, and a flicker of fire where a nose might be, if a Shadow needed one, but those eyes struck poison into her heart. It raised a whip of shadow that flickered with insubstantial fires to strike.

A Fire Shadow, among the more terrible of demons. And *real*.

Minth fainted, leaving her to face it alone.

Not alone. That was Songeth. And Veine. *Fight!* The weak, fierce thought was Airrock.

Shivering with fear, Silmavalien fumbled for her hunting knife. Her only hope was in the power and compassion of the Lord of the Light who would most probably act through her ring of light, and she summoned all her strength through the terror to cry, "O Lord of the Light, help me and fight for me against this Shadow!"

It laughed at her. Soundlessly. Cruelly. In her soul, where she should only ever hear her dragons.

Her dragons wrapped her in their song, weak as it was. She ignored the Shadow. The Lord of Light was her only hope. She had seen his power in the cavern, long ago, or so it seemed. She knew his voice. He was powerful enough to defeat even a Fire Shadow.

She stepped forward, determined. She could not let it touch Minth. All her weakness seemed to flee before that thought.

The Shadow's wings quivered and it struck with the whip of flame. She tried to move but she knew she was not fast enough. Somehow, the whip did not strike her, though for a moment she felt its heat. The Shadow drew its whip back.

She lunged at it, stabbed at a wing. Something that looked like lightning shot from her ring, ran the length of her hunting knife, shattered into a hundred streaks and stabbed at the Shadow. Vanished. The whip of flame arced towards. She twisted. Fell. Lay over the edge of the cliff. Screamed against failure. Terrible, impending death. "Lord of Light, save!"

A flicker of motion. A figure moved up the cliff below her, leaping upwards with amazing grace and strength. She turned her head and saw the Shadow descending … upon her? … or Minth?

She struggled to get away from the edge before she fell.

Someone or something leapt over her. Out of the corner of her eye she saw a sword of light flash in the darkness of the Shadow and it faded.

To Be Continued …

In **Return of the Dragonriders Book Two**
DRAGONWING

"Noren gasped as he saw the flag of Silrah spread out in the wind. The winged creature was a dragon. A crimson dragon with folded wings, perched like a hawk on a branch, and surrounded by a violet crown, a crown the color of the end of the rainbow. Both dragon and crown showed strikingly against the cerulean blue background that must surely represent the sky.

He recognized the flag. More than one bard had described it to the people of Treas, even though none of them had ever seen it. But he had never dreamed that the winged creature was a dragon. A dragon on the flag of a kingdom that persecuted dragons, and no one noticed!"

Sign up to be notified about new releases:
https://books2read.com/r/B-A-OUYQ-HMXXB

Follow me on Goodreads:
https://www.goodreads.com/author/show/20243136.Raina_Nightingale

Follow me on BookBub:
https://www.bookbub.com/authors/raina-nightingale

Or, if you like weekly reviews, ramblings of all sorts, and occasional art posts, you can follow my blog:
https://enthralledbylove.com

If you liked DragonBirth, *please leave an honest review on your favorite book platforms. It really helps readers and independent authors to find each other. I would deeply grateful and encouraged.*

See you again!